THE DARKLING ODYSSEY

BLUE PROMETHEUS SERIES #2

NED MARCUS

ORANGE LOG PUBLISHING

Copyright © 2019 by Ned Marcus

ISBN 978-986-95833-4-3

2nd edition (softcover)

All rights reserved.

No part of this book may be reproduced in any form or by any electronic or mechanical means, including information storage and retrieval systems, without written permission from the author, except for the use of brief quotations in a book review.

This book is a work of fiction. The characters, places and events are products of the author's imagination or have been used fictitiously and are not to be construed as real. Any resemblance to persons, living or dead, is entirely coincidental.

Published in 2019 by Orange Log Publishing

Cover Design by Damonza

CONTENTS

Chapter 1	1
Chapter 2	9
Chapter 3	19
Chapter 4	30
Chapter 5	44
Chapter 6	59
Chapter 7	67
Chapter 8	76
Chapter 9	80
Chapter 10	92
Chapter 11	103
Chapter 12	114
Chapter 13	129
Chapter 14	136
Chapter 15	141
Chapter 16	153
Chapter 17	164
Chapter 18	173
Chapter 19	186
Chapter 20	197
Chapter 21	206
Chapter 22	212
Chapter 23	218
Chapter 24	227
Chapter 25	233
Chapter 26	240
Chapter 27	249
Chapter 28	256
Chapter 29	262
Chapter 30	271
Chapter 31	277
Chapter 32	285

Chapter 33	295
Chapter 34	303
Chapter 35	312
Epilogue	322
Please Leave A Review	325
Free Stories!	327
Books By Ned Marcus	329
About the Author	331
Acknowledgments	333

1

Thomas Brand waited for the giant lift. Other prisoners jostled around him, and one man coughed repeatedly—no one wanted to remain in the hot, humid mine. Victor San and the rest of his team pressed against him. When the door opened, they pushed to the back. The gangers always stood at the front. Avoiding them was necessary for survival.

His thoughts turned to the dead—those he loved more than the living. Most of all, Aina. But Lucy, too, and Orange, the troll. All dead because they'd loved him.

Other losses weighed him down as well. He'd lost the Spirit Key, a pentacle that amplified magic—a magic that few in this world believed in.

He'd lost the magic of life itself.

He slowly breathed the stale air, hardly noticing the men squeezing against him as gangers of the Nine Planets, the most powerful gang in the prison, entered the lift. The lift shook as it ascended, and Drew Walker, the leader of the local faction, studied his reflection in the metal doors. His stubbly green hair was well-known, as were his men: Garret Pick, Joshua, and Buzz. Around them were others; all were loyal to gang and empire. They were its tools and proud of it.

One of the gangers pushed Thomas and a new convict in their faces, forcing them back—Thomas tasted the dirt and sweat from the man's hand, but he didn't react. The man next to him was obviously new—he glared at the ganger. Thomas knew the outcome before it happened. The ganger punched the man in his face. No one reacted to the assault, and the man moved away, holding his bleeding nose.

The artificially intelligent lift quietly laughed. When Aina had once told him that imperial machines did this, he'd thought it a joke. But it was true. Some, like this lift, were intelligent; they were also armed with small guns and fiercely loyal to the Empire. This lift had demonstrated its power: two weeks earlier it had shot a man for telling a joke about the Emperor. That single bullet had silenced all laughter.

The lift jolted to a stop, and the doors opened. Joshua led Thomas's team back along the dimly lit passages to the cavelike cells, cut from the rock by prisoners long dead. The metal door at the front of the cell slid shut as Thomas lay on his stone bed.

"Another day," Victor said as the lights dimmed. The old man lifted his artificial leg onto his bed.

"In hell." Thomas closed his eyes, and seconds later, he fell asleep, and the dream he'd dreamt so many times began again.

Thomas knelt and held Aina's cold body close, desperately wanting to warm her, but even his tears froze before they touched her face. The freezing wind numbed him further. These parts were familiar. But this time he was not alone. A shadow moved within the dark forest surrounding them.

He watched the trees move, wondering what had the power to enter his dream. Monsters were real, he knew.

Afraid of what might step from the darkness, he held Aina's body closer, hoping to protect her, but she dissolved into mist. Grasping the air, he tried to will her back, but she was gone. Usually he woke up at this point, but this time he did not.

A dark creature stepped from the forest, the ground trembling as it approached. Its eyes burnt red, and he felt its heat—just as he had on the day of her death.

He stood and faced it. "Why do you disturb my dreams?"

The red fire of its eyes brightened. "Aina lives."

For a second, Thomas hoped. Then the memory of that day returned, and Thomas shook his head. "She died in my arms."

"Her spirit lives."

"You're just a dream, and I'm alone." He knew what had happened—she was dead.

"You're never alone, even in your darkness."

Thomas closed his eyes, but the fiery eyes of the creature burnt into his mind. Again it spoke. "She lives."

"Leave me!" He turned to move away.

"Go to her; claim the Fire."

"She's dead!"

"Travel to the centre of the planet. Take the Fire!"

Thomas woke from the strangely lucid dream and looked around the dark cell. The forest was gone, and the dragon's words had been replaced by the sounds of the prison at night.

Its words took him back to happier times, sitting in a teahouse with Aina and Lucy when she'd first told them of the prophecy. He'd laughed in disbelief. He no longer laughed.

He remembered her words: "When a darkness spreads across the stars, and when the shadow of a dark leader stretches throughout the nine planets, a force shall arise to counter the evil. From the stars, Bright Ones shall come and claim the Keys and counter the darkness with fire." She had believed them to be the Bright Ones. He blinked away a tear as he remembered her earnestness. And she'd continued. "The Bright Ones shall descend to the inner sun, where their strength shall be tested and forged in fire. They shall raise the Fire of Prometheus, thereby raising the consciousness of all."

As he sat in his darkness, he questioned his beliefs. Could she really be alive? But then he remembered her death again. How could the dragon's words be true? A man's cough, the famous death cough of Min Flo—the most remote prison of the Empire—brought his attention back to the world around him. He guessed he had less than two hours before the doors opened for the shift in the mines.

The single bulb in the passage flickered, and he glanced at the silhouette of his cellmate on the bed opposite. The old man seemed to sleep even less than he did. Victor was a gaunt man of about sixty, an ex-politician from Palace Moon, and a survivor, but Thomas was still surprised he'd lived so long. The man was fiddling with his artificial leg.

While Victor fiddled, Thomas rubbed his hand along a groove a past prisoner had made in the stone wall. He enjoyed the feel of the grit between his fingers. He imagined a feeling of the old magic, but it was an illusion. The magic was gone.

"I had a dream," Thomas said.

"Everyone dreams the same dream, but dreams don't dig tunnels," Victor said.

"Not of escape. I dreamt she's alive."

"The girl you lost?" The bulb in the corridor brightened

again for a second, glinting in Victor's piercing green eyes. "Do you believe it?"

Thomas gave a shake of his head. He knew better, but even so, he said, "I wish it."

"She's in a better place than us," Victor said. They both went still as a sound came from the dark passage. "Maybe spiders."

Thomas had been here too long to care about the bots that cleaned the passages, though they sometimes killed prisoners as well. He was sure their look was designed to scare people; spiders were the size of a rat, with wiry legs that could span a table and red eyes that shone in the dark. But this was the second time that day the bots had come. That never happened—not in the nine months he'd been there; not unless there was a problem.

"Something's there," Seven, a prisoner in the cell diagonally opposite, said. His cellmate, Nigel, made ghost sounds, but everyone ignored him.

Thomas listened, but the sounds had stopped, although not the whispers of prisoners, which passed from cell to cell along the gloomy passage.

"Do you think the Empire listens?" He knew that Victor would understand. Imperial subjects throughout the nine planets were routinely tagged: nano-computers inserted into their brains at birth—a convenience for communication, entertainment, and the Empire, which gained billions of eyes and ears.

Victor grinned. "This was once my field; I used to monitor our subjects' moods."

His eyes widened in surprise. Victor was usually as secretive as he was. "And?" Thomas said. He was pleased he'd asked the question and hoped to learn more about his cellmate.

"We mostly looked at the average man. It's a game of statistics. Do you know how many billions of imperial subjects live on the nine planets?"

"I've no idea. Is that a no?"

Victor shrugged. "What can we say that will affect them?" Victor looked at him curiously. "Don't tell me you haven't noticed the lack of downloads? Most people complain about it all the time."

"I'm untagged," Thomas said, wondering whether his sudden impulse to speak the truth was wise. Victor's eyebrows lifted in surprise. "But even if they're mostly switched off, it doesn't mean the Empire doesn't listen."

"True enough." Victor watched Thomas, and Thomas knew he was considering how much he could say. "They say criminals are often untagged."

Thomas grinned. "I was once the most wanted man in the Empire."

Victor didn't smile. "I've wondered about that, and I don't think you're entirely joking. How did you manage that?" he asked quietly.

Thomas paused at the question. If anyone knew the truth, he'd be dead, and as bad as life here was, he wasn't quite ready for that. And the man sitting opposite him was not just another convict.

Acting on a gut feeling, Thomas switched from the imperial language, almost ubiquitous in the prison, to Silvan. "I'm not an imperial subject."

Victor grinned, and Thomas leant back against the wall, knowing that the old man loved any kind of intrigue. "That explains some things," he said in accented Silvan. "But Silva's probably a part of the Empire by now. You've been here, what, a year?"

"Near enough."

"And that makes you an imperial subject," Victor said.

"An untagged one."

"There is that." The old man paused for several seconds, and Thomas could almost see him thinking. "How did you guess I'd understand Silvan?"

"A hunch," Thomas said. "You were an imperial politician before they got rid of you. But you speak it badly."

"I speak Venusian. It's close enough to Silvan. I'm surprised you didn't know that." Thomas waited, not wanting to reveal too much. "I know you don't have a loose tongue . . ." Thomas's listening was sharp, but he only just heard when the old man whispered, "I'm untagged, too."

"How?"

"They deactivated my tag as a punishment," he whispered.

Thomas grinned. "A blessing."

"Perhaps."

"I heard it again," Ivan, the boy in the cell opposite them said. "Something's out there." The boy looked concerned. Stories of monsters living in the deeper parts of the mines were rife, but Thomas had seen no evidence. Yet his experience in the forests of this planet ensured that he never dismissed such stories as nonsense either. He listened. The boy was right, there was something there.

"I can't hear anything," Victor said, "and spiders never visit twice on the same night." Thomas sat up, feeling uncomfortable. "What?" Victor asked.

"A feeling," Thomas said.

Studying him closely, Victor said, "You get a lot of them."

"And they've sometimes saved my life."

"No doubt."

Thomas stood by the bars. Something hissed in the

darkness. He shivered in recognition, but it wasn't until he smelt it that he was sure. "Stand back from the bars!"

The men looked at him in surprise, and most obeyed. He was less garrulous than many, but when he did speak, the men listened. Victor looked at him in surprise. "Why? We're locked in our cells." Thomas waited impassively, and Victor struggled to attach his artificial leg. "You're making me nervous—and few men do that."

Thomas knew that wasn't completely true, but he chose to let it pass. He waited by the bars, ignoring his own advice to move away.

"What is it?" Victor asked. "Do you care to share your knowledge?"

A large shadow moved in the dimly lit corridor. It sniffed the air.

"Ice demon," Thomas said.

2

The reptile stood on two legs and watched them. Its head touched the roof of the passage, its frilled neck slowly opened and closed, and its tail stretched into the darkness. It wore a dark green uniform over its black and green body. Thomas recognized the colours: this one had been part of an elite unit, although it was no longer in good shape. It hissed, and its acrid smell reached him. It was a female, about seven feet tall—a male would need to crouch in this passage. But even the females he'd seen had been bulkier than this. "It doesn't look well," he said.

"What is it?" the boy asked.

"An imperial battlefield weapon," Thomas said.

"I've heard of them, but they were decommissioned years ago," Victor said.

"I've killed them," Thomas said. "And they're still used in the Tower and in the forests of the surface." It stared at him; he knew their hearing was good. "What do you want?" he asked the hissing reptile.

"Animals don't speak," Victor said, raising his eyebrows.

"They're not animals—not completely." Thomas

wondered why an ice demon was here in the mines; it didn't make sense. Surely the Empire had better uses for its weapons.

The creature walked its swaying walk to Thomas's cell. It thrust its head against the iron bars with a crash that sent Victor to the floor. "I think you were right about not standing too close to the bars."

"I was," Thomas said. But he refused to move back, even when it pushed its head closer to his. He only stepped back when it reached through the bars, pointing its curved dagger claw at him. It cackled, and he covered his mouth at its rank breath. "What do you want?" he repeated.

"Feedz," it cackled.

Victor breathed in sharply. "It spoke."

"They possess some words," Thomas said. They also possessed a rudimentary telepathic ability; a yoke attaching them to their leaders. Thomas had once spoken this True Language of ideas, images, and emotions to a higher level than any ice demon. He reached out to the lizard with his mind, expecting nothing—but something itched inside, although it was not the magic he remembered. However, the ice demon's eyes widened slightly; something had happened.

It sprayed a small cloud of acidic spittle onto the bars of the door, and the iron sizzled. Sniffing the air, it whispered, "Magic." Thomas wished. It pushed its head closer to Thomas, tilting it slightly. The smell was sickening, and he wanted to step back, but he was curious; the creature was in pain.

"Careful," Victor said from the back of the cell. "It's up to something."

"I know."

"It's ugly!" Doug, the boy's cellmate, said. His head was

pressed up to the bars. "And it stinks!" The reptile span round, its tail striking the bars in front of Thomas, making him jump. It flew across the passage, its talon slicing through Doug's neck. His body fell against the bars, and the ice demon lapped up the blood flowing from his open neck. For several minutes, they watched in silence as the ice demon pulled slices of body through the bars and ate. The only sounds were the reptile eating and Ivan retching.

Thomas stood at the front of his cell. Further down the passage, some of the men had started banging on the iron bars, and a few were shouting. He had a vague feeling that he should be angry, but he'd never cared for the snide man, and he'd seen too much death for it to be unusual. His main concern was that it'd want to feed again; it was the thinnest ice demon he'd ever seen.

Curious, he tried to probe its mind again. Why was an ice demon feeding here? Why was it here at all? Had the Empire really let it loose? And why weren't they feeding their killing machine?

He felt it mentally repel him, but it turned and walked towards him. "Thomas," Victor warned.

"I know." It pushed its snout against the iron bars of his door and sniffed. They stared at each other.

Again the magic stirred in Thomas, and without much thought, he pushed harder into its mind. It released its grip on the bars and mentally blocked him. "What are you?" it asked.

He didn't answer but waited for it to push back. It came suddenly, but Thomas had played these games before. The harder it pushed, the more it exposed of itself. Thomas saw flashes of memories: images of young reptiles lying dead in a pool of blood.

"Nooaass!" The ice demon pushed away from the bars; it

gurgled and then moaned, thrashing its tail against the bars of the opposite cell.

"What the . . . ?" Nigel said.

Eyes wide, Victor hopped to the back of the cell.

Thomas noticed the men's alarm, but he kept mental contact with the creature. A second image appeared. "You ate your children," Thomas whispered. He felt sicker as its toxic emotions washed over him. "And now you're alone. And somehow you found your way here." He had no idea how it had managed that journey.

"Not mine!" Its frilled neck fluttered open and shut rapidly.

"Why?"

"Hgry," it moaned. "They attcked me, too." Thomas glanced at the others; they hadn't understood. He wasn't sure whether they even knew it was speaking, but he'd made out the words. There'd been some type of fight; then it'd killed and eaten the young. His friends looked at it in revulsion even without understanding what it had just admitted.

"How did you get here?"

"Hunted," it hissed. "I found a way down." Drops of acid spittle sizzled on the bars, and Thomas edged back slightly.

It looked along the passage, and, still linked to its mind, Thomas heard through its ears. "Two guards are coming," he said, recognizing the sounds of their footsteps. So this was how ice demons heard—he was impressed. Despite what he'd seen in the demon's mind, he was unsure how it would react to imperial guards. Obedience was part of their nature—or so he'd assumed.

"I'll send you to hell!" a voice blared. It was the guard with a grudge; Thomas knew him too well. "I know the cause of this disturbance."

Thomas wondered if he did. He glanced at Victor. "He means us."

"He's been looking for excuses to beat us," Victor said quietly. "He doesn't like you." That was certainly true. "He's going to blame Doug's death on you, too."

"Even if they see the ice demon?"

Victor looked at the ice demon nervously. "They're not looking for truth, but at least they'll shoot the monster."

The ice demon hissed at Victor. "They're harder to kill than you think," Thomas said. He doubted pistols would be powerful enough to do more than sting. "Depends if they're carrying anything special."

The ice demon's ears twitched as it sniffed the stale air. Slowly, it crawled up the wall and along the ceiling, flattening its body as it did so. Its long tail flicked out, smashing one of the lights and sending broken glass to the floor.

"I'm coming for you, Brand," the guard with a grudge shouted. The pair of guards swaggered around the corner, hands resting on their pistols and batons. The one with the grudge drew his baton and hit the bars by Thomas's face. His eyes bulged with hatred, and in his emotion, he didn't notice the blood nor the pile of entrails in the cell opposite. The other, a laconic green man, watched. Thomas took a half step back. "Damaging imperial property carries a penalty." The guard stared into his eyes and slapped his baton into his palm. Thomas was determined to show no fear.

"I haven't damaged any property," Thomas said, watching him warily. He still ached from the last beating.

The man pointed at the glass on the floor. "What's that?"

"Don't stare," Victor whispered from the back of the cell.

Thomas knew the rules and the ways of the prison. The first was that there was no way out of a situation like this.

The first guard's face was flushed. He touched the keypad and ordered the door open. The motor whirred, and the door slowly slid back. The second guard grinned, his baton dangling from one hand, his pistol in the other.

"He'll kill me, unless I do it to him first," Thomas said quietly. He waited for the door to open and prayed for a touch of the old magic, but he felt nothing. He needed a distraction.

"Even if you escape, they'll hunt you down."

"Thank you, Victor."

The old man looked a little abashed, but then he stood straight and pointed. "What about Doug?"

Only then did the two men seem to notice the pool of blood in front of the cell opposite, immediately ordering the door closed again. "What's this?"

The other man shone a light into the cell. "Sir, one of the men is gone."

The guards were nervous. Thomas knew that the loss of a prisoner would be blamed on them. The first guard glared at Ivan. "Where's he gone?"

As soon as the words were out, Doug's head dropped to the ground, making them jump. And Thomas's hope returned. "Support!" the second guard yelled. Electronic ears within the man and around the prison would send his words to the command station. The guards stared at the bloody head and then looked up.

The ice demon's tail dropped and twitched. The second guard fell against Ivan's cell and moaned; the first guard drew his gun.

The ice demon dropped on the moaning man. He didn't move again. The first guard fired, but that only made the demon angry. Their bellies were even tougher than their backs—a special feature. It sliced off his fingers. His pistol fell just beyond Thomas's reach.

"Open!" The guard shouted as he tried to stop the bleeding. But nothing happened. Before he could speak again, it cut his throat.

"More guards will be here in a few minutes," Victor whispered.

The ice demon diced the bodies and ate. Thomas watched, sitting cross-legged on his bed. "It must be hungry."

"Don't be too satisfied," Victor said. "Trouble's coming."

He shrugged. "It's always coming."

The ice demon was watching him. Its long tail flicked slowly from side to side, clanging against the doors opposite. When it knocked the pistol towards Thomas, he picked it up.

"Thomas?" Victor said. "That wasn't wise."

"No."

The ice demon watched him, then it picked up the guard's hand and swiped it against the pad. "Open," it said, mimicking the dead man's voice. The door opened, and the ice demon stepped into the cell. "You should shoot me now."

"It's not for you," Thomas said, lowering the gun.

"Shoot it," Victor said. He was pushing himself to the back of the cell.

The ice demon pushed past Thomas and grabbed Victor's leg. Thomas shot its tail, and the demon turned and grinned. "You must do better, human."

"My name is Thomas Brand, and I said it wasn't for you." He kicked Victor's leg from the demon's grip, and the old man crawled away, cursing under his breath. "I have some questions." Then he noticed a red bullet hanging from its neck. He stared, and for a few seconds, he forgot where he was.

"My magic charmz." It rubbed the bullet with a claw.

He remembered the Red Bullet he'd ridden with Aina, and his heart jumped. The ice demon leant forward, pushing into his memories, using his emotion as a key. It saw secret parts of his life and used his feelings for Aina to go deeper.

He was within the dream again; he held Aina, and then the black dragon spoke. The scene changed: Lucy crying by Aina's body; Lucy had exhausted her magic and failed to keep her alive.

The ice demon's eyes widened. Thomas pushed the surprised creature from his mind. *"I've never experienced such strong psychic ability in an ice demon,"* he said in the True Language.

The demon answered in the same telepathic language. *"I am Chloris, and I was special, too. But like you, no longer."*

"What surprised you?"

"You dream of dragons."

Thomas doubted it was that. *"I dream of Aina. That she lives."*

"Dragons deceive."

"Then it's not true?"

"Even if true, they have their own reasons for coming to you."

"I don't care."

"You should. What benefits dragons seldom benefits humans."

Or you, Thomas thought. *"I don't care too much for humans."*

The ice demon snickered, spraying an acidic cloud from her mouth. *"We have something in common."*

"You saw something else," Thomas said. He was sure the ice demon had hesitated as it had watched his memories.

"The Bright One," Chloris said.

Thomas's eyes opened wide. *"What?"* But he already knew. It'd recognized Lucy.

"She's not dead," Chloris said.

"Lucy's alive?" he said aloud.

"Someone's coming," Victor said, taking the pistol from Thomas and hiding it.

But Thomas hardly paid attention to him. *"How do you know?"* Thomas asked.

The ice demon was already crawling up the wall. *"I smell her magic. I go to her now."* And then she was gone.

Thomas was stunned. Could she still be alive? For the past year, he'd hardly noticed the restrictions of prison life. He'd felt numb: he'd had nowhere to go, and no one to go to. If Lucy was still alive, this had changed. "I might need to escape."

Victor laughed. "You've only just thought of that?" The new guards stopped and stared in shock at the carnage. The guards ordered the door to shut. "The door?"

"I'll open new ones."

"With that monster?"

Thomas shrugged. "She'll do what she chooses. She's tough; she was bred for the battlefield."

"She?"

"Her name's Chloris."

Victor gave him an incredulous stare. "It's an imperial weapon—we can't trust it."

"I'd trust her more than some of the humans who live here." Thomas wondered if that were really true as he watched the prison guards checking the prisoners' tags. Only the boy had been close enough to see, and he'd been crouching in the corner with his eyes closed during the ice demon's attack. "They've no idea what's just happened," he said quietly.

A guard pointed some device at Thomas and Victor, then he shook his head. "Untagged."

"A monster," Victor said to a guard's question. "We hid at the back, like the boy." He gestured to the back of the cell nervously. Victor was quite a good actor when he wanted to be, Thomas thought.

Thomas was surprised they asked so few questions; mostly, they just left cleaning bots to do their work.

"Your girlfriend's given us a late start; I appreciate that," Victor said.

3

The first shift started a few hours later than normal, and Thomas felt more relaxed than usual as he climbed down a shaft with Victor and the rest of his work gang. "Is it really true that no one's escaped?" he asked quietly.

In between deep breaths, Victor gave a short laugh. "Escaping's not the problem. It's staying alive after that's the problem."

"Spiders?" Thomas asked.

"And guards, gangers, starvation, thirst, and death by accidents." Victor coughed and spat dust down the black shaft. "And that's apart from the ice demon and whatever other monsters lurk down here."

"So some escape?"

"No one passes the barrier."

"That's going up. What about down?"

"Death."

"I've heard of an underworld." He'd actually heard of even deeper levels. The rock magic and geology he'd studied didn't always correspond.

Victor rested on the rungs of the ladder above him for several seconds—the rest of the group took the chance to rest, too. "No one can live down there." Thomas glanced down into the black hole. The old man was right; it wasn't appealing. "The only way is to return to civilization, but no one's ever done that."

"Civilization?" He'd not thought of it in those terms for a long time.

Victor's reply was drowned out by the shouts of the gangers, and Thomas felt the anger of their supervisors—something was happening to him. He'd not felt any empathic connection to anyone for more than a year. He also sensed the anger and fear of the men. They resumed their descent, and Thomas thought about the small surges of magic he was experiencing. It was not that much really; not enough to escape easily, but the emotions of the men around him were becoming clearer. Although, he couldn't yet hear their thoughts, as he had with Chloris.

He rubbed his hand along the rock wall as he descended, feeling intermittently surging magic as he did so. Had the dream of Aina and the dragon's words awoken something inside him? He'd possessed the magic that Aina had taught him before he'd ever touched the pentacle. That magical weapon had only amplified his natural magic. Now, the rock attracted him like a weak magnet. Unfortunately, it was not the strong magnetic power he'd once felt; otherwise, he'd simply have escaped, with less worries of the things that would hunt him.

Theirs was the first team to reach the shaft bottom, and since Doug's death, there were only seven of them: Thomas, Victor, Ivan, Jackson, Nigel, Seven, and Jet. From there they followed Joshua down a final descending tunnel. Another ganger followed at the rear. The walls were sharp, and a challenge for Victor's artificial leg. Thomas supported him for part of the way.

"I appreciate what you did," Victor said. Thomas raised an eyebrow. "Stepping between me and the demon."

"I'd wanted to kick you for a long time," Thomas said.

"Cheers."

They continued on in silence. At some points, side passages left the main tunnel; some were no more than cracks in the rock. Thomas had asked about these before. Even Victor hadn't known where they went. A slight breeze from one of the cracks in the rocks attracted his attention. Thomas stopped by the narrow entrance and pretended to take a breath, his hand resting on the rocks. "It goes deep."

"How could you know that?" Victor asked. Thomas didn't try to explain what he just sensed. "No one could fit through anyway," Victor said.

"I could stuff you through."

"Charming," Victor said.

Thomas grinned as he imagined Victor's expression, which was hidden as the old man moved the lantern forward. The draught of air added to a lightness he'd felt since learning of Lucy. He thought again about the incident with Chloris. The prison authorities had hardly questioned him, and he wasn't sure if they would. The guards who had arrived to the scene of carnage had been obviously confused and concerned, but they'd not found the pistol, which was hidden in Victor's secret hiding place behind the loose rock. The rear ganger shouted, and they started moving again.

About half an hour later, Joshua called for a rest, purely for his own sake. Thomas rested his hands on the wall again and tried to listen to the rocks as he once had easily done. Then he called his rock magic. He doubted anyone in the mines could sense magic, especially not the vestigial amounts he possessed; that skill was rare. With surprise, his mind entered the rocks, and he was soon seeing thin veins of copper running through them. Then the ganger ordered them on, and Victor poked him in the side. "What is it?"

He must have sensed something in his slowness to respond. "Something's happening to me."

"Cryptic as ever," Victor said.

By the time he reached the rock face, Thomas was drenched in sweat. Fit as he was, it made little difference; the humidity of the mines was stifling. There were no cool breezes here. They were surrounded by the vein of copper ore Thomas had felt earlier. His friends had asked him about his ability to guess the location of minerals underground; he'd just said he was lucky. He wondered now if his natural magic had never actually left him; perhaps it was he who'd abandoned it. Feeling strange, he dropped the pick he'd just picked up and crouched on the ground. He was shaking—sweat soaked his clothes.

"What's wrong?" Victor asked.

"A tremor." He wasn't even sure if that were true. He just knew he didn't feel right.

"I felt nothing," Victor said.

It came again, stronger, and Thomas put his head in his hands.

"Are you okay?" Victor asked.

"I feel strange. Like I'm swimming." The men gathered around, but no one spoke. They didn't need to—he felt their concern. Again he felt a vibration. It was familiar. "Something's happening to me."

"This is not a good place for a medical emergency," Victor whispered. "Can you pull yourself together?"

"It's not that." Thomas had felt a vibration pass through the rocks straight into him—more intense than natural magic. He leant against the rocks, unable to speak whilst the low-level magic vibrated his body. Then it stopped. "I'm okay," he whispered. He took hold of the pick again.

He always worked at the front, knowing instinctively where the richest veins were, and the gangers were now happy to let him choose where to mine. Jackson dug the rock face beside him, while Victor and Nigel loaded the handcarts, and Ivan, Seven, and Jet pulled the rickety cart to a loading station further along the tunnel. From there, the second team took the ore back to the shaft, where the third team carried it, on their backs, up the long ladder to be processed.

Despite the technology of the Empire, the mine used old-fashioned equipment and physical labour; lives were cheap and plentiful. The two gangers played dice away from the noise and dust of the rock face, which suited Thomas fine. He worked in silence, and the morning passed quickly.

Victor possessed the only clock, and when he tapped Thomas on the shoulder, Thomas stopped and shouted, "Break!"

With Jackson just behind him, he crawled back along the low tunnel, helping Nigel and Victor move the flat cart of rocks. Victor used his one leg to propel himself expertly along. He removed his artificial leg when working in the low tunnels. They kept crawling until they reached the first cavern, where the rest of the team helped pull the cart across the cavern. "At last," Victor said, sweating heavily from dragging the loads of rocks up the tunnel. They sat on some of the larger rocks in the cavern, and Victor grasped the metal flask of black tea—the only luxury they were permitted. Thomas nodded and drank the hot tea. Three lanterns lit their underground space.

They drank in silence, listening to an argument further

up the tunnel between a ganger and men from the second group. "Is that Maxwell?" Victor asked.

"That's him," Thomas said. The second group had gathered in the second cave, about twenty yards from theirs. "I'll take a look." The way along the tunnel was easy to walk, and with his sharp sight, Thomas needed little light to find his way.

The lead ganger, Joshua, struck Maxwell's legs with a long cane. "Push!" The loaded ore cart had run off the bottom of the tracks; the metal stops had snapped. Maxwell and another man pushed, but the cart was too heavy. He shielded his legs and made a crude joke, quickly receiving another blow. But instead of crying out, Maxwell grinned.

Thomas didn't know why the man grinned, it was just something he did. He didn't mean anything by it, but it enraged the ganger, who hit him again. The other ganger pointed his cane at Thomas. "Get back to your cave and stay there!" But no one moved. The ganger looked at them, deciding not to back up his words. The gangers were feared, but they were not guards, and here in the deepest parts of the mines, things sometimes happened to them when they pushed too hard. But Maxwell was with another team, and Thomas didn't intervene. They had to sort it out. The second ganger turned back to Maxwell, who was crawling along the ground, and took his anger out on him instead. They watched silently as Maxwell moaned under the blows.

Thomas thought of his rock magic and wondered. He mentally probed the rocks around him as he'd used to. He felt a slight return of power again; this time stronger than before. Turning away from the beating, he leant against the slanting roof of the tunnel. His fingers tickled, as if small electric shocks were being applied. He felt a surge of energy and then a drop as the power fluctuated.

Before he had time to wonder why this was happening, his mind entered the rock. He moved quickly, seeing its strengths and faults, and he noticed a crack in the roof above the gangers. His power was like water alternately spurting then dripping from a tap, and although he tried to turn it to full, he couldn't. All his senses were now merging with the rock, and for an instant, he saw himself from the rock ceiling of the tunnel. He contracted and expanded the rock directly above the gangers until the rocks snapped. The gangers and prisoners started, apart from Jackson, who watched Thomas. The others nervously watched the roof. Forgetting the moaning Maxwell, the gangers moved back.

Within the walls were several cavities and Thomas hummed a rock song he'd heard a long time before in another world. The music vibrated within the rocks, creating strange sounds as the rocks responded with their own interpretation of the tune. The rocks rapidly contracted and expanded, pulsing in and out, to the rhythm of the music. A series of loud bangs directly above the lead ganger caused him to cry out, before running with the other ganger and the second team. All apart from Maxwell, who lay on the ground. A fault in the roof followed the narrow tunnel through which the gangers and the team ran, and Thomas followed the fault, cracking the rocks above them as they went. When he withdrew from the rock, he found his team staring at him.

"What did you do?" Jackson asked.

Thomas shrugged. "Just humming a song."

The big man laughed, while Nigel looked at both of them oddly. The bloodied Maxwell grinned, wincing as Thomas helped him stand.

"A strange tune," Victor said. "And was it related to what just happened?"

"How could it?" Nigel asked. "It was an earthquake."

Victor just looked at Thomas.

The slight return of his magic was something he didn't wish to discuss with anyone here. It was strange—even by Thomas's standards.

"What if the earthquake returns?" Nigel asked.

"It won't," Thomas said. "It was just a vibration in the rocks."

"Is there any difference?"

Thomas didn't answer. No explanation would be helpful. He remembered his own first reaction to magic.

"The rock's unstable," Nigel said. "We all heard it."

"It's safe," Thomas said.

Jackson gave Thomas a measuring look before saying, "I've heard rumours of men who can do odd things."

"What do you mean?" Victor asked.

Jet laughed. "He means magic."

"I wish we had some magic," Thomas said. "Maybe we'd magic our way out. But these rocks are safe." He preferred to draw attention away from what had just happened, but Jackson looked at him with narrowed eyes.

As they spoke, a piercing scream came from along the tunnel, and Thomas felt a surge in his power. And an old memory returned.

Victor raised an eyebrow. "You were saying?" More screams followed.

A dark shadow moved at the end of the tunnel. Others saw it, too. It watched them, and then it was gone. "It's the thing that killed Doug," Jackson said.

"I'm not sure," Thomas said. He spoke in the True Language, but if it was Chloris, she wasn't answering.

"It wasn't human," Victor said. "That was clear."

He nodded. "No, it wasn't." Thomas sensed something

calling him; something magical. Five of seven men from the second team ran back. Thomas recognized Pete, who lived much further down from Thomas's cell.

"The demon!" Pete said. Breathless, he came to a stop by the cart. "It came out of the darkness. Four men are dead."

"The gangers?" Thomas asked.

"It took them first."

Thomas smiled.

"Is it the same thing that killed Doug?" Victor asked.

"Yes," Pete said.

"You were too far away to see the ice demon in the prison," Thomas said.

"What else could it be?" the man said.

"Do you think there's more than one of those things wandering the mines?" Victor asked.

"I don't know, but it's given us an opportunity," Thomas said.

The men looked at him with raised eyebrows. "And that is?" Nigel asked.

"The chance to explore."

"Why would you want to do that?" Jackson asked.

Thomas wished to speak openly, but he couldn't take the chance that the authorities would be listening to this conversation at some future date. "I know the rocks. I want to find easier seams to mine," he lied.

Nigel snorted, and Victor watched him, his eyes narrowed, but some of the others seemed to believe him. "And you'd risk your life for that?" Pete asked.

"Too many of us die in the mines; it would be worth it to stay safe," Thomas said. Victor raised an eyebrow but remained silent. More of the men nodded their agreement. "Anyway, I think it's gone." He was sure it had gone—the magic had faded.

Thomas walked back up the tunnel. Carefully stepping over the remains of the dead, he reached the crack in the wall that had interested him earlier. He raised his lamp, but the darkness seemed to suck all of its light out—he could still see nothing. The only thing he noticed was that the narrow gap looked as if it had never been mined.

He wasn't sure whether the creature had come from this crack in the wall or one further back. Nor was he sure where it had gone. Though he no longer sensed the magic around the creature, he wished he'd brought a small pick for protection. He knew that magic could be concealed. He squeezed into the gap. The draught of air was slightly stronger here. He doubted that the creature had come this way at all; the gap was just too tight. Then he looked up and his stomach sank: the gap widened above him. Any creature even slightly related to an ice demon could easily crawl along the roof.

Despite surviving a first meeting with an ice demon, he didn't want to meet any similar creature alone in a dark tunnel. It had been a long time since he'd cared about dying. But the possibility that Aina might be waiting for him had changed that.

The rocks scratched as he pushed through the tight passage. It was slow work, and he had to stop to get his breath a few times, but eventually the passage widened enough for him to walk without further shredding his shirt.

The lamp didn't really help; it distracted him from using the little magic he had, so when he reached the first fork in the passage, he placed it on the ground as a marker for when he returned, and he felt his way along in the darkness.

The rock magic he'd once learnt had permanently altered his vision, especially his night vision. He'd noticed the difference between himself and the other men. Perhaps the slight return of magic would improve it again, but he soon realized he was not seeing at all, but sensing the presence or absence of rocks and their location.

Even so, he didn't sense the thing that hit him in his face. It was an effort not to cry out as it scuttled along his arm. The cockroach was the size of his hand, and he knocked it to the ground in disgust, then desperately kicked it away when it tried to crawl up his leg. He continued in the darkness, a little upset with himself at being so easily shocked by a roach.

The tunnel turned sharply, opening into a large cave. Two tunnels left the cave: one smelt stale; a fresher breeze came from the other. Thomas breathed in the air of the second tunnel with rising excitement. He'd found what he was looking for, or at least, this tunnel led somewhere interesting. What he didn't know was whether it would lead to an upward shaft with a downdraft, or whether it would lead deeper into the planet. Either would be worth exploring, but time was short. Bots would soon come to investigate.

"Just a little longer," he said to himself. He mentally reached into the rocks, feeling their small vibrations. A part of his mind travelled deeper down the tunnel, following a micro-fault along the roof. It twisted and turned a few times, then he entered a larger tunnel—deeper than any of the others. Leaving his body far behind, his conscious mind descended deep into the planet until he came to an open plain. A wet wind blew against his face, and a black bird perched on a fungal tree. Slowly he relaxed and reentered his body. Then he quickly returned to his friends.

4

Lucy left the cell and followed the other women along the passage to the hole in the floor. The prized work was in the imperial laundry, but she preferred the dirt of the farm; it was closer to nature, and she could be alone with her thoughts. More importantly, she could be away from the other prisoners. The women's section of the prison was controlled by a gang that reminded her of a pack of wild animals, with its own pecking order. She was outside the pack and had no wish to join.

Lucy climbed down the ladder within the shaft. It was an easy, if tedious, climb, and twenty minutes later she reached the damp ground of the fungus farm. The partially lit chambers were humid, and the smell of mushrooms was strong. The walk to the outer parts of the farm took more than half an hour, and she was surprised to see Maggie Green, the pack leader, with some of her friends following her. None of these women worked the farm. Even the lowest in her gang fought for positions close to the shaft to avoid carrying baskets of mushrooms from the deepest parts of the underground farm; the part Lucy preferred.

As she walked deeper into the farm, Lucy pushed thoughts of the gang out of her mind, assuming they had some business there; perhaps they'd received the punishment they deserved.

Instead she thought about her life. It'd not worked out as she'd wished. She was trapped with nowhere to go. Despite retaining her natural magic, she couldn't easily escape, and if she did, she didn't know what she'd do. There had been talk of invasion when she'd been arrested in Silva —perhaps it'd already happened.

With regret, she remembered how she'd persuaded herself and Thomas to donate the cup and pentacle, the Spirit Keys, to the Silvan Museum. She couldn't believe that she'd taken advantage of Thomas while he was still grieving over Aina and given possibly the most powerful magical objects in the world to a museum. She knew he'd blamed himself for Aina's death. She sensed that he still did. What else would explain the heaviness she felt around him? She sensed his presence, but in his depression, he'd blocked his own magic, and despite her efforts, he was closed to all communication. How wrong she'd been in her hopes that the world had become a better place. She focussed again on the farm around her.

The pack was still watching her, but she ignored them. They'd never follow her to the edges of the farm. Again, she turned inward. *"I need a sign,"* she said to anyone who could hear, but there was no one who could. She missed the tarot cards she'd lost in Silva. They'd connected her to a much bigger world. Perhaps she didn't need them; perhaps she could speak directly. Focussing her thoughts, she spoke the True Language to the Universe: *"Give me a sign; show me the best way forward."*

The ground was softer here, and she moved more carefully, not wishing to slip. Noticing something on the ground, she bent down and picked up a clump of unusual white spores. They were different from the usual mushroom spores. Anything natural was rare here, so she put it in her pocket to study later—perhaps she could grow it in her cell.

Hearing something, she turned and was surprised to see the pack had followed her into the final chamber of the farm. Nine of them in all, but they were clustered by the entrance, about thirty yards away—too far to have made the sound she'd heard. Turning back, she continued walking away from them when she heard it again. It was coming from the furthest corner, the place where she'd found a disused shaft three days before. She listened.

As she walked quietly towards the disused shaft, everything was quiet. Perhaps it had been nothing. Feeling nervous, she leant over the dark shaft, telling herself that if there was anything there, she would have sensed it. When an animal hissed in the darkness behind her, she cursed her foolishness.

Panic rose inside her as the familiar, bitter smell reached her nose, but she knew she had to remain calm if she was to have any chance of leaving this corner of the farm alive. She slowly turned and looked up at the dark shadow. The ice demon looked down at her. "What do you want?" Lucy asked.

"You," it whispered.

That was not the answer she wanted. She was trapped and alone with one of the most dangerous creatures in the nine planets and felt foolish to have walked into this trap—and without a weapon. Not that many weapons would stop one of these. "Why?"

"I am alone."

Again, this was not the reply she'd expected. "Explain,"

she said. And when she did, she felt the mental pressure of the ice demon press against her. It wanted to speak in the True Language. As she pushed back, she felt its pain, and for a moment she was almost overwhelmed. Empathy had its benefits, but sometimes barriers had to be established, and she was sure that opening herself to the emotions of a reptile bred to kill was not wise. But she realized that many things she'd done in her life were not wise.

Her intuition told her to make contact, and she did. As the creature's pain washed over her, Lucy cried. Her disgust at the murder and devouring of young demons was lessened when she understood the reasons. But cannibalism was still cannibalism.

"You saved my life," it said. Lucy saw herself in a past time with Aina in the Tower. This was the unconscious reptile she'd persuaded Aina to let live. *"I am Chloris."* Lucy could hardly believe this was happening. Then the ice demon surprised her again. Flashes of Chloris's encounter with Thomas flooded her mind. *"Your friend?"*

Lucy nodded. *"Aren't you hunted?"* she asked.

"I hunt the hunters. I was made for special work."

Perhaps she had an excuse for not hearing the creature. *"Who are the hunters?"* Lucy asked. She already knew that all the ice demons employed in the Tower were part of an elite group.

"My kind who hunt me for their imperial masters. Come with me."

"Where?" Lucy asked.

"To the surface of the planet. I know secret ways."

"Why me?" Lucy asked.

"You're the Bright One. I remembered you when I was alone. You saved me." Lucy remembered the prone and injured ice demon in the Tower. She'd hardly thought of it that way.

"And you're different. You see what I am, and you forgive." Lucy was stunned. This dangerous demon stood before her asking for friendship, and possibly seeking redemption through her. Was this even possible? The demon's revelations had shocked her, but she'd seen worse. And it was true that she didn't shun her for them.

"Is there life in the tunnels and shafts leading to the surface?" Lucy asked. She wanted to change the direction of the conversation until she'd had time to think about what she'd heard. *"Wouldn't we starve?"*

"The way is hard, but I'm more dangerous than the humans and animals there, and I can find food." Lucy absolutely believed her. But she shook her head. What sort of life would it be on the run with an ice demon? *"Your friend wants to go deeper."* Chloris seemed nervous she might agree with Thomas, and Lucy didn't want a nervous ice demon next to her. Chloris shared Thomas's dream of the black dragon. *"But we don't need to go where it wants. The dragons have their own motives for wanting this."*

"What the dragon wants can't be," Lucy said. *"He gave Thomas false hope."* Chloris lightly hissed her approval, but Lucy had returned to her memories of the day of Aina's death. She'd been with Aina when she'd died, and the dead did not just return to the world of the living.

"Humans come!" Chloris faded into the shadows behind her.

Lucy's heart sank as she watched the seven figures approach. She searched for the other two and saw them standing by the section entrance. She had no time for this kind of conflict; she had more important things to do with her life. Helping Thomas was one of those things. But most importantly, she knew her future was no longer in this prison. It was as if she'd just woken up from a deep sleep.

Maggie Green and six others formed a semicircle around her. Behind Lucy was the side of the shaft, which rose about three feet from the ground. In the distance, she saw the silhouettes of the other two women keeping guard by the entrance to this section. A natural empath, and strengthened by her magic, she clearly felt their sickness. A cloud of spite clung to Green, and sadly, Lucy realized there was no good ending. At one time in her life she would have tried talk, but their intention was murderous.

"Hello," she said, glancing to the tools and blades they carried. As they laughed, Lucy felt a loose rock on the side of the shaft behind her. She pulled it free and held it tightly. She knew she wasn't a fighter, but she was determined to defend herself. Both Aina and Thomas could really fight— she'd watched them many times, and they'd patiently taught her the basics of fighting. She imagined them standing by her now, ready to help. Tears came to her eyes as she remembered the lost companionship, but feeling their presence gave her more confidence. They would fight to the death.

"The Orange Witch is scared," Green said, grinning at her followers. "Anyone want to have some fun?"

The Empire had called her by the same name, but they believed that Orange Witch to be dead. "Go and calm down," Lucy said. "We can have peace." One of the women appeared to almost consider her words, but Green's laughter brought her back in line with her sisters. When a woman reached for her chest, Lucy smashed the rock in her face.

Maggie Green's mouth hung open. "She was defenseless."

"I'm not." Lucy kicked a metal spike away from the woman's hand. Her legs felt weak, but she was determined not to show her fear.

The woman sat on the ground wiping blood and dirt from her face. "Do something!" she shouted.

"I'll . . ." Green's words were cut short when Lucy stepped on her foot and pushed the rock into her face. They fell to the ground and the women formed a circle around them. Green was strong, but Lucy was determined. Imagining Thomas and Aina supporting her and shouting advice, she managed to get her legs between Green's and then flip her over. She hit the woman again with the rock before Green knocked it away. The woman fought hard, but choked when Lucy shoved a handful of mushrooms into her mouth. When Green whimpered, Lucy let her go.

She stood and watched while the circle of women watched their leader spit the mushrooms and dirt from her mouth. Green staggered to her feet. "Kill the witch!"

"Would you mind if I joined you?" Chloris asked from behind.

"Not at all," Lucy said. As the women came closer, she spoke to them. "I'm outnumbered."

Maggie Green glared at her. "It's your problem if you don't have any friends."

Chloris hissed.

Green stared into the gloom. "What's that?"

Lucy glanced back, and she could only just make out the ice demon moving towards them, her body flattened to the ground. She knew they couldn't see the ice demon. "My friend," Lucy said.

"So what?" Green said. "There's only two of them. Let's do them now."

As they moved towards her with spikes, small blades, and stones, Chloris's tail whipped out, sending several women flying. Green ran at the ice demon, and Chloris sliced her in two. Two of the prisoners lay in impossible positions, already dead. The four remaining women limped away.

"Come to the surface with me," Chloris said.

But Lucy knew she couldn't. Not yet, at least. "I need to help Thomas first," she said, speaking aloud.

Chloris watched the retreating women. "I can kill them."

"No, I don't want more death. I want to escape, but I need to think more about it."

"Thinking too much is a human weakness," Chloris said. "Just act. Escape now with me."

"And Thomas?"

"We can return for him."

But Lucy knew that was unlikely. They needed to escape at the same time. Lights were moving towards them; the guards were coming.

"We're wasting time, but if you want it this way, then I'll wait for you. But don't take too long." The ice demon dived into the old shaft and was gone.

Lucy stood in the bright light of the farm's main hall, facing her accusers.

"The Orange Witch killed them!" a woman shouted. "And a monster." She was one of the four who had limped away from the corner of the mushroom farm.

Two blue bots hovered above. Lucy knew they scanned their tags. They'd replay the incident through the eyes of the women. A bot hovered before her. "Untagged," it said. Her accusers stared at her with wide eyes.

"That's impossible," the woman said.

"She's Silvan," one guard said to another. That explained

her lack of tag to them, but not to the women who had probably never heard of the small country.

"I don't think she's capable of doing this," another guard said. "What really happened?"

"A monster," the woman said.

The guards watched a small screen on the side of a bot intently. Lucy sensed their nervousness; they seemed to recognize it. "It came out of the darkness," Lucy said.

One of the guards glanced behind himself into the recesses of the dimly lit farm. "There's not much we can do here. The spiders will report back." The other guards nodded. None of them were comfortable with what had happened.

"It's the witch," a woman said. "She's responsible."

The guard shook his head. "There's no such thing as witches." Speaking to the other guard, he said, "They can't stay here," before facing Lucy and the other woman. "We're moving you both to different blocks. We don't want you upsetting the prisoners."

Forty minutes later, Lucy was descending to a deeper level without a single regret at not returning to her previous cell. She followed the guards along the passage while women watched her from behind their bars. The cell they stopped outside stank, and Lucy prayed that they had stopped for another reason. Seconds later, the door opened; she took a breath and stepped inside. Objecting was not an option. The door closed behind her. Two women watched her from a rotten mattress in the corner. A stained sheet partially covered them.

"Dix's got a new friend," the woman in the cell opposite said. Lucy's stomach sank. Polly Dix, if it was her, was notorious. She wondered if she should have gone with Chloris, but it was too late for that. Apart from the stinking mattress, there were two bunks carved into the rock. She took the one furthest from the women.

"That belongs to me. You sleep on the floor."

Lucy threw a few pieces of rotten clothing to the floor. "It's empty." She sat on the bunk and waited for the inevitable, but the woman was half-dressed and fumbled with her clothes.

While she waited, Lucy ran her hand along the stone bed she planned to keep. It was dirty from lack of use, but it was natural dirt from the rocks, which she didn't mind—the stink of the lovers' mattress was something else. She'd already sensed the life crawling inside it.

"Are you grinning?" the woman said.

Lucy had no idea. Perhaps she'd smiled at the thought of telling the mites and bugs to bite the women. She focussed on her natural magic instead.

"What's your name?" Lucy asked as the woman walked towards her.

"What's that to you?"

"Just being friendly," Lucy said, without any feeling of warmth whatsoever.

"Friendly, is it?"

"My name's Lucy." She still hoped to stall the inevitable confrontation.

"Lucy, that's a sweet name. I'm Polly Dix." She stood in front of Lucy's bunk. The woman on the mattress made a strange sucking sound. Lucy assumed she was simple. "She's Smalls. You can have her if you're good." She looked down at Lucy. "Stand up!"

"I'm happy here," Lucy said.

"I didn't ask if you were happy!" Lucy tensed as Dix tussled her hair and touched her face. "Soft and white." Dix and Smalls were green, of course—like most in the Empire.

Lucy was calm by nature, and she waited to see where this would go. She looked at the large face, inches from hers, as it examined her. She knew she was not reacting as Dix had expected. Dix rubbed her cheek. That was enough. Lucy stood.

"She likes it," Smalls said.

Lucy didn't want to be caught sitting in any conflict. The soles of her feet itched as energy trickled into her. If only she could call a fraction of what she'd once had when she'd held the cup, it would be enough. If not, she'd have to use her wits, as she'd done so far, and her strength, which might just match this woman's.

When Polly Dix caressed Lucy's breast, Smalls whistled. But Dix stopped smiling. Lucy had touched the woman's mind. It was toxic, but she persisted. The woman couldn't speak the True Language, but her mind was open to suggestion.

Lucy delved deeper to where Dix kept her fears, and then she showed the woman the face of a roc. The bright bird's eyes pierced the woman's mind, and Lucy added their strong but not unpleasant scent. No more than a handful of humans would know what it was, and Dix certainly didn't. She let go of Lucy and moved back in horror. "You're a witch."

"What's wrong, Pol?" Smalls asked. Dix staggered back to her dirty mattress and sat down. "What's she done to you?" Smalls put her arms around the woman and glared at Lucy.

Lucy absently watched them, but her mind was elsewhere. When she'd shown Dix the image, she'd felt a surge of power separate from her natural magic. She was sure something significant had caused this, but she had no idea what. Now, she wanted to test it more fully. She not only listened with her ears, but with her inner ear, and she heard the murmurings of True Language being unconsciously spoken throughout the prison.

Images and emotions from the two women washed around her, but she tuned them out as the rocs had once taught her. She avoided Dix's toxic thoughts and Small's stupidity, instead listening for life. She noticed a line of fire ants crawling along a bar in the door of the cell and some kinds of simple plants, almost invisible to the naked eye. Then her mind pushed further, expanding beyond its confines.

She hardly noticed the prison lights turn off. An image appeared quickly. She sat up straight, sweating and shocked but alert, as she focussed on the mental picture. A dark figure moved towards her, and she recognized his magic. He carried the Keys, the magical weapons she'd left in the museum. She understood: the surge of magic she'd experienced was the power leaking from the objects this man bore.

Taking a deep breath, she calmed herself. Whoever this man was, he was close, and if he carried the Keys, he was dangerous. She knew that if she tried to see the bearer, he might in turn see her. But only if he possessed magic. It was hard to believe he didn't, not when he carried objects of such power. She hesitated, not knowing what he would do if he saw her, but the risk of not looking was higher. She closed her eyes and concentrated on the cup that had once been hers. It called her, and she was drawn to it like a moth to fire.

But something else watched her in the darkness—and it wasn't human. Its vertical green irises glowed with magic. She gasped and broke contact. Lucy leant against the wall of the cell, shivering despite the heat. She was tired, but the magic burnt inside her. She'd asked for a sign, something to help her decide what to do, and the Universe had answered twice: with Chloris, and the creature bearing the Keys.

She remembered the prophecy and Aina's words: "The Bright Ones shall descend to the inner sun, where their strength shall be tested and forged in fire." She knew what she had to do: retake the Keys and descend to the centre of the planet to take the Fire.

"Thomas!" She called several times before she felt his presence.

"Lucy?"

She breathed out in relief at having finally contacted him. They spoke briefly of Chloris and magic, but before she could speak of her decision, Thomas continued. *"I've found a way out."* He told her of the passage. *"It leads to an underground world."*

"Is there life?" she asked.

"I saw a bird in a tree." Then he was quiet for several seconds. *"And I've been dreaming of Aina. She's waiting for me in the centre of the planet."*

She sighed quietly. *"Do you believe it?"*

"I don't know. I mean, I held her when she died."

She sensed the conflict within him: he still hoped for the impossible. Lucy believed in reincarnation—but even for her, and she believed in really strange things, being reborn fully formed, as in a previous life, was impossible.

His hope in the impossible upset her, but the thought of destroying his hope upset her more. He described the dream Chloris had shared with her. Then she spoke. *"We must complete our part in the prophecy."*

"Chloris says that the dragon isn't to be trusted, that it wants something from us."

"That could be, but we must travel to the centre of Prometheus and take the Fire, anyway," Lucy said.

"Do you think the dragon is only showing me images of Aina to make me want to go?"

"Perhaps, but Aina wanted us to complete our part in the prophecy."

"You're forgetting one thing," Thomas said. "We don't have the Keys. Without them, we could never travel there. Our natural magic isn't enough, we need the Keys."

"The Keys are moving towards us," she said, feeling his surprise.

"What?"

"I've felt them; their magical signature is unique." She described the reptilian eyes bright with magic.

"So it's not human?"

"No." She shivered at the thought of the eyes she'd seen. "And it's seen me."

5

Thomas sat in his cell, gazing at the fragments of crystals glittering beneath his fingernails as the men gossiped about the latest killing, but his thoughts were neither on rocks nor death. It was two days since he'd spoken to Lucy, but her words had stayed with him. He knew she didn't believe Aina could be alive—not in this world. But he wanted to believe it, even if the dragon's words were impossible, or even if, as Chloris had said, dragons acted for their own reasons.

Since the magic had stirred, he wanted to take action. Although the prophecy, purported to be true by the black dragon, didn't interest him, avenging Aina's death did. And retaking the Keys would make that much easier.

"Your girlfriend's been busy," Victor said.

He knew the ice demon would happily kill humans for food, but he didn't think the latest killings were her work. They were too finicky: organs laid out in particular ways, parts eaten and parts not. Ice demons were not fussy eaters. His gut told him it was the creature in the mines. Perhaps the same one Lucy had seen in her vision.

"She's got to eat."

Victor shook his head. "What would you do if you met it in a dark tunnel? It might not be so friendly next time. Or do you think you have a special relationship?"

"Ice demons kill to eat, but they're not fussy—you saw that yourself. They don't impale victims on rocks and eat them alive; they don't lay out the entrails. That's not their style."

Victor was watching him carefully. "The ice demon we saw wasn't a finicky eater, I agree with that, and you seem sure of yourself, but if you're right, our situation is worse. That means we have two monsters hunting in the tunnels."

"Yes."

Victor became subdued at the thought. "But why now?" he asked quietly. As he spoke, Thomas felt another surge in his power. The magic had returned with strength. "Are you okay?"

"I think something bad's going to happen." Thomas held out his hands and stared at them.

"You're shaking," Victor said. "Are you ill?" Thomas heard concern in Victor's voice.

"Someone's coming."

Victor stood and looked down the passage. Seconds later a whisper rushed along from cell to cell. Victor turned and looked at Thomas. "How did you know?"

Thomas shrugged. "A lucky guess." He leant back against the wall, and again he rubbed the fragments of dust and rock. This time he infused them with power, watching them coalesce in his fingers.

Another whisper came, but it was clear enough for both to hear: "The governor."

Victor's skin turned to a paler shade of green at the words. He looked nervous. Surely a visit from the governor was no worse than a visit from the guards. "What's happened between you and the governor?"

At first, Thomas thought he wasn't going to speak. But then he looked up. "I knew him a long time ago. We were both exiled."

"You must have upset someone a lot." Victor didn't answer, and Thomas wondered whether this visit was about Victor, himself, or something else.

Four guards marched in a square. In the centre walked two cloaked men: the governor wore black, the other—a knight of the Imperial Order—wore crimson. A black attack bot flew a few yards behind the tight formation.

"Stand for Governor Hardy!" a sergeant ordered. All prisoners stood.

The governor smiled coldly at Victor. "Baron San's been my guest for a long time." The man in a crimson cloak waited impassively. "How are you enjoying Min Flo?"

"After my previous life, solitude suits me, Baronet Hardy," Victor said.

The governor watched him, his eyes cold. "I doubt it. And I'm Governor Hardy here."

Thomas studied the man in the crimson cloak. He was shielding himself, but Thomas felt magic around him. Although he heard the conversation between Victor and the governor, and he wasn't really surprised by the old man's previous rank—most politicians were members of the aristocracy—he continued to focus his attention on the crimson knight.

"So you've come to pay a visit after all these years, Governor Hardy."

"No. I have other business today." The governor turned to the figure in crimson. "Is he the one?" He gestured to Victor.

The man in crimson shook his head and pointed at Thomas. "I want him." Thomas tried to make out the man's face, but the hood hid his features. The accent was strange.

"I don't know why Imperial Intelligence wants a common criminal," the governor said. "Scan him," he ordered the sergeant.

The sergeant pointed a device at him, then shook his head. "He's untagged, Governor." The other prisoners watched him.

"Ah, Silvan Resistance," the governor said.

"Possibly, Governor," the sergeant said. "A few hundred protesters were arrested in Silva about a year ago. Prior to the crackdown, Governor."

"The Empire was more merciful in those days, Sergeant." The guard nodded nervously, and the governor turned back to Thomas. "Welcome to the Empire." Thomas felt sick. Was it true? Had the Empire annexed his adopted country—Aina's home? If they had discovered his previous role in the Resistance, he would soon be dead.

"I wish to speak to him alone," the crimson knight hissed. There was something familiar about the accent.

"What's this about?" Victor whispered. Thomas shook his head; he wasn't sure.

When the governor ordered the guards to step away, the crimson knight again said, "Alone." The governor nodded curtly and joined his men. The bot hovered several yards to the other side.

Magic flowed from the knight towards Thomas, probing him. He stood by the bars, feeling a little strange. Moving closer, the crimson knight raised a hand, revealing a patch of skin. It was scaled and mottled in green and grey.

"Thomas!" Lucy was with him.

"Lucy, it's a basilisk." He allowed her into his mind.

She saw through his eyes and felt through his body. *"The basilisk has the Keys,"* she said. *"Kill it and retake them."*

He was surprised at her vehemence. *"I know, but how?"*

"I don't care!"

"Tell me about the Keys."

Thomas sensed the desire in its voice, but what was the motivation? *"It has the Keys. What does it want?"* Thomas asked Lucy.

"I only feel its greed," she whispered.

"You were once a bearer."

"Pass them to me, and I'll demonstrate," Thomas said.

"That would be a mistake, but I can improve your life here." Victor was looking at the basilisk wide-eyed as it rattled under its hood.

"He's lying," Lucy said.

"Naturally." Thomas studied the three strands of magic radiating from the crimson knight: its native magic, the black magic of the Empire, and the magic of the Keys—the pentacle and cup. Quietly, he drew the loose strands of the pentacle's magic into himself. The knight didn't seem to notice. Thomas gasped. Looking closely, he saw the crystals under his nails had grown. He pulled them out and watched as they grew. The dirt was unaffected, but the tiny crystals were growing fast—his fingertips were bleeding.

"Thomas, your fingers?"

"They're okay." They'd stopped hurting; he rubbed the crystals between his fingers.

"Sir Val, do you require assistance?" the governor asked.

Ignoring the governor, the knight took a step closer to the bars. "Tell me what you know."

"What exactly do you want to know?" Thomas asked. He needed more time to loosen the strands of magic. He felt the basilisk's native magic tighten around his throat, but pulling a single strand of magic from the pentacle relieved the pain.

Thomas pretended to choke. "Are you all right?" Victor asked.

Gaining confidence, the knight stepped closer. "How could a human use basilisk magic?" It called the magic of the Keys basilisk magic, as the high priest of the Black Nest once had.

"It wants the magic for itself," Lucy whispered, *"but it doesn't know how to use it."*

Thomas could see it clearly now; it wasn't drawing on the magic of the Keys at all.

"Draw the power into yourself," Lucy whispered in his mind. *"It doesn't understand its danger."*

"I'm trying, but it's tangled," Thomas said.

"Who is this prisoner, Sir Val?" the governor asked, shifting restlessly eight or nine yards away. "What do you want from him?"

"What I want is a matter for the Empire," Sir Val said. "My orders come from the highest levels."

"He's lying," Lucy said.

The idea that an imperial knight and basilisk lied was hardly surprising—and Thomas trusted Lucy's intuition—but why lie to the governor?

Sir Val now stood next to the bars. Thomas wanted to reach into the knight's robe and take the Keys, but its magic pushed hard against him, giving him a headache. Its hooded head was inches from his, and its energy pushed harder. But just as he would sidestep a punch, he turned its two magics away, pulling on the power of the pentacle. The deflected magic rushed past him into the stone wall above Victor's bed, sending a cloud of dust into the air. The stone had grounded the magic. He heard Victor gasp from the back of the cell, but he had no time to turn to him.

Sir Val belatedly attempted to block the power of the Keys; perhaps the knight hadn't considered that they would attempt to reach out to him. Fragments of magic forced their way through the magic shield Val had hastily constructed and slowly trickled into Thomas. He sensed that a further stream flowed towards Lucy.

Probably unconsciously feeling its toxic magic, the guards and governor edged away. Thomas sensed its confusion and frustration. Sweat poured heavily down his back as the basilisk's magic pushed into him, and as he was compelled to allow it access to certain parts of his mind, he, too, gained access to parts of its mind.

As Thomas directed it away from sensitive memories, he himself sought answers in its mind. Lucy was right, it didn't know how to use the Keys, but he found more: the basilisk was frightened. It had travelled to the prison, unsure if he even lived, in search of knowledge. But why the fear?

Thomas felt Lucy gently pushing deeper into its mind. *"Thomas, it's terrified of something very powerful."*

When it magically attacked him again, he stepped back in surprise. He'd been overconfident. It was stronger than he'd thought, but when the magic of the pentacle flowed around him again, protecting him, he breathed out in relief. It was using the black magic of the Empire and not its native magic—a mistake that weakened it.

Sir Val's attack paused. Thomas knew it wondered why its attack had not had more effect. Drawing more power from the hidden key, Thomas tried to take the pentacle. It roared wildly, but he lacked a reliable way to transform the raw magic into physical power. It had been too long since he'd wielded such magic. His power surged intermittently and then was reduced to a drip.

Again, the power of the pentacle swelled and pushed aside the basilisk's magical block. Thomas raised his hand towards the knight, power flowing freely. Realizing something was wrong, the basilisk began fighting harder, but Thomas struck the knight with invisible magic. The crimson knight was caught off guard and flew to the floor on the far side of the passage. The governor, guards, and prisoners stared at Thomas and the prone knight with their mouths open.

"What happened?" the governor asked.

No one answered. Thomas tried desperately to regain the connection he'd had to the pentacle, but his power once again only came in tiny spurts.

"I've just had an idea . . ." he heard Lucy say as her voice faded. He felt himself alone in his mind again, but before she'd left, she'd shared an image. He smiled to himself. "Thank you, Lucy," he said quietly.

Remembering the crystals he'd grown, Thomas focussed his magic on the fragments still in his hand. They shone in the dim light, and he gently rubbed them against the metal bars of the door. Questions and threats sounded around him, but he thought only of the energy that pulsed through his fingers and into the crystals. The rocks and earth had once been his friends and had responded to his calls. He called on them again.

A guardsman crouched down and pulled back the knight's hood. He fell back into the wall with a curse. Mouths open, everyone stared at the serpent man. It had only slits for ears, and its mottled grey and green skin was glossy and heavily tattooed with magical symbols. Only Thomas was unsurprised.

"What's that?" the governor said. His hard face crinkled in disgust.

"A basilisk," Thomas said, grinning as he tried again to draw power from the pentacle, hoping to take advantage of its loss of consciousness. Some of that power flowed around the half-broken magical shield the basilisk had tried to use to protect itself. Thomas fed this energy into the quietly growing crystals beneath his fingers.

Its eyes opened, revealing a pair of vertical irises. Hissing at the humans, it stood unsteadily on its feet. A tail dropped from its dishevelled robe. Its forked tongue flicked from its mouth as it tried to block his access to the magic. Slowly, Thomas's power was reduced to a small but steady flow, which he fed into the crystal garden beneath his fingers.

"You should ask it whether it serves the Empire," Thomas said, still hoping to gain more time.

"Do you?" Governor Hardy asked. "Do you serve the Empire?"

"I'm Sir Val, Knight of the Empire." Then it pointed a long green finger at Thomas. "Kill him!" When no one obeyed, the basilisk drew a gun from its cloak.

"You may or may not be a knight of the Empire, but you're not the governor of this prison. Only I issue orders here." The guards pointed their weapons at the knight, and it lowered its gun.

"Fool!" Sir Val hissed. "Kill him!"

"He's not going anywhere," Governor Hardy said. "If he was, he'd have gone by now. But I intend to learn what's happening here. And I have my own ways of learning the truth."

Thomas knew those ways, and he continued to rub the crystals onto the iron bars. Many of them stuck to the metal and glowed faintly. A guard was watching him. "Governor, the prisoner's doing something strange."

The governor snatched an electric baton from the guard and struck Thomas's hand with it, but the electric shock merged with his magic and added to his strength. The tiny crystal garden grew around Thomas's fingers, and the green and orange growths were spreading along the surface of the metal bars. The governor struck him repeatedly. Each time, Thomas transformed pain into power. No one understood what he was doing.

The governor tossed the stick back to the guard with a complaint and snatched a longer, non-electric one. The governor grasped a metal bar to steady himself, and the tiny crystal growths touched his fingers. "That's better," he said when Thomas stepped back. When Governor Hardy scratched his face, the crystal growths spread to his cheek.

"We're going to escape," Thomas said to Victor. "Attach your leg." Victor stared with wide eyes at his cellmate. Thomas grinned. "We learn something new about each other every day, Baron San."

"Who is he?" the governor said. "It's impossible to take that pain." He was breathing heavily and sweating from the beatings he'd given to Thomas. For the first time, he appeared disconcerted.

"You must kill him!" Sir Val said, staring at the crystal growths that now covered about a third of the iron bars.

It was time. "Root," Thomas said aloud and in the True Language to the growing crystals. He was vaguely aware of Victor and the others staring at him in horror, but his attention was on the crystals. As simple as they were, they did possess a basic intelligence, and they rooted into the governor's arm and face. The governor dropped the baton and screamed. Crystals pierced and burrowed into his skin. As more growths sped along his hands, guards pulled him away from the bars. He screamed as pieces of his skin were left hanging from the door.

"What have you done to me?" the governor cried, falling to the floor.

His face was flushed, and he was breathing heavily. He stared at his crystalline hand, and when he touched his face and neck with his other hand, he moaned. The guards had moved away from him. Even Thomas was disturbed by the man's appearance. His screaming continued as green, orange, and red crystal flowers sprouted from his cheeks. When a crystal spike grew from his eye socket like a fruit tree with his burst eyeball on its branches, he lost consciousness.

Sir Val fled. Three other guards stared in horror and confusion while a fourth sat on the floor trying to stop the crystals sprouting from his arm. The others watched the crystal garden grow from the governor's head and neck. Long blue blooms now broke from his skin, and wherever he bled, fresh flowers grew in sudden spurts.

Thomas kicked the bars and the brittle metal shattered, sending a cloud of dust into the air. The black attack bot that had been waiting for orders flew directly at him and into the cloud. Thomas again spoke to the crystals as they attached themselves to the bot.

It quivered in the air, then crashed into the remaining bars of the door. The crystals had blinded it. Slowly, it sank to the ground. Thomas stepped into the passage and snapped a crystal growth from the dying governor's chest. "Do you like flowers?" he asked the three guards. He offered them the single blue bloom, and they fled.

"What about me?" the remaining guard asked.

Thomas looked at the man, but it was too late for him.

He took the pistol from the governor's body and shot the man. Nigel looked at him in shock. "He was dying. This way's better."

"What the hell just happened?" Victor asked.

"We're escaping," Thomas said. "Get the other pistol."

"I'm not sure I want to," Victor said, eyes wide at the scene in front of him. "Escape to where?"

"Hell, probably."

"What did you do?" Victor repeated.

"Rock magic," Thomas said.

Victor shook his head. His team and the other prisoners watched him warily. "They're scared of you," Victor said.

Thomas saw another bot flying fast along the tunnel. "They're going to feel worse in a few seconds. Victor, stand back." When the old man moved back, he kicked the governor's body.

"What—" Victor began.

Thomas prayed his timing would be right; the bot was getting closer. The governor's chest shattered, sending a crystal cloud into the air. "Surrender!" the bot ordered.

Thomas raised his hands and slowly stepped backwards towards his old cell. The bot decelerated and flew straight through the cloud. Particles stuck to its metallic skin and grew fast; soon crystals sprouted from the machine. It crashed into the glowing crystal wall and slowly fell to the ground, becoming a part of the growing crystal garden.

Thomas bent down and snapped off the governor's head. He held it up by the grassy spikes that grew from the top of the skull. The governor's face was covered in small crystal flowers.

"A souvenir?" Victor asked.

Thomas gave him a cold grin. "It may be useful." He pocketed the man's hand, too. Thomas looked around to the other prisoners and held the head for all to see. "Does anyone wish to join me?"

With eyes wide, they stared at the head, but no one spoke, apart from Jackson, who cleared his throat before saying, "That's something I never expected to see, but I'm staying here. They're going to have everything they have hunting you. Nothing good will come of this."

Thomas nodded, looking to Victor. He knew that, being Thomas's cellmate, this would be a death sentence for him, even though it was Thomas's doing.

Victor did not look enthusiastic as he said, "I was almost killed for what I saw; they sent me here instead. They'd kill me just for knowing you. They'd assume I knew your plans." Victor nodded to the colourful crystal garden growing in their cell. "That's if these things didn't kill me first." The crystals had made it too dangerous to stay.

"Then it's the baron and me."

"Whoever you are," Victor muttered. He gingerly stepped over the remains of the governor.

Ivan looked as if he were going to cry. He stared at Thomas and Victor. Thomas guessed that the boy had no other family, but he was glad he hadn't volunteered; he didn't want the responsibility of looking after him in an escape like this.

Thomas and Victor ran down the passage in the direction the basilisk had gone, and away from the team they'd worked with for the past year. Thomas swore that if he lived, he'd return to free these men.

Victor could move surprisingly fast on his artificial leg, and he did so now, clacking along the passage, past men in cells who he recognized but hadn't spoken to.

"We have a problem," Thomas said. A group of gangers stood in the passage, pointing at them.

"Already?" Victor said sarcastically. Thomas noticed that his pistol was in his hand.

Still holding a pistol in one hand and the head in the other, Thomas looked around for a way out, hoping the basilisk hadn't taken a lift. "We can't take a lift." The artificially intelligent lifts would immediately trap them.

"We'll have to use the old system of shafts," Victor said.

"You're a natural climbing down those, like a monkey swinging from rung to rung."

Victor frowned. "I'll have to be."

A few blooms of tropical colours had followed them, but otherwise, the prison here was normal. Waiting for them in a central chamber, the gangers watched them approach.

"You're not allowed here," a man said. Thomas had never been here before. The cells were larger and more comfortable; some had women inside. The man blocked their way. "This area isn't for prisoners."

"You're prisoners, whatever you think," Victor said.

The man shoved Victor, and Thomas pushed the governor's crystal head in his face. The men backed off.

"We're just passing through," Thomas said.

The group made way for gang boss Drew Walker. His enforcer, Fulk, stood by him.

The ganger boss looked at the head. "What's that?"

Thomas held it up by its grassy crystal hair. "The governor's head." When the man didn't move, Thomas slipped his gun into his pocket and snapped a strand of hair from the head. He stabbed at the boss.

Walker jumped back just in time. "You're dead."

Thomas jabbed again, forcing the man further back. "No time to chat."

"Bot," Victor said.

Another black bot flew from a hatch high in the wall. Its

red eye-like lights were on, and it dropped towards them. The gangers quickly fell back.

Thomas threw the governor's head at the bot, hitting it directly. The head exploded into a cloud of dust. The bot flew into the wall where it fired, and bullets ricocheted around the tunnel. It flew erratically along the tunnel wall, slowly getting closer.

"Surrender before you get us killed!" a ganger shouted.

Thomas took out his pistol and shot the injured bot. It fell slowly to the ground. He grinned at the startled ganger, then moved back along the tunnel.

"Where are you going?" Drew Walker said.

"Escaping."

"No one escapes." But no one tried to stop them. "Fools. They can switch on your tags and read your minds. They'll know where you are every step of the way," Drew Walker said.

"Lucky we're not tagged then," Thomas said quietly. Victor nodded. They ran away from the main area with the lifts towards the older part of the mine and the old shafts, moving quickly through forbidden parts of the prison. The governor's hand came in useful, opening and shutting many of the security doors—luckily, only the back of the hand had transformed to crystal.

"This way," Thomas said. The basilisk was still in the prison, and it still fed him with magic, making the route it had taken clear.

"It leads to the old shaft," Victor said. Thomas nodded. The old man had spent decades inside, and he knew the tunnels better than almost anyone. They ran faster along the dark, dusty, and disused tunnel.

6

Lucy watched a mouse run across the dirty floor and out of the bars. She, too, wanted to leave, but running with an ice demon did not seem the way to go. Taking the white spore from her pocket, she brought it close to her face and studied it. *"What are you?"* she whispered. Her vision altered, and she wondered whether it had hallucinogenic properties and whether she should put it back in her pocket. Then an image of a white web appeared. Seconds later it vanished, but it had left an idea—although she was unsure where it had come from. Putting the spore back in her pocket, she closed her eyes and meditated.

For hours she sat and listened with her inner ear—open to any messages. Then she opened her eyes in shock. The magic was flowing freely. Something had happened. *"Thomas!"*

He welcomed her into his mind. Her dark cell faded as she saw through his eyes and felt through his body, almost becoming overpowered by the magic of the Keys. Blinking, she regained control, and then she saw the dark creature of her vision. The Keys were hidden beneath its clothing.

"*A basilisk*," he said.

Through his eyes, she saw the mottled green and grey skin, too. She was worried that something like this had sought them out. She watched the events unfold in Thomas's cell, and she tried to help, sharing the idea the hallucinogenic spore had given her.

Sudden pain broke the connection. She opened her eyes, blinking tears onto her stinging face. Polly Dix's fat face was inches from hers.

"Did I make you cry, darling?"

Lucy gasped for breath, and the woman sniggered. The broken telepathic contact hurt her more than the slap. Her anger with the woman was rising, but this woman's childish attack was unimportant compared to retaking the Keys.

Ignoring the woman, she closed her eyes again. Again she reached out to Thomas, and the basilisk glowed before her. She saw its mix of magic, and she slowly drew power from the golden cup. Her head snapped back as Dix slapped her a second time. Her cheek was stinging, and the connection was completely broken. Smalls cackled from her rotten mattress.

She knew it was time to go. Slipping from her bunk, Lucy pushed Dix. The woman seemed to have forgotten what had happened earlier and didn't expect her to do anything. Dix staggered backwards a few paces and glared at her. Moving to the door of the cell, Lucy took out the white spores and placed them on the metal bars. Magic was still pulsing through her, and she focussed it on the spores.

Dix and Smalls watched her, but they couldn't see what she was doing. She held the iron bars tightly and only thought of the flow of energy through her body and its effect on the spore.

A crunch from behind made her turn. Smalls had

stamped on a mouse and broken its back. She picked it up by the tail and waved it at Lucy. The stupidity of the situation and the woman angered her more than it should, but escape was still her priority.

"Ginger Witch," Smalls said.

The name, in one form or another, seemed to follow her. She turned back to the spores—they had germinated, and slender stems were growing. Lucy rubbed one between her fingers. Perhaps the women thought that she was cowed because she looked away and didn't rise to their provocation, but when something hit her in her back, making her snap a stem in her fingers, she'd had enough.

She turned, still holding the broken stem of the unknown fungus. Lucy moved the dead mouse away with her foot, and then she infused the stem with magic. "A gift."

Smalls glanced at Dix, who nodded, giving her more confidence. She stepped closer, until her face was a foot from hers. "What did you say, witch?"

"A flower." Lucy touched the stem to Smalls's face, and the stalk instantly took root in the woman's skin. Screaming, she pulled at the rooting stem, which only caused her to scream louder and let go as drops of blood ran down her cheek. Lucy was surprised at the speed of growth.

Smalls stepped back, but Dix shoved her. "Get away from me!"

"Witch!" Smalls shouted. She ran at Lucy in rage, but as she got closer, Lucy stretched out her palms and the plant on Smalls's face grew faster. Its root system spread under her skin, and above the surface it was already inches long. Smalls whimpered and ran back to her mattress.

A horrified Dix stepped back from her. "What did you do to her?"

Lucy was surprised by what she'd done, too, but not

shocked. She'd done worse when threatened. Lucy returned to the door of the cell. At least neither of the women approached her. Each of the white spores she'd placed on the metal bars had become slender stems several inches long and still growing.

Anxious that her connection with her energy source would be removed, she drew more magical energy from the cup the basilisk bore. To do so meant focussing on her power to the exclusion of all else, and that risked an attack from Dix or Smalls; she hoped she'd scared them enough to keep them away from her.

She put her hands around the white stems, creating a mini-hothouse, and her palms itched as the energy flowed. The stems pushed through her hands and spread to other bars. Soon the door had become a white fungal mass.

Strands of the mass pushed between her fingers and wrapped themselves around her fist. The fibres grew quickly along her forearm. Her hand was now hidden within a white fungal hand. She waved long fibrous fingers at Dix and Smalls, who now crouched in the deepest part of the cell and stared at her in horror.

Lucy studied the growing fibres. They appeared to follow her thoughts, so she turned her thoughts back to the bars and soon they were covered in white fibres. She pulled, and one by one they snapped until the door was no more than pieces of metal on the passage floor.

Smalls whimpered, and immediately white fibres wrapped around her ankle and grew along her leg. The woman screamed. Lucy pulled back, but the plant was strong, and its fibres wrapped around Small's neck. It was strangling her. Dix dashed past her and along the passage. Lucy tried to pull the plant off Smalls, but it only stopped when the woman was dead.

Lucy hadn't intended to kill her, but the white fungal mass that now covered her had a mind of its own—and it was a cold one. Lucy spoke to it, but its voice was distant and strange—it seemed to call her. Its communication was nothing like the simple images she'd received from flowers or trees in the past.

As she stepped into the passage, she noticed many of the prison cells were covered in white slime, and some fungal fibres were spreading from cell to cell. A few of the doors were broken, and some of the prisoners wandered in the passage, but when they saw her, they ran or hid inside their cells.

Feeling close to panic, Lucy looked down at herself. She had disappeared, and covering her body was another body, a fibrous white body that writhed around her, and hands extended from her like pale snakes. A guard ran towards her, drawing her gun. Lucy flicked out a fibre, and the gun fell to the ground. Another fibre whipped out, of its own volition, and took off the guard's head. Now covered by the fungal growth, she felt claustrophobic. She told it to leave her, but it refused; she felt sick and desperately tried to calm herself. She only had partial control. Although she was able to direct it, it defended itself aggressively, and several prisoners lay dead on the ground around her.

Enclosed in a fungal ball, she floated down the passages; it used its own fibrous legs to move like a strange white octopus. All around her, metal groaned as it was pulled away by the white fungal forest, and although much of it was physically separate from the fibrous mass around her, it was connected psychically, and it also responded to some of her wishes.

Struggling and failing to keep calm, she tried to slip out

of the fungal sphere, but as she tried to squeeze out, it tightened its grip.

"Come," it said coldly.

She struggled, but it squeezed. She screamed. Her world was now dark, and with no other choices, she waited in the heart of the giant octopus.

She no longer saw the world with her eyes, but sensed it through the fungus. She was a part of its mind and felt its body as she strode through the prison, wreaking havoc. It had already killed a dozen or more guards and prisoners.

A simple grey bot attacked, and she wrapped her arms around it. It shot off three of them, but she overwhelmed the machine, and it fell to the ground covered in white slime. She grew new arms at will.

Three of the more aggressive blue bots flew in formation along the passage towards her, and their bullets cut through her fibrous arms and legs. She whipped out in pain and anger, slamming the first bot into the second. Lasers melted her body, but she grew new arms and soon two of the bots were buried in fibres. The third attacked again, and she formed a lumpen fist with several of her strands and punched the bot into her sisters, who were growing in the shape of an open hand from the wall. The fungal fingers closed and smothered the bot.

Clouds of spores filled the passages, and they found homes in the smallest of crevices. Her pale garden glowed in the dim light. *Use it to escape*, she told herself; at least it appeared to be helping her get out.

"Down," she said in the True Language. She wanted to find Thomas, and she showed it mental images of the old shafts. It seemed to listen, moving faster along the passages. When they entered a part of the prison that was off limits to prisoners, the alarm rang.

She sensed rather than saw the old shaft ahead of her. She descended into the darkness like a spider, sending fibrous arms out to find a grip on the rough sides of the shaft. An old, partially broken ladder ran down one side, and she used that until it fell away. Then she lost her grip and tumbled down the shaft, ripping off arms and legs as she dropped.

The loss of legs and arms wasn't painful—more of a relief. But she felt panic as the speed of her descent seemed to be out of control. She desperately grasped at the sides of the shaft and more appendages were violently wrenched off. She left them hanging to the sides of the shaft above her. They had slowed her descent, and again she moved under her own control. With some relief, she climbed slowly down another section of ladder she'd found using her remaining fibrous hands. Her white fungal skin was now thinner than it had been, but she still had five arms besides her own.

Several minutes later there was a change in the air, and after several more minutes, she felt an opening in the side of the shaft. She squeezed her fungal body through the gap and was covered by red dust from the tunnel. It stuck to her, changing her outer white body pink. The fungal body stumbled on, taking her away from the shaft entrance.

"What do you want?" she asked the thing that had enclosed her.

An image of a strange forest appeared for a few seconds, and a woman with golden brown skin stood before her. Lucy sensed her magic immediately. *"Bring me the white fungus."*

"Why?"

The vision vanished and her fungal body exploded. She strained to see in the dark tunnel, aware that her clothes had fallen apart with the fungal covering. She was alone, and wearing only a thin covering of dust. Feeling too tired to care, she lay on the ground and was about to close her eyes when something moved in the darkness. Suddenly very alert, she sat up slowly and felt on the rocky floor around her for a weapon.

7

Thomas followed the magical trail through the tunnel. The only light bulb was about ten yards down the tunnel, but with eyes permanently sharpened by his previous use of magic, he needed little light to see.

He called Lucy again, but she didn't answer. He'd been debating within himself whether to go to the women's section of the prison to help her, or to follow the magical trail and retake the Keys instead. He decided that if she needed rescuing, going empty-handed would hardly help—and might make their situation worse. Ahead he saw a deeper darkness, and a cold draught of stale air came from it. As they got closer, he saw it was the entrance to a shaft. Two other tunnels converged at the same point.

"How did you find that?" Victor asked.

"A benefit of magic."

Victor didn't look convinced. "Well, somehow you've found one of very few back doors deep into the mines. I'd almost forgotten that it existed, but I don't like the feeling of this—no one's been here in years."

"There's nothing to like," Thomas said. "It's the way the basilisk went."

"Thanks for giving me confidence," Victor said. "All I need is something waiting inside to kill me." He wiped something sticky from the entrance. "What's this?"

The cracked muskin that lined the old shafts was brown; here it was completely white. Thomas rubbed it in his fingers and smelt it. "Mushrooms," he said.

Victor smelt it. "Why would an old shaft smell of mushrooms?"

Thomas looked inside the shaft and pulled out a shrivelled strand of white fibre. "It looks like this shaft has been busy. The basilisk went down, but something else has come out."

"Nothing came in our direction," Victor said.

"I know." Thomas smelt traces of magic. He walked along one of the other tunnels that radiated out from the old shaft.

"Don't you want to follow the knight?"

"I want to know what happened here first." He crouched down and picked up a blue rag. "A woman's shirt." He thought of Lucy, but was unsure—there were traces of magic that felt like hers, but there was something he didn't recognize, too.

Victor came closer. "Look. There's more." They searched the area and found shreds of clothing on the ground. "If a woman's walking around these tunnels half-dressed and she meets one of the men . . ."

"I know. I'm worried that it might be someone I know. I need to find out."

"Well, it's better than chasing a monster," Victor said.

They walked along the tunnel, and Thomas found more

of the fungal material as they went. He walked ahead, while Victor followed as fast as he could, his leg clanking on the hard ground.

"It goes back in the direction of the prison," Victor said.

Thomas had already noticed that. With a sinking feeling in his stomach, he realized it might lead to one of the gangers' sections. "If you want, you can wait for me here. I need to run." He knew Victor couldn't keep up.

"Stay here in a dark tunnel by myself with the stuff that's hunting us? I'll follow as I can."

Thomas ran down the tunnel, and Victor raced behind him. The old man could move almost as fast on his artificial leg as most prisoners could on their original legs, but Thomas was not just another prisoner; he was fit and could see in the dark.

Magic had sharpened all of his senses, and he listened as he ran. He heard voices ahead, and then a woman screamed—it was Lucy. Sprinting down the tunnel, Thomas pulled out his pistol. Far behind him, Victor's artificial leg was clacking on the hard ground; the old man was moving at a fair pace, but he was still too far behind. He'd be helping his friend alone.

FEELING around the floor for a potential weapon, Lucy edged backwards. Her fingers touched something warm and alive. She pulled her hand away and breathed deeply. This was getting worse. She turned slowly. A white orb about twice the size of her fist glowed in the darkness—the remains of the fungal creature. She touched it again, but nothing happened. For a moment, she felt like throwing it down the nearby shaft entrance, but it had helped her escape, and it might be of use again. She picked it up before turning her attention to whatever else lurked in the tunnel. She prayed it was just her imagination. The last thing she wanted to deal with was a prisoner or guard from the male section of the prison—especially without clothes.

Whatever it was in the dark tunnel shifted its position again. "Welcome," it hissed.

And she felt sudden relief. "Chloris."

"I followed you here." The ice demon approached and sniffed the glowing orb. She hopped back and hissed. "Leave it."

Although it made her uncomfortable, Lucy didn't want to leave it—it still might have a use. Men's voices came from along one of the dark tunnels, and Lucy cursed. She was relieved she'd found Chloris, but she still didn't want to meet any prisoners, and she felt around for anything that could be used for clothes; even the oldest rags would've seemed good. All she had was the white orb. She squeezed it, and it vibrated.

It pushed an image of her being covered in the fungal matter into her mind. "Not again!" she shouted.

"What?" Chloris asked.

The ice demon had been right. She dropped the orb, but it rolled towards her and stuck to her bare foot. She screamed as she felt a dampness crawl up her legs. She tried desperately to rip it off her, but it kept growing. "Get it off me!" It had stuck to her and was now rolling up her legs. Chloris sniffed it but seemed uncertain what to do. The thing had now reached her thighs and was still rising up her body.

"She's down there!" a man shouted. Several men were running towards her.

She shuddered as it ran between her legs and then around her waist and up to her belly. Chloris rubbed her leg. "May be okay," she said.

The stuff had reached her chest. *"What do you want?"* she asked it, but it just continued to spread a sticky substance over her body.

"A woman!" a man shouted. Chloris disappeared into the shadows as three men ran towards her. The men stopped and stared as they shone their torches on her. One of them made lewd remarks and the others laughed.

She stepped back and found herself stuck to the wall. When she struggled to pull away from the sticky substance, the men laughed again. Two more men walked around the corner. "She's stuck to the wall," one man said.

He touched her and pulled his finger away, now covered in the sticky stuff. "She's naked."

Pulling harder, Lucy realized that the sticky substance had hardened and was no longer sticky. She broke away from the wall and smelt her arm. It smelt like fresh muskin —the mushroom leather. She looked down at herself as the men shone their lights over her body and realized that she was clothed in muskin pants and jacket. Unfortunately, the orb had forgotten a shirt and she pulled her jacket closed. She was still barefoot.

"Where am I?" she asked.

"You're safe with us," the first man said. "We'll take care of you."

Lucy had no wish for their care; she read their intentions clearly. Chloris had disappeared, and she looked at the slightly shrunken orb, wondering whether it could become a weapon.

"Help me." She remembered her magic, and it woke. Again the fungal matter became hot. She hated it crawling

over her hand and up her arm, but she had little choice. The men now pressed closer to her. The white substance had wrapped itself around her forearm, but this time it was thick and hard—like a protective glove and arm pad.

She pressed back into the tunnel wall, partly because of the stink of the men. The first man reached for her chest, and when she pushed him away, he cried out in pain, clutching his chest where her protective white glove touched him. Blood seeped through his fingers.

As the others noticed the wound she'd inflicted on their friend, their faces darkened and they grabbed her roughly, thrusting her back into the wall. She fought, but they overpowered her. One man held her right elbow tightly and kept the fungus from touching them. "That should do it," he said.

Lucy cursed them. "After what you've done, I'll be a bit rougher," the first man said. He slapped her hard. The pain focussed her magic, and her fungal arm pad came alive.

Snakelike heads pushed out from it and looked at the men, but they'd pulled her jacket apart and didn't notice the small heads watching them. The fibrous snakes bit the man who held her. He screamed and let go, but two of the white snakes had detached and one of them had coiled around his arm. It quickly crawled up to his neck. The men watched in shock as it strangled him. But not one of them tried to help. So much for friendship, she thought. She pulled her jacket together and faced the men.

"Go now if you want to live!" She watched the second white snake crawling towards them.

"Don't tell us what to do," the first man said, pulling out a long knife.

Lucy saw the dark shadow moving towards them. It was too late for them. She called the snakes back, and she was surprised when the first one unwrapped itself from the dead man's neck and slithered across the floor towards her. The other followed. The second man made some comment, but she wasn't listening; instead, she watched with interest as the other snake heads merged back with the white substance around her arm.

The dark shadow rushed forwards. Chloris decapitated two men in one smooth motion.

The third man stared at the ice demon in terror. "Let me go! I didn't mean to hurt you." Lucy doubted that, but before she could do anything, Chloris decapitated him, too.

While Chloris fed, she used the white gauntlet and the remains of the orb to make a pair of boots, a shirt, and a bag. She put the two snakes into the bag.

Lucy was thankful for the dark—not wanting to see any more of Chloris's eating habits than she had to. By the time Chloris had finished her meal, Lucy was fully clothed.

THOMAS RAN TOWARDS THE SCREAM, Victor clacking along the tunnel behind him. He'd heard the men in the distance and knew nothing good would come from such a meeting. Then the men screamed and there was silence. Scared by what that might mean, he sprinted around the corner. And stopped suddenly at the sight.

The ice demon crouched in the shadows, licking blood from the ground. "Chloris? If you've harmed Lucy . . ." Chloris hissed her displeasure.

"Thomas!" Lucy said. "I'm here!" She hugged her friend, then pulled back. "You smell bad."

"I know. You smell like a mushroom. What's the ice demon doing?"

"We met earlier, and she followed me here." Thomas

looked at the remains of the bodies. "My snakes got the first man." He looked confused, and she pulled one of the snakes from the bag. "Chloris got the others." Chloris hissed at the approaching clacking sound.

"That's my friend," Thomas said. The old man ran around the corner, stopping suddenly at the sight of the ice demon staring at him. "This is Victor San," Thomas said, "my cellmate." The man hobbled into view. "Lucy Thomson."

"Nice to meet you," Victor said, still eyeing the ice demon.

"It's been a long time since anyone's said that to me," she said.

"I've not forgotten how to speak to people, despite the poor environment."

"Baron San," Thomas said.

"Not anymore," Victor said. "My connection with the Empire ended a long time ago."

Chloris leapt at Victor and pushed her large head against his. He yelled and jumped back, hitting the wall. "Nice to meetz you," Chloris said.

"Get this thing away from me," Victor said.

"Shall killz itz?" she hissed, pushing a curved talon to Victor's throat.

"He's our friend," Thomas said.

"He's too noisy. Too slow." She shaved a sliver of hardened muskin off his artificial leg with her razor claw, tasted it, then spat it to the ground. "Tastes bad."

"Help me," Victor said. His artificial leg involuntarily beat against the rock like a drumstick hitting a drum.

"She's just playing," Lucy said. She touched Chloris's arm. "*Let him go,*" she whispered.

"Already eaten anyway," Chloris said, letting go of the shaken Victor.

"What now? Lucy said.

"The basilisk's trail is back there," Thomas said.

"Then let's go," Lucy said. The four companions ran back towards the old shaft.

8

At the bottom of the old mining shaft, Thomas climbed over a rusty pump and then up a few feet and out of the open entrance—parts of an old rusted door lay on the tunnel floor.

"It feels very deep," he said.

"Deepest level," Chloris said.

Thomas touched and listened to the rocks. Victor started a snarky remark, but Lucy put a finger to his mouth. "He's listening."

"To?"

"The rocks."

Victor shook his head irritably, but he waited until Thomas looked up. "Well?" Victor said. "What do you hear?"

"We're close to the tunnels we worked, and we're being followed," Thomas said.

"I can't hear anything," Victor said.

"Spiders and people."

"I've escaped with a lunatic. Hearing things that no one can hear," Victor said, sighing.

Lucy grinned. "How long do we have?"

Thomas shrugged. "Ten minutes for the spiders to reach us, perhaps."

"I hope you have a plan," Victor said. "They're faster than us, and they never give up."

"I have an idea, but we need to find a tighter part of the tunnel, and we need to gather any objects we find. We're going to block the tunnel."

"Block the tunnel! Spider bots won't care about that; they'll rip apart any blockade in seconds!" Victor said.

"Peg Leg is right," Chloris hissed.

"A special trap," Thomas said. "Chloris, do you know a narrow tunnel leading deeper into the mines—one with a draught? The entrance is wider at the top."

"I know it, but we should go up. I know secret ways."

"We descend," Thomas said.

"To death."

"Perhaps we should listen to the lizard," Victor said.

Thomas ignored him. "It leads to a damp plain. Chloris?" She hissed and bounded away along the tunnel. "I take that as a yes." They followed, and after ten minutes, they heard sounds from behind. No one spoke until Chloris stopped by a side tunnel. They'd entered the main passage from a different angle, and Thomas might have missed it, but he recognized the freshness of air. "We need something to block the way."

"Wasting time," Chloris said. Then she stilled and pointed at a shadow moving towards them.

Thomas took out his pistol and shot it repeatedly. With the final bullet, it stopped moving. "We block the tunnel. Lucy and Victor, you squeeze through first and try to find something on the other side. Me and Chloris will look here."

"Take this," Victor said, passing him his pistol.

Thomas looked and felt his way around the tunnel for scrap metal or pieces of wood. He found a few pieces of metal, including the dead bot, but not enough. "Here," Chloris said. She passed him something the length of his thigh.

"What's this?" Then he stopped himself. It was a human femur. He didn't like it, but there was little choice, and the spiders were close. The men could help one last time. Thomas and the ice demon wedged metal and bones across the space, climbing over the blockade before they completely covered the entrance.

"That won't stop anything!" Victor said.

Thomas put his fingers to his lips and pointed at shadows moving along the tunnel roof. Thomas then rubbed crystal from his hands onto the pieces of metal, but nothing happened. Perhaps there's another way, he hoped. He couldn't directly draw power from the pentacle, but he could still communicate silently with the world around him. He spoke to the crystals and was a little surprised when they answered in musical notes. He hummed and they chimed. The spider stopped to listen.

"Whatever you're doing, keep doing it," Lucy said.

A glowing lattice of crystal stems and flowers formed between the iron and bones. Thomas continued to hum an old song as the spider bot crawled onto the web of crystals.

As soon as the bot touched the crystals, it became stuck. Its legs quivered, but otherwise was still. "Let's go," he said. They moved quickly along the tight tunnel, and just before they turned a bend, Thomas looked back. A second spider had become entangled in his web.

Thomas sensed the spaces around them, but Chloris was a natural at finding the best ways through them. She found new holes to climb down in unexpected places. He doubted that the spiders, even after they'd broken through his trap, could navigate their way any faster. They'd left the mines behind and were now moving though the natural spaces of the planet. After eight or nine hours descending, including a couple of hours sleep, they stopped.

"We're here," Chloris said.

They stood on the edge of a damp plain that stretched into darkness. It was a drab rocky world, but at least here there was a carpet of mossy plants. Drizzle fell against Lucy's face. "Salty rain!" she said, wiping her lips.

"We may be beneath an underground lake," Thomas said.

"Let's hope there's little seismic activity here," Victor said.

The roof of the underground world was about twenty feet above them. A few lightstones shone from what looked like a night sky; a few more glittered from boulders on the ground, but they gave out little light.

"Where exactly are we going?" Victor asked.

"To the deepest point," Thomas said. "And from there we go deeper."

"Days of walking," Chloris hissed. "This is the most dangerous part of the journey."

"So you know it," Thomas said. She hissed in reply.

"How is it dangerous?" Lucy asked.

"The plain's open. They'll come with men and robots, and once here, they can move faster than us."

"Cutters?" she asked, referring to the flying bikes.

"Perhaps." Chloris ran into the misty moor. "Come!"

9

"The basilisk's trail goes that way," Thomas said, pointing across a large hollowed piece of land.

Lucy nodded her agreement. The scent of magic was faint but clear.

"Dangerous," Chloris said. "Too open."

"It's all open, but the trail goes that way. I can still smell it," he repeated.

"He's right," Lucy said. "I can sense it, too. The trail enters the wetlands." She glanced at Thomas. *"She's uneasy."* Turning to Chloris, she said, "Where do you think the basilisk's going?"

Chloris's tail twitched. "Don't know."

"She's lying," Thomas said. He spoke the True Language so softly that only Lucy could hear.

"Yes."

"This is insanity," Victor said. "We should have listened to the lizard. It could have taken us up, not down."

"Agreed with Peg Leg," Chloris said. "We go to the surface."

Lucy shook her head. "The magical trail leads this way."

She pointed across the hollow land. "Chloris, where will that take us?"

"To a stinking corner," Chloris hissed in distaste.

"With a way out?" he said.

"No," Chloris said.

"Then, how do we descend deeper into the planet?" Lucy asked.

"We can't. We kill the snake and take the magic."

"The basilisk must think there's a way," Thomas said. "It's running fast, without hesitation. That's not a sign of being lost."

"Fools. It's death to enter the faerie world."

"Faerie?" Lucy asked.

"Elemental magic."

"So there is somewhere deeper, and humans live there," she said. "And there's elemental magic?"

"Perhaps," Chloris said, "but dangerous."

"We must go," Lucy said. "Do you know where the entrance is?"

"There's no entrance, just holes and rocks. To enter, you must walk through the rocks like the elemental creatures."

"Then how did the humans reach it?"

"A way before—not now."

"Take us as close as you can," Lucy said. The ice demon moaned. She continued. "When we return, we'll come with you to the surface."

"Promise?"

"We do," Lucy said.

The frills on Chloris's neck expanded, then flattened, as she looked at them as if gauging their seriousness. "I'll show you the way to the edge of the faerie world. But humans live in those holes."

"That's good," Lucy said. "Have you spoken to them?"

"I've eaten them," Chloris said.

"You've eaten them?" Victor asked, staring at the ice demon.

"They don't care."

"They don't care about being eaten?" Lucy asked, feeling annoyed with Chloris's evasion and ignoring the look of amusement on Thomas's face.

"They don't like me eating them, but they don't care—I've seen them eat each other."

"Cannibals!" Victor shook his head.

They followed Thomas through the drizzle. They'd hardly spoken a word for the last hour, and the monotonous journey seemed endless. When they reached a flatter part of the moor, Chloris stopped and put her ear to the ground. "They're coming."

Dropping to his knees, Thomas did the same. His feelings of boredom had vanished. He nodded at Lucy.

"What's coming?" she asked.

"Humans and robots. Many of them," Chloris hissed. "Forty or more men, and over twenty robots. They're spread across the plain. They're coming towards us. We must run."

"Stop," Thomas said.

"What?" Chloris asked. She stopped, her long tail flicking from side to side.

"I can smell it, too," Lucy said.

"Smell nothing," Chloris said.

"The basilisk has been here," Thomas said. "I can smell the magic of the Keys."

"Are these keys weapons?" Chloris asked.

"They can be used as weapons," Thomas said.

"If we can take the magic and use it, then we might live," Chloris said. Her nostrils flared as she spoke. Thomas wondered whether this was a sign of anticipation.

As they ran through the wetlands, Thomas felt the vibrations of their pursuers, but they needed to rest. When they stopped, Chloris confirmed it. "How much further to the caves?" he asked.

"An hour," Chloris said. "Less if we run."

"And our pursuers?" Lucy asked.

"They'll reach us in less than an hour," Chloris said.

"We won't be here then. We'll be in the cannibal caves," Thomas said, ignoring Chloris's hiss of disapproval. "And when we're there, we'll find a way."

"I don't like it," Lucy said.

"Neither do I, but what else can we do but try? If Val is trapped there, then we retake the Keys and fight. With magic like that, even a small army of humans and robots could be defeated, especially in such a restricted space."

"What if it's not trapped there?" Victor asked.

"Then it's found a way through, and so will we." He was aware of many holes in his logic, but it still seemed the best choice.

For the next hour, they ran across the damp underground plains.

THEY STOPPED at the edge of the world. They could now almost touch the lightstones that had looked like stars. "We've made it," Lucy said, feeling relief to be entering the hills after the wide plain.

"Only just," Victor said. The red lights of the approaching spider bots were about a hundred yards away.

"We're approaching the cannibal caves," Chloris said.

"Once we find Val, we'll have other options," Thomas said.

"Yess, magic," Chloris said, appearing excited by the thought. "The snake can't escape; there's nowhere to go. We're at the end of the world."

"Unless it's found a door to the elemental world," Lucy said.

"No door!" Chloris said. She sniffed the stale air. "Humans move with the robots."

"Look," Lucy whispered. "The other way." She pointed at the caves. About eighteen ragged men and women moved towards them.

They grinned to themselves as they came closer, seeming to believe themselves hidden in the darkness, but Lucy could see them clearly enough—as could Thomas and Chloris. The ice demon crouched behind a small ridge that ran across the cavern floor. Some of the cannibals wore rags, but many were naked. All were heavily tattooed.

The smell was strong. Thomas spoke to them, but she didn't want to get much closer. They stopped and spoke rapidly amongst themselves. "What language are they speaking?" she asked.

"I never speak with my food," Chloris hissed from the shadows.

The people moved closer. Thomas knocked away the hands of some of them. "Can you take us into the caves?" Lucy asked. A woman cackled and started to feel her flesh. Lucy pushed her away, and a larger man raised his fist; Thomas knocked him to the ground, but more cannibals surged forward.

Chloris leapt into the air and slashed a man. The ice demon screeched, and the cannibals ran back to the caves.

"I'll show you a way," Chloris said. They followed her into a cave entrance.

"Is there any way out of these caves?" Thomas asked.

"A vertical flue in the cave ceiling."

"That's useful," Victor said sarcastically. He ducked as her tail flicked over his head.

As they followed Chloris through the narrow tunnels, Lucy caught glimpses of children watching them from dark passages. Chloris led them to a slightly larger smoky cavern. A fire burnt in the middle. Lucy saw the importance of the flue immediately. An ancient naked man, wearing only bones attached to a string around his neck, danced in front of them. Others watched from the four tunnel entrances in the sides of the cave.

"A charmer," Thomas said.

Lucy looked at the naked old man who danced towards them, shaking his bones. "I don't feel charmed."

The old man grinned, showing a pair of yellow teeth. Then he started jabbering. Lucy couldn't understand a word. The charmer didn't seem to care about Chloris; he was only interested in Lucy.

As he danced on, more humans, almost all of whom were naked, crept out of the tunnels. They were grinning as wildly as the old man. The smoky space stank of rotten flesh, excrement, mushrooms, and roasting meat.

"I feel sick," Lucy said.

Chloris screeched and cleared the cave of people in seconds. Only the old charmer remained, dancing to music only he could hear. They searched the cave, walking from tunnel to tunnel, feeling for traces of magic.

"Thomas?" Lucy stood by one of the tunnels leading out of the chamber. "I can feel the Keys; he was here earlier."

She stepped back quickly. "Something's coming down this tunnel." She quickly moved back to stand by him.

"From all tunnels," Chloris said.

THOMAS CHECKED HIS PISTOL: it had three bullets left. Not enough to fight a small army. Dozens of cannibals rushed into the chamber. They came from every direction, pushing Thomas, Lucy, and Victor back to the wall. Many carried stones, and all were agitated, but they kept well away from Chloris.

"We're trapped," Thomas said.

Chloris cracked her tail against the ground and sprang into the air, sticking to the roof like adhesive and then crawling into the vertical flue.

The sounds of machines came from the tunnels, and the cannibals started shouting. Two bots flew into the cavern and shot at the cannibals. Thomas shot at the nearest bot, but they were armoured, and they hardly noticed. He threw the empty gun away and silence fell in the cavern. A dozen guards ran in through three of the tunnels, followed by some of the worst gangers.

Lights swept around the cavern—they'd been seen. One of the blue bots already hovered yards from their heads, its gun barrel pointed down at them.

"The end to our great escape," Victor said.

"Why are gangers here?" Lucy asked.

"Bounty hunters," Victor said. "The prison uses them sometimes for dirty work; they're expendable."

"We got them!" Drew Walker shouted. The gangers ran at them; they all carried guns. Fulk, the biggest of the gangers, held Thomas, while Buzz and another held guns to his chest.

Garrett Pick, the gang's deputy, held a pistol to Victor. A woman approached Lucy. "Dix," Lucy whispered. He'd already heard enough about her.

She glared at Lucy. "The Orange Witch." Another woman watched her curiously from a distance as Dix slapped her.

Drew Walker ordered a man to tie them up. Only when they'd been bound were the pistols lowered.

"Our reward's bigger if you're alive, but you're worth something dead, too, so don't get any ideas," Walker said.

"We found them," a sergeant said.

"We caught them," Walker said. While the ganger and guard argued, Thomas felt something cool crawling up his arms, and only Lucy's faraway expression kept him from flinching. She was speaking in the True Language, but even he couldn't hear her.

"Be still," Lucy said. He nodded. Something was chewing through the rope; it then slid down his leg and climbed up Victor's. "Quiet!" she told him. Soon his bonds fell to the floor, and the fungal snake returned to Lucy.

"Useful," Thomas said.

"Yes, but they can only do so much."

Thomas drew on what magic he could and extended his mind into the rocks around them. At least he could listen and speak the True Language. He'd noticed the stalactites hanging from the ceiling of the chamber, and he searched for cracks anywhere in the roof. If there were, then he might be able to shake them loose, but the roof of the chamber was solid. Then he remembered Chloris.

"Chloris, please kick some of those stalactites loose—the ones furthest from us." Her dark shadow moved across the roof,

but none of their pursuers noticed anything. Then she snapped one from its place.

One of the gangers looked up as a stalactite pierced his chest. *"That's not one of furthest ones,"* Thomas said. Lucy was listening, too.

Chloris hissed and span around; her long tail dislodged several more stalactites. Two guards died instantly; another was badly injured. She snapped a stalactite from the ceiling and threw it like a spear at an approaching bot. The other fired at her, but it didn't carry the heavy weapons of a battlefield bot, and its bullets bounced off her. She leapt into the air and caught it in her talons, and as she hit the ground, she smashed it into pieces and threw them at the guards.

A ganger moved in close to shoot her, but she span around again and her long tail whipped out and split his face open. Her claws cut through more of the guards. She hissed, her frilled neck fully expanded as the guards fired with their pistols, but again the bullets bounced off her.

Thomas noticed that some guards carried heavier weapons, the kind that could kill an ice demon. He warned her. When those guards rushed forward, she leapt to the ceiling. They fired, but by then she'd disappeared up the flue.

"Idiots!" Thomas yelled. He pulled Lucy and Victor down.

Bullets ricocheted wildly around the cavern, killing a guard and injuring another. One of the gangers lay dead. Nobody seemed to notice the cannibals who lay on the ground dead or moaning. And, for a few seconds, they'd forgotten about their prisoners.

Thomas tried to merge with the rocks, as once he'd been able, but the source of his power was too far away. Instead, he probed the surrounding cavern for life.

"I couldn't find any life here," Lucy said.

He silently called for help. "It's worth a try." She didn't look convinced. Then, something moved inside the rock. "There's something there."

"What?" Victor said.

Standing still, he concentrated on the movement, but nothing happened. Thomas almost doubted himself for a moment, then he felt it again. Something was moving inside the rock. He saw a green light in the wall of the chamber. Then vibrations shook their world.

"Earthquake!" Walker said.

"Thomas?" Lucy whispered.

He shook his head. He was convinced the rock here was stable; this was something else. The rock face in front of Thomas opened, and a green light shone from the gap. Something moved inside the gap.

"I saw it, too," Lucy said.

The crack widened enough for a man to pass through, and as it did, the cavern groaned and snapped. The gangers and guards were now concerned. A tiny figure watched them. Thomas couldn't see exactly what it was, but it clearly wasn't human.

"Thomas, what is it?" Lucy whispered.

"I don't know, but there's a passage through the rocks, and if we remain, we're dead." He pulled Victor to his feet and stepped inside. Chloris ran down the wall towards them. "Come," Thomas said. When they hesitated, he pulled them behind him. Chloris followed. Thomas prayed the narrow crack wouldn't snap shut with them inside. It was tight, sharp, and unstable.

"Is this wise?" Victor asked.

"No!" Shouts from the cavern told him their disappearance had been noticed.

Ignoring the cuts, they pushed harder through the crevice. Thomas could no longer see the tiny creature, but several minutes later, he felt a draught against his face. "Quickly!" Pushing even harder through the narrow space, his threadbare shirt ripped apart, but he hardly noticed. The rocks around them groaned and vibrated.

"This could close up on us, just as it opened," Victor said.

"I know!" The space got smaller, steeper, and hotter. Soon they were climbing down a shaft. Shouts and screams came from behind them as the rocks shook. When he reached the end of the shaft, he dropped to the floor below and found a tunnel that descended further.

"Faster!" he shouted as the others hesitated at the jump. He caught Lucy, taking a kick in his jaw as she fell.

"Thanks," she said as he put her down. The ground shook harder, and Victor lost his footing. Thomas caught him, too. Only Chloris needed no help.

They ran down another tunnel. "We're almost there," he said. A faint red light came from ahead. When he finally stepped through the mouth of the tunnel, a wave of heat hit him; it was as if he'd just arrived in a tropical country. They were on a ledge about ten feet above the ground. Another vibration shook their world, and he half fell and half scrambled down.

Lucy dropped again, and Thomas just caught her in time. "Thank goodness you've got good reflexes," she said.

"My leg's stuck," Victor shouted. Thomas quickly made his way back to Victor, catching him as he lost his balance, this time avoiding being kicked.

"Much appreciated," Victor said. "But, unfortunately, I think I've cracked my leg."

"We'll find you a new one," Thomas said. Chloris

dropped silently to the ground beside him. Thomas turned to where Lucy stood.

A dark underground world, partially lit by glowing red fires from volcanic vents, stretched out in front of them. In the distance, an orange river of lava flowed across the plain.

It looks like hell, Thomas thought as a smoky breeze blew into his face. From the vibrations in the air and rocks, he sensed that it was far larger than the rainy plains they'd just left.

"More stars," Lucy said, her face tilted upwards.

"Lightstones embedded in the roof," Thomas said, looking around. He was secretly impressed by the scale of this underground world.

"Thomas?" Lucy said slowly.

A tiny figure watched them from the ground. Then, with a green flash, it ran straight into the rocks.

10

"What was that?" Victor asked as the green glow slowly faded into the rock.

"Part of the faerie world," Thomas said. He'd seen similar things before. Lucy exchanged a glance with him—he knew she'd dealt with them, too. Victor stared at the rocks with wide eyes until a blast of hot wind made him look away.

"Is it still there?" Lucy asked Thomas.

"It's gone," Victor said. His sharp green eyes glinted as flames flared nearby.

"Thomas can listen for movement within the rocks," Lucy said.

Thomas noticed Victor's questioning look as he placed his hands on the rock. He listened, then shook his head; there was no sign of the creature. However, he sensed something else. "We have company." Another tremor shook the ground and shouts came from the gap in the rocks. He recognized the voices of the gangers. "We should move back behind those boulders."

"We should leave," Victor said once they'd retreated into the shadows. "They have guns."

"We have Chloris, and I want to see exactly what's coming after us. Besides, where would we go?" Thomas gestured towards the dark world with its red glowing fires. "I'd like to question the green creature in the rock. I think it may know something."

"We know what's coming after us," Victor whispered. "Robots, guards, and gangers—all armed."

From the screams in the rocks, Thomas doubted they'd all make it through, but they were dangerous. He turned to Lucy. "Can you sense Val?"

She shook her head. "I don't think it entered the world here."

Thomas nodded. He felt the same, and he was tempted to take Victor's advice and run, but they were lost in a vast underground world, and he wanted local knowledge. He suspected the tiny green man had answered his silent call. For it to have happened by chance seemed too remote a possibility. But if it had let them in, why? He'd dealt with faerie creatures before—they were not altruistic.

He bent down and picked up several suitable stones. "For throwing," he said to Victor. He grinned at the man's expression. "Throwing stones is a part of rock magic."

Drew Walker's head appeared from the mouth of the passage. Walker looked around but didn't see the four figures standing in the shadows. Vibrations shook the ground, and the gaping mouth of the tunnel groaned again. They watched him slip and fall. As he stood, the feet of a ganger kicked him in his head; cursing, he knocked the man's legs away and stepped away as the man tumbled to the ground. He mumbled something under his breath, but Walker was looking up as more of the gangers came through. Pick and Dix dropped to the ground. Buzz and a thin woman with unusually large eyes were next.

"I understand the prison using bounty hunters, but why the thin woman?" Thomas asked. "She doesn't look like a fighter."

Following his gaze, Lucy said, "Adela. I don't know much about her. She's a bit strange. Some people say she's psychic." The woman squealed as she hit the ground. She sat alone, examining her cuts.

"Fulk! The weapons!" Walker shouted. The ground still shook. "It's an earthquake." But Thomas knew it wasn't. He felt the green creature's earth magic manipulating the rocks.

Fulk's large head poked through. "Got them." A woman cursed the giant from behind; he half turned and spoke to her.

"Eve!" Adela shouted.

"Throw them down!" Pick yelled. A green light flashed from the rocks. "Give us the guns!"

The giant man squeezed his left shoulder through the narrowing gap. Then the rocks snapped shut. Fulk's head fell to the ground. The weapons were sealed inside. The four men and two women stared at the rock face.

"Eve!" Adela shouted, watching the rock wall with a deeply troubled look on her face.

"I don't care about Eve!" Pick said. "I need those weapons!" As Thomas watched and listened with the True Language, he felt Adela's hatred. Lucy glanced at Thomas and nodded; she'd picked it up, too.

"What happened?" Victor asked quietly.

"The faerie creature removed its magic, and the rocks returned to their natural position," Thomas said. "The question is why it opened a passage in the first place."

A snap from Victor's broken artificial leg as he shifted weight caused the gangers to turn and stared into the gloom.

"It's them!" Dix said.

Thomas stepped out from behind the boulder. Lucy and Victor joined him, but Chloris remained hidden in the shadows. "You should be dead," Pick said.

Drew Walker pointed at Thomas. "You're responsible for my friends' deaths."

"You don't have any friends. You just let a woman die because your guns were more important to you—and you still failed to get them. We didn't ask you to follow us," Thomas said. He massaged the stones in his hand. He'd hurt them if they attacked.

"You're dead," Pick said.

Thomas threw fast. The first stone hit Pick on his forehead. Before they could react, Thomas spoke again. "We've killed guards and robots; we can kill you." That shut them up for a few seconds. They became more aware of their surroundings.

Dix peered into the plain. "Is the monster with them?"

"Let's go," Lucy whispered.

"I agree," Thomas said. The gangers were looking into the shadows for Chloris, but she remained hidden.

"You're not going anywhere," Walker said.

Their talk was empty, and Thomas focussed on the rocks behind the gangsters. *"I can feel it too,"* Lucy said.

Thomas felt something strong and earthy. *"It's there."* His thoughts interrupted hers. He looked at the rock face behind the gangers and had the feeling of movement. "Something's coming through the rocks."

Too far away to hear their private conversation, Drew Walker misunderstood their hesitation. "That's better; you can't run from us."

Thomas was looking at the spot behind the gangster's legs. The green light had reappeared.

A pale green man, eighteen inches high, walked out of the rocks. The light flared, then faded. He was thin, wiry, and looked like a miniature human, except for his silver eyes. He wore a red and green jacket; his boots, pants, and hat were all brown, and a short sword was strapped to his back.

"What are you?" Lucy asked in the True Language.

"I'm a gnome." He looked directly at Lucy and Thomas.

"What is this place?" Thomas asked.

"The Underworld." He showed his teeth in what might have been a grin. A glint of light sparked in his eyes.

"You've scared them, Drew," Polly Dix said. "Look at the old fool's face." Then she looked down. "Eek!" She fell back into Buzz and pointed at the tiny figure.

"What the . . . ?" Buzz said.

"Stamp on it, Buzz!" Dix shouted.

Buzz put his hands on his knees and bent down. "What are you?" he asked.

The gnome silently stared at Thomas and Lucy. *"Why did you help us?"* Lucy asked. Lucy glanced at Thomas. *"Something else came into your world, didn't it?"*

"Show us where it went," Thomas said.

"If you're what I think you are, you'll find it. If not, you'll die."

"What do you think we are?" Lucy asked.

"You may be the Fire Bearers—the ones that some call the Bright Ones—or you may be thieves." Thomas felt the gnome pushing lightly against his mind. *"I sense traces of magic, but a different magic from the crawling snake."*

"Crawling?" Thomas asked.

He grinned again. *"It lost its legs in the rocks; it now crawls on its tail."* His grin vanished. *"But I was too slow."*

"What is it?" Walker asked as a few of the gangers surrounded the tiny creature.

"It's dumb," Pick said.

"Kill it, Buzz!" Dix said. "I can't stand little things like that. It's not normal."

"Leave him," Thomas said.

"It killed our friends," Pick said. "It's not going anywhere until we know what it is." The ganger rushed at the tiny creature and kicked, but the gnome moved fast, right under his legs. And as the tiny man passed beneath his groin, he punched upwards. Pick collapsed to the ground, gasping and cursing. The others stepped back and watched.

The creature walked up to Thomas and Lucy. *"Why do you hunt the serpent man?"*

"It's stolen what belongs to us," Thomas said.

The gnome seemed satisfied with his answer. He spoke in Silvan. "It's an infestation of the earth. Are you able to retake what it's stolen?"

"We have to," Thomas said. He was distracted by shouts from the gangers, and when he looked down again, the small man was gone. "Where's the gnome?"

Lucy shook her head. "We should go, too. The gangers are afraid, and that makes them dangerous."

"You're outnumbered," Walker said. "And we're going to collect the reward on your heads. Besides, we have the means to find you wherever you go."

Thomas grinned. "And what's that?" He assumed they meant tags.

"We have locaters." He glanced at Dix and Adela.

Thomas raised his eyebrows at Lucy and Victor. Victor shook his head.

"There's a rumour that one of the prisoners can psychically locate people," Lucy said under her breath.

"Is that even possible?" Victor asked.

"It's possible," Thomas said. "But that doesn't mean this pair can do it, nor does it mean they're accurate."

"I don't know about Adela, but Dix is a fake," Lucy said.

Even if Adela could locate them, Thomas didn't feel too concerned.

Walker turned to his men while Buzz and another man broke from the group and rushed at Thomas. Dix grinned as she strode towards Lucy.

Chloris shrieked, and Thomas cringed at the sound that could probably be heard a mile away. The gangers almost toppled over in their attempt to stop. They slowly edged back.

There was nothing left to say. Thomas turned to his friends. "Let's go." They walked out into the dark plain.

"I WISH we could navigate by the stars," Lucy said.

"We probably could if we knew them," Thomas said. "In this world, they're fixed."

"There's a bright star in the distance," she said. "Perhaps we should walk towards it."

"It's a good a direction as any," Thomas said. "We may pick up the scent of magic on the way."

It took almost three hours of walking across the monotonous plain before they reached any water. The only thing they passed on the way was the bones of a long-dead animal, the remains of a harness attached to it. When they finally reached a hot water spring, Lucy bent down, sniffing the water. "I think it's okay."

Her thirst was so strong that the smoky water tasted good. They filled their water bottles. Seeing a patch of mushrooms, she walked over to them, knelt down, and spoke.

Thomas and Victor joined her. "Are they edible?" Thomas asked.

"Yes." She picked some and began to eat.

"How do you know?" Victor asked.

"I asked them."

Victor took a bite and then hesitated. "Isn't this like eating your friends?"

"The first time I spoke to animals was the time I stopped eating them, but plants are a bit different. They don't object as much to being eaten." She grinned at the look of perplexity on the old man's face. "You don't know what to make of me, do you?"

"That's the truth."

"Perhaps you can develop your intuition; perhaps you can learn to listen to life around you, too."

"I can listen to people; I've learnt that."

Before departing, they picked as many of the mushrooms as they could, stuffing them in their pockets, and Lucy filled her muskin bag.

There was no life apart from the moss beneath their feet and the few insects that crawled there. Then Lucy noticed movement on the surfaces of the puddles and ponds that were becoming more frequent. "We have company," she said. "Get ready to run."

"Where?" Thomas asked.

"Everywhere."

"Hostile?" Victor asked.

"Unfortunately, yes."

Dark masses of insects rose from the puddles of the

humid plain and swarmed around them. "Insects?" Victor said, swatting them away. They bit hard, and Lucy desperately knocked them off, but hundreds more came. She spat the things from her mouth, blew them from her nose, and wiped them from her face, but still more came. They ran.

"We're their first meal in a long time," she shouted. The black flies pushed themselves under her clothes and crawled to softer areas to bite, even at the cost of legs or wings. Each puddle and pool added to the swarm. Soon, tens of thousands of biting flies followed them.

She spoke to the insects, telling them to go, but they were too hungry to hear. She did manage to plant the seed of a thought in their collective swarm mind that she was less delicious, but the weight of flies landing on Thomas and Victor increased, and Victor disappeared in a black cloud. When she heard him stumble, she just let the flies be and was bitten as much as the others. Only Chloris was unaffected.

"Thanks," Thomas said, attempting a grin but giving up when dozens of flies crawled into his mouth. He spat them onto the ground.

So he'd noticed her attempts to influence the flies. And she thought she'd been particularly subtle in sending her suggestions.

"Any ideas?" Thomas asked.

"Run faster!" Lucy yelled, holding her hand over her mouth. As she led the way, she sensed another change. She pointed towards the edge of the giant swarm and ran straight towards it. Thomas and Victor followed, but she didn't look; she only heard Victor's heavy breathing and his leg clacking as he ran.

As soon as they left the wetland behind, the flies were gone. It seemed they were even more attached to their damp homes than to their food. Lucy breathed heavily in relief and looked at the pinpricks covering her arms and legs. Thomas and Victor wiped the remaining flies from their bodies. They used up the water and walked on.

Hours later they still walked, but now they were thirsty as well as tired and bored. "Does anyone know where we're going?" Victor asked.

"Towards the bright star," Thomas said, "but we seem to have reached a mountain." He pointed at rock formations ahead.

Lucy felt embarrassed by her lack of observation; she'd been so focussed on searching for any black flies to avoid that she'd not seen the looming form in front of them. "Shouldn't we change direction? Or do you think we can climb over it?"

Victor groaned. "I can't climb that; it's a sheer rock face."

Thomas turned to Lucy. "Have you noticed?" he said.

"Noticed what?" The only thing she'd noticed for the past half hour were the itching bites all over her body.

"The basilisk was here," Thomas said.

"Yes," Chloris confirmed, sniffing the ground.

Some of Lucy's tiredness fell away, and she listened to the magic again. Thomas was right. "The trail's old."

"But better than nothing," Thomas said.

She walked closer to the rocks that rose from the flat plain. "The trail seems to go into the mountain."

"Tunnels?" Victor said.

Thomas looked at them. "You two rest here, I'll scout ahead with Chloris." She was happy to let them go. They were the best suited anyway; they both had an ability to blend into the landscape in a way she couldn't.

Feeling more tired than she'd felt in long time, Lucy

found a sheltered place between some boulders, sat down, and closed her eyes. Victor rested nearby.

As she drowsed, she listened to the land around her—which was as much as she could do with magic at the moment. When she briefly touched the group mind of a cloud of gnats hovering twenty yards away, they buzzed, and she quickly redirected her attention away from them. A pair of small rodent-like creatures were playing in the rocks above her. Although she tried to fight it, tiredness came over her, and she closed her eyes.

A dark shadow was prowling in the darkness at the edge of the mountain. She shook Victor but couldn't wake him, and she called Thomas, but her voice was gone. The shadow looked towards her, and she was as quiet as she could be, and then it faded into the darkness.

11

"Lucy, wake up!" Thomas shook her. She opened her eyes. "You were having a nightmare."

She sat up straight. "Something's hunting us."

"You were just having a bad dream," Victor said.

"No," she said to Victor. "It's stalking us!" She looked at Thomas. "It had magic."

Thomas felt uneasy, remembering her previous dreams well enough. If she was sure it was a premonition, then he believed her, but her certainty gave him an empty feeling in his stomach. "The basilisk?"

She shook her head. "It was more powerful. And it walked on two legs."

If she was right, they'd just have to wait for it to show itself, if it ever did. He decided to change the subject. "I found a trail through the mountain."

"But?" she asked.

She was too good at reading his mind. "Thieves are using the caves.

"How many?" Victor asked.

"I counted ten."

"They're nothing," Chloris said.

"They have swords and knives," Thomas said. Chloris hissed her contempt. "And the smell is almost as bad as the cannibal caves."

Lucy wrinkled her nose. "If they're thieves, who are they stealing from?" she asked.

"The people of Tartaros. I heard them talking. Paths lead through the mountain and into the heart of the city. Val has been this way, and we need to follow before the trail disappears, and before the Keys are too far to draw magic from. With the magic we have, we should be able to hide ourselves. Perhaps we can find a way around them. I don't think they're expecting anyone to enter from this side; there are no guards. It may be trickier on the other side."

"Not tricky," Chloris said. "We just kill them."

Victor chuckled, but Lucy shook her head. "Not unless we have to."

"Val doesn't know we're following. I'd like it to remain like that," Thomas said. It took about twenty minutes of them edging along the mountain until Thomas found the narrow gap he was looking for. "Down here."

Eyebrows raised, Victor asked, "How did you find this?"

"I still have a little rock magic."

Chloris ran straight inside, while Thomas and Lucy helped Victor scramble through. Lucy looked at the crack down the middle of his wooden leg. "We'll really have to find a way to fix his leg," she said.

"Perhaps in Tartaros."

They squeezed into the narrow cave. It was hotter than the wide open space they'd left, and the air was stale. "Where are the thieves?" Lucy asked.

"You'll smell them soon," Thomas said.

"I think I already can."

"That's us."

She grinned. "It's not; it's worse than us," she said. "I've seen no sign so far."

"There are too many caves and tunnels for them," Thomas said.

"They're superstitious," a voice said from behind. It spoke in accented Silvan.

They turned around just as the gnome stepped from the rocks. All they could see were its silver eyes shining. "They're scared of wandering from the path; they think the mountain's possessed."

"Do you have anything to do with that?" Thomas asked. He sensed more than saw the gnome's grin. "Have you been following us?"

"I watched your progress. To be sure."

"Of what?" Thomas asked.

"Of what you are."

"And?" he asked.

"If you hunt the crawling snake, then I'll guide you."

"Why?" Thomas asked.

"I was working in the barrier between our worlds when I left a way open, and it entered. I must right my mistake, and you can help me."

"And that was why you helped us?" Lucy asked.

"I was curious about your magic, too."

"Can't you do this by yourself?" Thomas asked.

"I'm unfamiliar with its magic. It's better to have help."

"Haven't you made another mistake by letting us in?" Lucy asked.

"It was a risk, but I think I made the right choice."

"What about the ones who followed us?" she asked.

"They're nothing more than animals and make no difference to the balance; it's the magic that disturbs the world."

"And the thieves?" Thomas asked.

"Likewise," the gnome said. "You needn't worry about them." His eyes glinted in the dark.

Thomas knew that elemental creatures lacked human morality, but sometimes humans lacked it too. *"How far do you think we can trust him?"* he silently asked Lucy.

"I don't know." Lucy frowned as the gnome turned and grinned at them. "What's your name?" she asked.

"Odran." The gnome's head tilted to one side as he listened. "Those who came with you have followed."

They let Odran guide them through the tunnels. And he was fast. Soon, they left their pursuers far behind. The gnome kept to the bigger tunnel until they were blocked from going any further by a wooden barrier. Odran squeezed through a tiny gap near the ground and vanished.

"Can you open it?" Victor asked.

"It's not a door," Thomas said. "They've piled boxes against the entrance." He pushed.

"Who's there?" a man said. A second man spoke to the first. They were clearly nervous.

Chloris's mouth widened into a kind of grin, and Thomas stepped back. She screeched for several seconds. He grimaced at the volume, and Lucy put her fingers in her ears. There was silence on the other side, and then Chloris pushed hard, and the boxes flew out into the inner chamber. Two thieves stood frozen on the far side of the cavern. They looked only at the ice demon, then, without a sound, they turned and fled in terror.

The gnome approved. "Not bad." They followed Odran as he sprinted through the tunnels. With the constant twists in the tunnel, as well as the many places they were forced to squeeze or crawl through, Thomas wasn't surprised when Odran said the thieves hardly used them.

"Do you think Val will stop in the city?" Lucy asked.

"I do," Odran said.

"Why?" Thomas asked.

"Where else will it go? It will want to access the magic of the Keys, but it will fail. It lacks the skill."

"What do you mean?" he asked.

"There's harmony between your magic and the bigger magic of the Keys—you're matched. It would need more power to master them, something it lacks."

"It's scared of something," Lucy said. "We felt it when it came to the prison; it doesn't know how to use the Keys."

"The Keys responded to you, not to the basilisk," Odran said.

"How do you know?" she asked.

"It would have used their power if it could. Do you know what it's scared of?"

Thomas shrugged his shoulders. "Something worse than a basilisk, I imagine."

"The thing in my dream."

Thomas nodded. He wasn't happy at the thought that something worse hunted them. "Do you know where this thing was?" Lucy shook her head. "Then the best thing is to keep moving, before anything worse shows up." They resumed their march through the tunnels.

"Where did you learn your Silvan?" Thomas asked the gnome. "It sounds like an older version of the language."

"When humans first arrived on Prometheus, we watched. At first, they protected the planet, so we were interested. Some of us learnt their language, which was different then—although most of them were not even aware of our existence." Thomas had long been aware that many elemental creatures protected the environment, and for that he respected them. He continued asking questions as they walked.

After some time, the tunnels widened, but the roof dropped drastically. Thomas studied the open space cautiously.

"I sense movement," Thomas said.

The gnome nodded. He disappeared in the direction of the sounds; several minutes later, he returned. "It's strange. They are waiting in ambush thirty yards from here."

"Why strange?" Lucy asked.

"They didn't track us, they just knew we'd be here."

Thomas wondered whether Adela was really a psychic capable of locating people. "How many?" Thomas asked.

"Ten," the gnome said. "The ones that came through with you, and others."

"It doesn't make much sense," Victor said. "Why would the gangers care? They must know by now that they can't return to collect their rewards."

"I don't know," Thomas said. "Perhaps they're making friends with the locals, helping them catch intruders. Who cares?"

"Something doesn't feel right," Lucy said.

Thomas gave a short laugh. "A lot doesn't feel right, but we can't wait here, and I don't see why we should care too much about some killers." He laughed when Lucy looked at him. "We're just as dangerous. But I agree that avoiding an ambush would be better.

Odran shook his head. "We can't avoid it unless we go back and circle around, but it would take us seven or eight hours, and they might be waiting there, too."

"I assume no one wants to go back?" Thomas said. No one answered. "Then we need a plan."

"No need," Chloris said. "We just kill them."

"She's right," Odran said. "We can see in the dark; they can't." Thomas felt a chill inside. He'd killed before, but killing in cold blood was hard. At his silence, Odran said, "They'd kill us." Thomas wondered how much of his mind the gnome could read.

But there was no other way, and neither the gnome nor ice demon had a single qualm about murder. "Then let's do it. But I only have stones; they have blades."

"You have us," Odran said, indicating Chloris.

Lucy began to speak, but Thomas, Chloris, and the gnome were gone. They took the two nearest men; they died quietly. No one should have noticed, but Drew Walker was staring at him. He shouldn't have been able to see in the dark.

Chloris attacked Walker, but he struck the ice demon hard. She fell to the ground with a grunt.

"Thomas. Get away from him," Lucy called.

"Torches!" Walker's voice quavered.

"Thomas!" Lucy warned again. But he already knew something was very wrong. Walker's men lit their torches. This was not going as he'd hoped. Chloris was motionless on the ground, and Garrett Pick had tossed a limp Odran against the wall. All the gangers and two other men were there. They menaced Thomas with knives and short swords, and Dix shouted obscenities at Lucy. Adela stood at the back, watching silently.

Thomas moved the throwing stones inside his closed hands and sought to gain time. "Bounty hunters?" he asked Walker.

The man looked at him with glazed eyes, then laughed. His reaction seemed delayed. "I need no bounty."

"What then?"

Drew Walker stared at Lucy. "Her."

Thomas shivered. *"Lucy?"*

"I don't know what he's talking about, but he's making me uncomfortable."

"Can you look?"

"I'm not sure I want to go into his mind." Walker was grinning as they spoke telepathically. *"But I'll try."*

A second later, Lucy screamed and staggered back, holding her head. Walker ran straight at her, pushing Thomas away and causing him to gasp. He shook his stinging arms. The man was infused with magic.

Garret Pick ran at him, but this time Thomas was ready. Two stones hit Pick's forehead in rapid succession, but the man didn't appear to notice. Thomas's natural magic deflected the forced magic of the man, but the man turned and slashed with his knife. Thomas ducked under the blade, then rose quickly, punching the man in his heart. He staggered back in the same oddly disconnected way Walker moved.

Lucy screamed from behind, and Thomas heard Victor struggling, too, but he had no time to turn as Pick, joined by Buzz, attacked. But the men were not used to fighting together, and they got in each other's way. Thomas sidestepped Buzz's thrust, striking his temple with a stone clenched in his fist. He then locked his arm and took the knife.

Thomas pushed the dazed Buzz into Pick and got ready to fight again. But Garret Pick staggered, blood coming from his mouth, then he fell to the ground. Adela stood behind him with a bloody knife in her hand. "That was for Eve!"

Dix stared at her openmouthed. Then she turned to Buzz and, pointing at Thomas, yelled, "Kill him!" Buzz opened his mouth to speak, but Thomas thrust his knife into the man's throat. "Do something!" Dix shouted at the others, but they stood several paces back, silently watching.

A black mist came from Pick's body and rushed along the ground, passing where Victor lay bleeding, and moving towards Lucy. Walker sat astride her with his mouth gaping and dark vapour pouring out and covering her face.

Thomas glanced towards a sound, expecting another attack, but it was the gnome sitting up. "It's too late." He was looking at Lucy. "She's possessed by a powerful magic. You must kill her."

Thomas had no intention of killing Lucy, nor would he let anyone else try. He pulled Drew Walker's neck back and slit his throat, dragging his limp body away from her. He knelt next to her, glancing back at the gangers.

"Don't worry about them," Odran said.

But he was—they were already too close, and Dix was goading them on. The gnome hardly seemed to be in a position to help; neither did Victor, who was groaning on the ground, nor Chloris, who at least was beginning to stir. He shook Lucy, but she didn't respond. He cursed.

"It's not good. Leave her," Odran said.

"She's dying," Polly Dix cackled.

Chloris staggered to her feet and bit off the back of Dix's head, before vomiting it out again, along with the contents of her stomach.

"You're leaving, now!" Thomas shouted at the remaining gangers, who were already backing away and whispering to each other. When they didn't leave, he threw his knife into the heart of one of the locals. Adela and the two remaining men fled from the cavern.

Thomas sat on the floor next to Lucy. Chloris was sitting on the far side of the cavern; Victor and Odran were by him. He looked at Victor. "I have to do something risky. I need you three to watch over us. I won't be able to speak or move for several minutes."

"Why?"

"I'm going in." Thomas held Lucy's hand, which was like ice. He closed his eyes and slowly pushed at her consciousness. He'd done this before, and he waited until he heard her call. Then he entered her mind. He felt a tightness—a pressure pushing back at him, but he couldn't see where she was. Dark images appeared. Things he didn't recognize. And then he saw brighter images of Lucy's life: her home and her childhood; he saw her playing with her dog.

Then he saw a dark figure sitting in a library reading her memories like books. The figure looked up, his face concealed by a cowl, and Thomas heard a small noise— perhaps of surprise. From a bookshelf, an arm stretched out. Lucy was trapped in a space inside the wall.

Thomas reached towards her, and her hand closed around his. Dropping the book, the man strode towards him, but Thomas pulled Lucy clear before he reached them. She stood beside him with her head down.

"Who are you?" the man asked.

Thomas punched him as hard as he could, and the man staggered back. "You've just made a grave mistake," the man said. Thomas could smell his magic and was almost overwhelmed by its power, but he knew from experience that allowing any fear would make him vulnerable to further attacks. Thomas let go of Lucy and attacked again, but this time the man blocked his punch.

Dark magic oozed from the man's skin, and Thomas realized he'd need to do more than hit him. He felt a hand grip his again. "We fight," she said, glowing with golden light in the darkness. In her right hand was a bright sword.

With relief, Thomas drew on his own magic, and in this

non-physical space it came to him more easily. A bright sword appeared in his left hand, and they faced the intruder. Green light crackled around the man, and then he attacked; lightning forked towards them, but their swords absorbed the energy. They struck back. The figure retreated and began to speak, but Lucy stepped forward and stabbed him. He fled deeper into her mind, but they followed.

As they hunted the dark figure, they ran past many of her early memories. But he couldn't escape Lucy in her own mind—she knew where he hid. She pointed to a dark corner. "There."

She shone a light in the corner, and they saw a creature with the body of a giant baboon but a human head. It glared at them with red coal eyes. They attacked, and flames crackled around it as their swords penetrated its body. It screamed and burst into flames, but before it vanished, Thomas saw an image of a man dressed in black.

"Tell me your name!" Lucy demanded. And Thomas felt something pass between the man and her. "I know it."

Thomas opened his eyes. His clothes were soaked in sweat. Lucy opened her eyes and stared at him. She looked shaken. "What did you do at the end?" he asked.

"I took his name."

"Who is it?" Victor asked.

"Lord Frore is hunting us," she said.

"Then I suggest we move," Victor said, looking visibly shaken. "He's one of the worst they have." Odran led the way to Tartaros.

12

They moved quickly through the tunnels and eventually reached a river. The road ran next to it, and according to the gnome, it led to the town of Darkport, which faced Tartaros, on the far side of the river. Further down the road, they passed shacks with small lights inside. Their fronts were open, and groups of men and women with reddened eyes squatted on stone floors smoking rolled up leaves of some substance—Thomas guessed it was some sort of local narcotic. Some glanced up as the four of them passed, but avoided eye contact, and none of them saw the gnome running by their side, nor the ice demon running by the river.

"Prudent people avoid the eyes of those who enter Darkport from the mountain," Odran said quietly. A row of boats were moored by the side, and workers unloaded boats of what Thomas assumed were goods stolen from Tartaros.

"Can we just walk out?" Victor asked.

"We steal a boat," Thomas said. He'd seen the one he wanted: a large rowing boat with a covered section. It appeared to be unoccupied.

"Why not?" Victor said. "It'll save my legs from walking."

"I just want to get out of here," Lucy said.

Some men were unloading a nearby barge, but no one challenged them when they boarded the boat. A man was sleeping in the covered section—he stank of alcohol.

The gnome sniffed him. "Rotgut red." He shook his head. "Never drink it. This one won't be awake for several hours."

"How far is Tartaros?" Victor asked.

"Less than that."

They left the man sleeping and untied the boat. Thomas took the oars, though the current did most of the work. He kept the boat in the centre, where it was darker, and half an hour later they left Darkport and joined a much larger river.

Lucy crinkled her nose. "It's like an open sewer."

Thomas nodded; he hoped the city would smell better.

Odran pointed to the lights in the distance. "The Old Port is over there." The river was a few hundred yards wide, and Thomas rowed steadily towards the city, avoiding the small purple flames burning on parts of the surface.

"You'll need a guide for the city," Odran said.

"I was hoping you could help," Thomas said.

"I'm a gnome. I know a little of the city, but you'll need a human guide."

Thomas took the boat to the quietest part of the docks, but he misjudged the final stretch and crashed into the quay. Nobody in the docks above seemed to notice, but the sailor opened a pair of bleary red eyes. "Who are you?"

"What should we do with him?" Lucy asked as Victor climbed up the short ladder to the quay.

"Nothing." Thomas nodded towards the gnome, and then climbed up with Lucy behind him to where Victor waited.

Odran's eyes shone in the dark, and the man whimpered, crawling deeper into the stern of the boat and cursing the rotgut before collapsing. The gnome joined them on the docks.

"I cannot be seen on the streets," Chloris said. "I'll use the roofs to move. And I need to feed."

"We need to do something about her feeding habits," Lucy said once Chloris had disappeared onto a rooftop.

Thomas nodded, but he wasn't sure what. "Apart from humans, there's probably nothing bigger than a rat here." He doubted that Chloris would restrict herself to rats.

Lucy was staring up at the buildings. "Why do the houses need roofs?"

"Rockfalls and thieves," Odran said.

"That makes sense," she glanced up at the dark sky, "but it doesn't ease my mind."

Thomas had already probed the rocks and felt their stability. "I think it's fairly safe."

"This part of the world is not too bad," Odran said. "That's why they chose to build the city here."

They quickly blended into the crowd. It was a dark city of stone, lit by torches strapped to the walls and open fires in almost every square; their smoke added something cloying to the mix of smells.

"Tartaros hardly smells any better than the river," Lucy said as they walked past spice sellers lining the side of the road. "Now it's a fragrant sewer."

And a smoky one, he thought.

"Look," she whispered. Thomas followed her gaze; a child was defecating by the side of the street, yards from a vendor cooking spicy mushrooms. The man didn't appear to notice. "I feel sick."

"We have to be careful with the food," he said. "Despite

what the gnome says, we should keep an inch of rotgut red in our stomachs at all times." Victor laughed, but Lucy pulled a face at the idea. They followed the crowds and soon ended up in a market. "We don't have any money," Thomas said.

"A few coins." Victor jangled a purse.

"Where did those come from?"

The old man shrugged. "The dead don't need coins."

Thomas nodded; he'd noticed Victor checking the pockets of the dead in the caves. "True. In that case, I'm hungry."

They looked at the stalls as they passed. Varieties of fungi seemed to be the predominant food in the market: they came in many exotic shapes. Lucy peered into a coarse linen bag of long wriggling grubs and quickly let go.

Eventually, the street connected to a square. On the corner, an ornate temple stood. Inside the temple stood a carved statue of a goddess, surrounded by what looked like offerings of dirt. Incense burnt in her hands, adding a perfumed scent to the air. Next to the temple was a busy eating place where men and women squeezed along a long wooden bench. They found spaces at the end. In front of them was a rough wooden table made of planks resting on columns of stones. Along the table was a line of stone flagons filled with mild—a weak, dark beer.

They sat, and soon they had a large plate of black mushrooms and three mugs of mild. "Not bad," Thomas said. Lucy pulled up her nose at the beer in front of her and approached a water seller who quickly poured her a cup from his large pot. He stood grinning—apparently waiting for her to return the cup.

Lucy spat out the water. "What's wrong?" Victor asked.

"Something's swimming in it. Lots of somethings."

Thomas looked inside. Scores of tiny crustaceans swam about the stone cup.

"Protein," Victor said, drinking the mild.

Lucy threw the remains of the water on the ground and gave the grinning water seller his dirty cup back. She drank the mild instead. "Better for your stomach," Thomas said.

The vendor was watching them. "Not from round here."

Victor shook his head. "We're from outside the city."

The man nodded. "I have friends in the marshes."

Thomas didn't mention that they came from much further away than the marshes.

"What temple is this?"

"The Goddess of Filth." Thomas raised his eyebrows. "You're really not from around here. It's Lazolteotl's temple."

Shouts distracted them. Turning, Thomas watched bound men being dragged across the square; an excited crowd of people followed.

"Execution day. The king's getting rid of some of his staff." The man laughed. "He's hired a new assassin."

Thomas nodded at the man and smiled. "Let's take a look," he said to Lucy and Victor.

"Thomas?" Lucy said.

"I want to see what's happening."

They pushed through the crowd until they were close to the pair of gallows. Nine prisoners stood by the gallows. Several guards tried to keep the crowds from getting too close, but that didn't stop the occasional punch being thrown at the chained men.

"Which one's the king's assassin?" Thomas asked a man in the crowd.

"The one in blue."

There were two in blue, but Thomas chose the younger one, a man of about thirty. Thomas approached the man and a guard watched him suspiciously. Victor was at his shoulder.

"Are you the king's assassin?" Thomas asked. Not appearing to notice him, the man stared vacantly into the crowd. Thomas repeated the question in Silvan, and the man turned his gaze on him.

"I was," he said in Venusian. "I was fired."

"I know the feeling," Victor said. "I spent decades in Min Flo for being in the wrong place at the wrong time."

"Who are you?" the man said. The guard shouted something, and Victor punched his arm. The man winced. "What was that for?"

"The guards."

"Oh. Well next time aim for the other arm. Did you come to chat?"

"We need a guide," Thomas said.

"Tourists. That's nice."

"Does the new assassin walk strangely and hiss?" Thomas asked. The man stared at them, but Thomas saw recognition in his eyes. "We want to find him."

"And then?"

"Retake what he stole from us."

"And if he doesn't like that?"

"Killing him would be best. And I promise you he won't like it."

The man gave a slight smile. "I'd love to be of service, but as you see, I'm rather tied up."

"Agree to help us, and we'll free you."

He motioned to the big man next to him. "Agreed. And I'd like my companion here to come with me."

Thomas nodded. "If we had to leave this square quickly, which would be the best direction to go?"

The man smiled. "The second alley behind to your right. But you'll have to be fast. They plan to hang us soon."

"Don't react if you hear or feel anyone loosening the ropes."

"He'll have to be small and nimble."

"He is." Thomas stepped back and pretended to take an interest in the rest of the condemned. *"Odran?"* The gnome appeared by his knees, and the assassin's eyes widened in surprise. Thomas explained what he needed.

"Victor, get Lucy and wait in that alley. When we move, start running." The guards had already moved the first two prisoners into place. The ropes were around their necks, but before they died, a town crier read a long list of crimes. Thomas was sure that half of Tartaros heard it. The second two were the assassin and his accomplice.

Unseen by the guards and crowds, Odran waited at the bottom of the gallows. As soon as they moved both men into position, the gnome ran up the gallows and untied the rope from the top, then slid down and untied their hands.

As Odran worked, the town crier read the lists of crimes. It took longer than before. The crowd stared at the men with open mouths, and some spat at them as their crimes were read out. Thomas wondered whether he'd made the right choice saving these men, but the assassin would know the city better than most. As the time for the execution drew closer, Thomas focussed on the rocks around him, attempting to create a tremor with his rock magic. He played a guitar riff in the ground—or at least imagined it playing. That was enough. The crowd and the guards were distracted by the odd noise, and no one noticed when the ropes fell away. Thomas, the assassin, and his accomplice were halfway to the alley before the guards began their pursuit.

They ran for twenty minutes without stopping, the

The Darkling Odyssey

assassin leading them deeper into the old town. Eventually, they stopped, with the assassin checking carefully for signs of pursuit. All was quiet. "This way."

As they walked along a quiet alley, the assassin stopped and opened a door. "In here." His large accomplice entered last, locking the door behind him.

A candle burnt on a table, and the assassin lit two more. Then he faced them. "I don't know what you did, but it was good. My name is Alain Gardinier. This is Frank." The big man placed water on the table, and then sat impassively by the door. Alain looked around the room. "Where is your tiny friend?"

"He likes to wander," Lucy said.

"I'm not often surprised, but humans mixing with one of the little folk is unheard of." Alain then turned to Thomas. "What exactly do you want?"

"The new assassin has stolen some of our possessions, and we want them back."

"If they're of value, which I presume they are, then the only safe place is the king's castle, and even that is not completely safe."

"What kind of person is the king?" Thomas asked.

"Fearful. He never leaves his castle. He used to be a fighter, but now he's older and hides behind advisers. Unfortunately for them, the new assassin killed them and made himself the new advisor, too.

"We might have to kill this new advisor," Thomas said.

A slight smile passed over Alain's face. "Frank's proven himself invaluable in many such situations." The big man sitting silently gave a curt nod.

Thomas could easily imagine. "Does the new assassin leave the castle often?"

"He only appeared in the castle a few days ago, and he's

only been the assassin for half a day. But after what's just happened, I think he'll come looking for me. Does he know you're here?"

"He will do by now," Thomas said.

Alain took a sip of water, watching them all the while. "You're an unusual team, and if I'm right, you've lived on other planets." He looked at Victor.

"In another lifetime."

"I know all about those. What I need to know now is if you have any special skills. I know you have the gnome, and that's special, but is there anything else? What were those strange sounds?"

"I know some tricks and illusions," Thomas said. The man's face was unreadable.

"A powerful illusion, if that's what it was. And if you recover these stolen items?" Thomas was unsure how much to say to this man.

"We'll leave the city," Lucy said. "We have no reason to remain." She glanced at Thomas. *"He's not trustworthy, but he wants the king and new assassin dead."*

"And we can help," Thomas said silently.

"You've saved my life, and I appreciate that. As does Frank. Tomorrow, we hunt the new assassin."

THE NEXT DAY, with weapons hidden under their clothes, they walked through the dark streets of Tartaros. Thomas felt more comfortable carrying the short sword. He glanced ahead at the assassin, who was wearing a cloak with a hood, which hid his features. Alain led the way. Lucy walked with Victor, whose leg sounded on the cobbles, but less since the repairs Alain had made the night before. He and Frank walked at the back. Lucy had sensed the magic in the old town.

"Why can't I sense it?" Thomas asked.

"I'm not sure, but it's faint. It seems to have changed," Lucy said.

"In what way?"

"Less open. As if it's being blocked."

They passed a vendor selling saddle-shaped fungus. "I can smell something," Lucy said.

"The goblin's saddle or the open sewers?" Alain asked.

She looked at the yellow fungi being fried by the street vendor and shook her head. "It's coming from the alley—magic."

Thomas focussed on the alley, then narrowed his eyes. "I can't sense anything." He wondered if he was losing his touch. "What's up there?"

"The Smoking Bird," Alain said. "We could take a beer." Frank looked up, hopeful. "Not for you, my friend; I'll need you outside, just in case."

"In case of what?" Lucy asked.

"Just a precaution," Alain said.

"If you're right about magic, then the basilisk might be waiting for us," Thomas said. She frowned as they walked along the alley.

Before they reached the inn, they passed an open frontage, where a small group of people stood around an open coffin—the body of a boy lay inside. A priest was giving a simple service, and Frank stopped and stood quietly at the edge of the group.

"Why did he stop?" Victor asked.

"Life is hard in Tartaros. Frank lost his only child very young. He's paying his respects."

"He's an assassin," Lucy said.

"Death is an everyday experience here and not as special as in other places, but each person is different. Frank has killed many people, but never a child." Lucy glanced at Thomas. He shrugged. As the assassin said, it was a part of life.

The wooden façade of the narrow inn was carved to show birds surrounded by flames. Similarly, the sign above the Smoking Bird showed a large bird surrounded by fire.

Thomas pushed the door of the Smoking Bird open, and they walked into the smoky taproom. Torches on the walls lit the room, and people laughed loudly. A woman shrieked raucously at a joke. A pair of birds were being roasted over a large fire. Many of the men and women smoked pipes, and their smoke added to that of the cooking birds.

"Over there," Alain said, pointing at an empty table by a window. Before sitting, he opened the window.

Thomas noticed that it was the only window that opened, and it had a view of the alley. "Nice." He was sure Alain had picked this table with an escape route in mind.

A boy approached the table but avoided eye contact with them. "Porter or mild?"

Thomas liked the porter, but its strength made it unsuitable for applying magic. The boy soon returned with four mugs of mild, and the ubiquitous fried fungus usually served with beer.

"The boy's nervous," Victor said.

"I sometimes have that effect on people," Alain said.

"Do you think he recognized you?" Lucy asked.

"No."

"It might not be that," Thomas said. "I can sense something in here," Thomas said. *"But not the Keys."*

"I know," Lucy said. Then she spoke aloud. "With our rags, we blend in quite well."

"Not so much," Alain said. "We're being watched." Four men sat apart from the rest of the drinkers, not speaking. They appeared to be focussed on the drinks in front of them. Thomas listened in the True Language, and he noticed they were straining to listen to Thomas and his friends.

"They're violent," Lucy said. One of the men disappeared through a door behind the table and up a narrow set of stairs.

"Not just them," Alain said. "In the taproom, too." Thomas had noticed. The once loud taproom had become quiet since they sat down, and more eyes studied them intently from behind glasses of porter and mild. "This is starting to feel bad," the assassin said.

The gnome hopped out of the wall, and Victor spat a mouthful of mild onto the table. "At least give me some warning," he said.

The gnome grinned at Victor, then spoke to the group. "The basilisk is here."

"Basilisk?" Alain asked.

"The new assassin's not human," Thomas said.

Alain raised his eyebrows.

"A serpent person," Lucy said.

Thomas was unsure if Alain believed them, but it didn't really matter. Without looking up, he said, "We have company."

Twelve men moved towards them. They looked like brawlers, and most of them were armed with knives and clubs. Thomas had already seen them, and he'd drawn his short sword under the table.

"I think we're outnumbered," Victor said as the tables around them emptied of drinkers.

"Perhaps," Alain said, "but ability counts, too."

Which was exactly what Thomas was trying to judge.

There were five of them, but Lucy and Victor were not the best fighters, despite Lucy having improved since he'd known her. He judged the assassin and gnome as lethal.

A large man approached the table. "You're under arrest for murder." The assassin laughed and pretended to drink his beer, but when the man reached for him, Alain smashed his mug in the man's face and followed up with a punch.

The men attacked. Thomas stabbed the first one in his chest, and he saw Alain do the same. The two deaths taught their attackers to take more care. With a pair of short swords, the assassin fought two men who slashed at him with long knives. One fell back, bleeding from his forehead, but another took his place. Less than a minute later, another man lay dead on the floor. A man rushed at Thomas, who sidestepped the knife thrust and stabbed him in his throat. The man died with a confused look.

The narrow door crashed open, and a tall figure in a crimson cloak slid into the room—Thomas recognized the basilisk immediately. Their attackers pulled back. Breathing heavily, Thomas realized he'd become separated from the others, who were near the window. The armed men looked at the new assassin expectantly. "Twelve of you and you haven't taken them yet?"

"Only eight now," Alain said.

Thomas rushed forward, killing the man who had just fetched Sir Val with a single thrust of his sword. As the crimson-cloaked figure span around, Thomas pulled away its hood. When a whipcord of basilisk magic cut into his hand, he tripped and fell backwards, still holding the serpent's crimson cloak.

Their attackers stared at the basilisk in shock. Even Alain stared in shock at the mottled grey and green serpent man who stood before them, raising itself on its tail. Its slit eyes and vertical irises flicked around the room before returning to Thomas.

The creature was now alive with magic, and a grey cloud came from its hands and drifted towards Thomas. Thomas called his rock magic and the rock walls snapped. For a moment, Sir Val's eyes widened, then it cackled in relief. Again Thomas called on his magic, and this time a little more came to him. But it was not enough.

"I am the king's chief advisor. All will obey the will of the king!" he hissed. "Take this man and the girl; kill the rest." Men rushed towards Thomas, but they mysteriously fell, grasping their legs. Thomas saw the green light moving underneath the tables and chairs. Thomas attacked again, but the creature's magic flared—protecting it. It knocked the blade from his hand and stalked towards him. "Take them!"

Lucy and Victor were throwing broken furniture at anything that came close, and near them, Alain fought fiercely with two blades. Their attackers had learnt not to get too close to him, and they now seemed to be aiming to tire him out. It was working. Thomas knew it was just a matter of time before they were taken or killed.

His heart sank when more men ran into the inn, surrounding them. He'd found another sword, but if they'd not been trying to take him alive, he might have been be dead.

Lucy and Victor were knocked against the opposite wall, and they quickly disarmed Lucy. Alain tried to grab her but was forced back at sword point, and she was dragged to the far side of the inn. Alain then pulled Victor to his feet. He whispered something to the old man, who started to argue until a knife flew past his head. Victor ran and leapt out of the open window; Alain followed him.

Thomas looked for Lucy. He could no longer see her, but he did notice Odran by his feet. The gnome was still unnoticed by most of their attackers, until he slashed the nearest one across his ankles. Thomas finished him with a rapid jab to the throat. They now had their backs to the wall.

"It's over," a man said. But Thomas still felt some rock magic giving him extra strength.

"Thomas!" Odran said. The pale green man was walking into the wall near his knee. *"Forget your sword. Come with me!"* He felt the gnome gripping his leg, and he felt the elemental magic merging with his. He'd walked through rock with magical creatures before. Thomas lowered his sword, and the men hesitated, looking towards their leader.

"No!" the basilisk rattled loudly as Thomas fell through the rock and into the street beyond. Only his sword remained, imbedded in the wall of the inn.

13

Lucy pulled her chains, but they were securely attached to the dungeon wall. All she could do was stand or sit. So she sat against the wall and looked around the damp room.

Even with her sharp sight, it was difficult to see in the gloom. A glint of light entered the chamber from the viewing hole in the door at the top of a small flight of steps. It was enough to make her aware of a skeleton in one corner. And the rats—they were hostile and refused to speak, but at least they kept away from her.

She listened to the sounds of the castle. Since being brought here, she'd tried to contact Thomas, but something had stopped her. Possibly something in the strange-tasting water they gave her, although perhaps it wasn't strong enough, because she could still hear the life around her. They hadn't touched the white snakes that coiled around her wrists like bracelets, their heads swallowing their tails. But they didn't answer her either.

Lucy pulled on the heavy chains. If they'd used the electronic locks, she might have been able to free herself with the limited magic she had, but not the heavy iron padlocks. Intuitively, she knew she was closer to the Keys, and she knew that Thomas would come—perhaps some of the others, too.

Animals scampered away—someone was coming. A key rattled into the door, and it opened. An armed guard carrying a torch walked down the steps and unchained her. "The king wants to see you." Hoping she wouldn't meet the king's new assassin, she followed him up circular stairs. They went through a guardroom and then through a large hallway to another twisting flight of stairs. By the time she reached the top of the tower, she was out of breath. She had to warn the king that his new assassin was not what he seemed. They stopped outside a pair of heavy, engraved doors.

At the guard's knock, a sound came from inside, and the guard pushed open the doors. King John sat on an ornately carved wooden chair at the head of a long table. A fire burnt nearby. The king was probably in his forties, but he looked older. He was overweight, and his skin was pockmarked and an unhealthy yellow. Lucy realized that he was the first fat person she'd seen in this world. And that there was something seriously wrong with him. "Your Majesty, the girl," a guard said, and then the guard left the room. At least that was a good sign.

"Come!" the king said. He leant back and watched her. A slow smile spread across his face until she could see his yellow teeth. Although nothing appeared wrong, a chill passed through her; her intuition urged her to run, but she approached slowly, taking in as much of the room as she could. Swords and spears decorated the walls, and unwashed cups lay on a table in front of the king; the room smelt of stale beer. It was not what she'd expected.

"I have to warn..."

He interrupted. "Who are you?"

"Lucy Thomson. I'm passing through..."

"Why?"

She hesitated; she didn't want to talk about travelling to the centre of the planet, and certainly not about Thomas's dreams of finding Aina. "I have to warn you about your new assassin. He's not what he seems."

A faint smile passed the king's face. "No?"

His reaction was strange. "He's not human. He's a basilisk—a magic user."

"What do you know of magic?" As he spoke, Lucy felt a tremor of magic. He'd spoken telepathically but had guarded his words.

As a door at the back of the room opened, a heavy feeling settled in Lucy's stomach. She sighed as the basilisk slid across the stone floor—she should have read the signs. He still wore his crimson cloak, but his serpent's head and tail were both clearly exposed. He coiled up before the open fire and waited. Had he drugged the king? For several seconds, the three of them watched each other in the silent throne room.

The king looked at her coldly. "What did you have to warn me about exactly?" He sounded strange; perhaps he was drunk, but his eyes contradicted that. When she didn't respond, he said, "Tell me again. Why are you here?"

"This thief stole something of mine, and I want it back."

"If I remember correctly, you gave them away freely," the king said, "but they don't belong to you; they belong to the one who has the power to take them."

"You?" she asked.

"In a sense." The king laughed.

"The basilisk won't give them to you."

"He already has," the king said. She was confused as to why the basilisk would hand them over to this underworld king.

"They're designed to be used, not exhibited in a dusty museum. And I have a use for them."

"What use?"

The king stood and walked straight towards her. His physical condition contradicted the energy he gave off. She now knew the king was not what he seemed, but she was still uncertain what he was, apart from clearly being a magic user. Scared, she reached out for her magic.

"No!" The king punched her and then pushed her hard onto the stone table, knocking cups to the floor.

Leaning against the table, dazed, she brought her hands to her face. Her nose was bleeding. Wiping away the blood, she said, "What do you want?"

"Everything," the king said.

"You can just ask," she said, pushing away from the table.

"I don't ask. I take." There was something about his words that was familiar.

"You're in danger," she said, hoping to distract him. "Your assassin doesn't work for you."

The king grinned, and she shivered at his cold gaze. "He's mine. Like you." He gripped her neck and squeezed while Sir Val watched from the fireplace. Her skin stung, and she felt faint. Then, before she could block it, his mind penetrated hers. She'd never experienced such power and was helpless as he pushed her aside in her own mind and studied her private memories. She felt violated and dirty. Then she knew why he was familiar. "Frore!" She fought back, but he'd infused the king's body with his magic. He was too strong for her, both physically and magically.

"Thomas!"

"He's not here, and if he was, I'd kill him."

He flicked through her memories as if her mind was a picture album. Hidden secrets of her life flashed before her mind, of her family, of Earth. And those interested him most. She struggled and mentally pushed, but he repeatedly knocked her back. She felt the white fibrous snakes come to life, and she sensed his surprise, but the man ripped one apart with a burst of magic. The other fell lifeless to the floor.

She felt faint and could no longer feel her body; she was trapped again in a small corner of her mind. She saw the real king for a second; an outsider in his own mind as she was in hers. She called the real king for help, but he laughed at her.

Lucy felt Frore's surprise and curiosity at his discovery that she came from another planet. He went deeper and became lost within her memories. He studied its history, science, and technology. And he sought a doorway to Earth. Then his focus changed: he looked for ways to access the magic of the Keys. She sensed greed. He had no need, but he wanted more—he wanted to surpass the Emperor's power. But as he searched, he left spaces for her to exploit. His mind opened to hers, and as he took from her, she silently took from him.

Searching his memories, she found what she wanted. She saw the location of the Keys, and she saw how the basilisk had attempted to insulate the magic. She went deeper and entered hidden chambers—those protected by magic she left alone—but she observed the scenes in others. She saw him enter the Emperor's throne room. Magicians of great power watched her. Scared by the dark magic radiating from them, she searched other memories.

She saw the concealed knife in the king's robes. And then she saw three dark riders on giant hellhounds with burning red eyes—the first one was Frore. They approached Tartaros. Sensing that he had almost finished, she searched harder, seeking a smaller memory; one that no one else would know. And then she saw the forgotten place she wanted, and she planted a seed deep within his mind.

Lord Frore pushed away in shock. "What have you done to me?" he shouted. She'd been acting instinctively and wasn't sure exactly, but she sensed that one day, she could call upon that seed, and that it would germinate and grow for her.

Their minds were still connected by a grey, nebulous thread that extended from her to the king, and then on to the real Lord Frore who rode towards the gates of the city. Again he attempted to enter her mind, but this time she was ready. She imagined a fiery knife, and it appeared bright in her mind. She cut the wispy grey thread and Frore screamed. He was gone.

King John collapsed to the floor. He was having a heart attack, but she felt no sympathy for the man; she'd been too deep in his mind. While Sir Val tended his lord, unaware of what had happened, she ran to a safe hidden behind a hinged picture of the king, cursing quietly when she realized she couldn't unlock it.

The basilisk knocked her to the floor, and as it closed the picture door, she took the knife from the king's clothes. Sir Val slid across the room, stopping midway between the table and the doors. She knew the guards waited outside—she sat on the carved chair and waited.

"You killed the king," it hissed.

"Not much of a king." It watched her. It was deciding what to do, but when the white snake the king had killed came back to life, Val hesitated. "Why would a basilisk work for the Empire?"

Its mood changed, and she sensed discomfort. Subtly, she touched its mind and, unbeknown to it, listened to its thoughts. Nothing she learnt surprised her: desire, greed, rejection, and self-doubt. Frore would have seen the same as her and used them to his advantage.

She needed time to think of something. Magic flowed from the safe to her, but not enough. And she felt light-headed after Frore's attack. She was in the strange position of not wanting it to leave; she wanted time to gather her strength. She focussed on one of the main anxieties she'd found in its mind. "Will Frore really share magical knowledge?"

"He's already shown me magic."

"A little, but nothing significant." She was guessing, but a sudden spike in its emotions showed her she'd hit the truth, or close enough to it. "You can't trust him."

"I know."

"Are you of the Black Nest?" Lucy asked, remembering the only basilisk tribe she'd heard of. It rustled as its coils tightened. *Perhaps not*, she thought, *but it didn't feel comfortable with the name*. "What now?"

"We wait," it hissed. "Lord Frore wishes to reacquaint himself with you." She listened without feeling any emotion, nor any particular urgency, despite knowing that she only had hours before Frore and his riders arrived. "Otherwise I'd kill you immediately."

But even its threats didn't disturb her. She leant forward and poured a glass of cold tea from the jug on the table while the white snake watched the basilisk. She had a few hours to find the key to its mind and then the key to the box. "Shall we drink tea?"

14

Drawing on both his natural magic and the elemental magic of the gnome, Thomas walked deeper through the rock. Each step hurt; the rock was already hardening. He pushed harder through the rock. He'd be dead soon if he didn't quickly get to the other side of the thick wall.

His right leg sprang out of the stone, and he pushed on his left foot, crying in pain as rock ripped skin as he left the wall. The magic had gone.

"I've never seen anything like that," Alain said. Victor was with him, while Frank was stabbing the hands of the men trying to follow through the window. Thomas stood unarmed in the narrow alley, with tattered clothes and a bleeding foot. His boot had disappeared. He breathed heavily as the pain almost overwhelmed him. "I need new clothes. And skin."

Alain examined his leg. "We can find new clothes, and your skin will regrow." Thomas cried out when the gnome touched his wounds, but then the pain subsided. He looked down to see a green light around the gnome's hands.

"A healing magic, but you still need time to fully heal. And it needs dressing."

Armed men ran along the alley towards them; more pushed through the window, forcing Frank back, and others came out of an entrance at the back of the inn, behind them. Thomas backed away—his energy gone as well as his weapon. They faced twenty men, and despite their fighting skill, there were just too many swords facing them. The gnome had magic, but Thomas wasn't sure it was enough.

"Surrender," a sergeant of the guard said. "You can't win this fight."

The assassin looked at him, and Thomas knew what he was going to do. "I need a sword," Thomas said under his breath.

"That I can get you; more than that I don't know."

The sergeant turned to his men. "I want that one alive." He gestured to Thomas. "Kill the rest."

A screech came from above, and then a shadow fell on the soldiers. The odds had changed. The ice demon had killed several men. "Alain! A sword!"

The assassin stabbed a startled man in the chest and scooped up his dropped sword, tossing it to Thomas. "What . . . ?"

"No time to explain." Thomas stabbed at the basilisk.

"Lucy?" Chloris said.

"She's been taken prisoner."

"I saw a carriage," Chloris said. "The serpent was inside."

The fight lasted a few minutes longer, but the appearance of Chloris had taken away the soldiers' will. Soon they were backing away, and when Chloris charged, the last of the men turned and fled down the alley.

"The only place they'd take your friend would be the castle," Alain said as Chloris returned to their side.

"Then that's where we go," Thomas said. They ran down the alley after Alain, Frank bringing up the rear. With every step, the pain in Thomas's foot increased, and he started to slow.

"Frank can carry you," Alain said. Thomas was heavy, yet the big man picked him up and ran with him over his shoulder with ease. "I know somewhere to get your leg fixed." He glanced nervously at Chloris. "Who is our new friend?

"An ice demon," Thomas said. He was pleased to let Victor continue the conversation. It was hard to chat when bouncing over a running man's shoulder. Saying something about scouting in the True Language, Chloris disappeared up a wall.

They ran through the back alleys. The people they passed moved quickly out of the way, but Thomas noticed a man following them. He told the assassin.

"I've seen the fool." Alain span round and slapped the man; his other hand placed a knife at the man's throat.

The man's eyes widened in recognition, and his mouth opened wide. "I'm sorry. I didn't recognize you." He quickly stepped away from the assassin.

They quickly walked away. Alain shook his head. "The quality of thieves has deteriorated since I was young." He continued leading Thomas along the poorly lit alley.

A few moments later, they stopped outside the dingy entrance to some kind of shop. Alain pushed the door open and a bell rang. It was a primitive surgery.

"What do you want?" a woman yelled from a back room. Seconds later, a thin woman of about forty stepped through the door at the back of the room. She glared at Alain. "Where have you been for the past year?"

"Not that long," Alain said. The woman looked at Thomas, immediately noticing his bleeding foot.

"My friend needs help."

"I can see. You have money?" Alain placed coins on the wooden table. The woman pocketed them and pointed to a rickety wooden chair. Thomas sat, wondering what type of treatment he'd get in a place like this.

"Molly's the best healer in Tartaros," Alain said.

"You mean I'm the only one to do business with you." She stared across the room as the gnome disappeared through the door and blinked. "What was that?" No one answered, and she frowned before gathering the things she needed.

Thomas wondered if there was any point staying, but she cleaned up his heel and dressed the wound. The dressing she used was almost clean—probably the cleanest thing in the room.

"It's already started healing," Molly said. "It should be right soon enough."

The woman left the room, soon returning with a pair of cheap muskin sandals. "Someone left these." She dropped them in front of Thomas, then left the room again, leaving them to talk.

"You think Lucy's in the castle?" Thomas asked.

"Almost certainly," Alain said. "I assume you want to pay a visit?"

"Yes."

Molly screamed from the back of the shop. The assassin stood, his sword already drawn. The woman rushed in and grabbed hold of him. "Save me!"

He pushed her away and stepped towards the door to

the back of the shop; Frank was at his side. They stopped when Chloris pushed her way through the open door. She was bleeding from several cuts.

"Let me introduce Chloris," Thomas said. Turning to Chloris, he asked, "What happened?"

"I found some guards with pikes."

"And?" Thomas asked.

"I killed them."

"A new patient, Molly," Alain said. He walked over to a cupboard and took out a bottle of dark liquor and some dirty glasses.

"I can't help that thing," she said.

"Do you need help?" Thomas asked.

"Stopping the bleeding would be appreciated," Chloris said.

"Help her or she'll kill you," Thomas said flatly, wondering what he'd do if she refused.

Alain raised an eyebrow but nodded as Thomas spoke. "Molly specializes in exotic injuries." Molly was tougher than she appeared, and soon she was cleaning the ice demon's wounds.

Alain poured drinks for Thomas, Victor, and himself. "I know a way in, but it's going to be a dirty trip."

"What do you mean?"

"The best hidden way into the castle is through the sewers."

15

The boat Alain arranged was dark, sleek, and smaller than the fat barges that navigated the river. Alain steered the boat, Victor and Odran sat together, Thomas and Frank were next to them, and Chloris rowed with steady, powerful strokes. The boat glided quickly over the surface towards the castle, which lay half a mile upstream. In many places the black water bubbled as gas rose to the surface. Thomas wondered if anything could live in it; Lucy would have been able to probe its surface and see.

The castle sat on a promontory at the conflux of two rivers; both were cleaner than the rivers combined, but not by much. When they got nearer, Chloris stopped rowing, and the boat slid up onto a small beach. Despite the yellow stream seeping out from the castle sewers, the smell here was not as bad as at the docks.

Frank secured the boat. The gnome disappeared on the beach, while Thomas, Chloris, and Alain followed the shallow stream up the beach to the sewer entrance in the base of the cliffs beneath the castle. A gate blocked the tunnel, but a small section had broken away. Alain pulled two of the bars out, revealing a hole. "When you return, put these back in place. I'd like to keep this entrance a secret." He'd already given Thomas directions for finding his way inside the sewer. "I have to go. If we keep the boat here, it'll attract attention from the guards on the walls. We'll wait for you within shouting distance." He pointed to a small beach upstream from the smaller river.

Thomas and Chloris slipped through the hole, and Alain replaced the bars and was gone. They ran along the pathway by the side of the sewer. It smelt no worse than the docks, but it wasn't sweet. He mostly felt his way along, but the directions were fairly simple, and he ran straight for much of the way. Chloris remained silent, as usual. After about half an hour, he noticed a change in the atmosphere; smoky air blew down the tunnel—it came from a dark shaft above them. The royal toilet, as Alain had called it, and it also served the kitchens and the keep.

Thomas found the cracks and holes in the wall that served as steps, despite the dirty slime that oozed out of them, and soon reached the shaft. Once there, he found the metal rungs embedded in the wall. The secret that Alain had told him. A good climber could have climbed up slowly, but Thomas had a natural affinity to the rock. Feeling the rock's magic, he stuck to it like a mountain goat and moved rapidly up the shaft, with Chloris at his side, and he was pleased to discover that the slime on the side of the shaft was actually lichen.

He passed the narrow holes for the kitchens and guards' room, and then the shaft narrowed to about a yard across. At the top was a small circular hole: the king's toilet, he hoped. He waited and listened. He heard voices, but no one was in the room itself. The wooden toilet seat had a latch, which he knocked back. Slowly, Thomas pushed the wooden seat up and climbed out into a small torchlit chamber. A stone tub stood on legs to one side of the room. He'd have loved to soak there for the next few hours, but he knew it'd be a long time before he even saw a bathtub again.

He opened the bathroom and listened carefully. The room looked like one of the king's chambers, but it was unoccupied. He walked past a set of stairs and towards the solar, the king's personal chamber. His feeling was clear; there was magic in the room.

With Chloris at his side, Thomas pushed the doors open and walked in. The orange flames from the open fire and the hanging torches lit the room. The king lay dead on the floor. Lucy sat on a large chair with a dagger in her hand; dried blood caked her face. She looked calm, but the energy coming from her told a different story. He'd once thought he'd lacked empathy; now it almost overwhelmed him. *"Lucy!"*

"Hello, Thomas."

Sir Val was coiled by the fireplace watching them—a fresh cut ran across his face. Lucy's eyes were glazed, and Thomas searched for the source of magic.

"Behind the picture of the king," she said. "But the box is locked, and Sir Val won't share the key."

Thomas noticed a broken white fibrous snake struggling to raise its head, and the basilisk hissed as it moved. "Is that stopping it?"

"I don't think so. I think it's playing a waiting game. Three very unpleasant sorcerers will arrive soon, and when they do, they'll take the Keys and try to kill us."

He wondered whether she'd been drugged. Her reactions seemed slow. "I'm just tired," she said. He supposed that her reading of his mind was a good sign.

But Thomas had no time for stalemates. He approached

the basilisk. "The key to the safe." The creature called on its magic. Lucy tossed Thomas the dagger.

"Just stick it in it. I tried, but I feel a little weak to be chasing a serpent person around the room." Chloris hissed her approval.

"You wait because you have no choice," the basilisk said. "My master will take care of you soon."

"Take care?" Lucy said. "Is that what you call it?"

"There are worse things."

From Lucy's blank eyes, Thomas didn't think she could think of many. He rushed it, and Chloris attacked from the other side, but they were thrown back by a magic shock. Thomas threw the dagger, his hands still tingling from the basilisk's magic. His years of training helped, but the basilisk still knocked it away.

"You've cut it," Lucy said. It was true—more blood dripped from Sir Val.

Thomas noticed signs of a second fight, after the king had died. Lucy had weakened the creature, but weakened herself, too. She looked at him and nodded. Her reactions and mind reading unnerved him slightly, as did the brief smile that her eyes did nothing to support.

"It's making a mistake," he said to Lucy.

She watched Sir Val. *"Take advantage—I can't."*

Thomas jumped forward and slashed it with his own knife. When Sir Val attempted to draw magic from the box behind the picture, perhaps to aid his struggling magic, he opened the way for Thomas, who was bathed in a richer magic than he'd felt for years.

He called on the power of the pentacle and the picture flew from the wall. Sir Val shrieked as the safe burnt with white heat. He tried to press it shut with his magic, but he'd waited too long. The door of the safe melted, and the pentacle flew into Thomas's hand. He was bathed in bright light.

The basilisk rushed at Lucy, a knife in hand, but she stood and reached out, too. The golden cup that was hers flew faster than the serpent could slide, straight to her hand. She rubbed it, manipulating its magic, and it shifted its form, enlarging then shrinking onto her hand like a golden gauntlet. She punched the basilisk, and it flew across the room, hitting the wall by the door. It began to call on its magic, but when Lucy walked towards it, it gave up and desperately tried to open the main door.

She strode towards it, golden light pouring from her. The serpent frantically opened the main door and rushed out as fire burnt its tail. It screamed as it slid along the corridor, falling down the stairs.

Lucy reentered the king's solar. "Frore used the king to force himself into my mind, and now he comes with two more sorcerers," she said, looking towards Thomas and Chloris. "I plan to kill them."

This was not like Lucy, despite the man's attack on her. "What was he searching for?"

Lucy was silent for several seconds, then spoke. "He searched my childhood memories. It was as if he sought something he'd never had." Her expression was pained. "And he hopes to add to his power—that's why he wants the Keys. He wants more power than the Emperor."

"So he's ambitious."

"Thomas."

He was disturbed by the tone of her voice. "Yes?"

"He knows we're from Earth; he was searching for ways to reach it."

"I think Earth is safe. I don't even think there is a way. Not from here."

"He might find one, one day. He's dangerous. We must kill him."

This was so unlike her, although his mind hadn't been violated by the man. But he didn't disagree. To finish it now made sense—if they had the power.

Hounds bayed beyond the walls. "They come," she said.

"We fight?" Chloris hissed.

"Yes," Lucy said.

Thomas was less sure. "I have no problem killing Frore, but he's more powerful than any sorcerer we've met."

"Thomas, so are we! We have the Keys again. Can't you feel the magic?"

He could. It pulsed through him. He felt all the stones of the castle down to its foundations, and he felt the earth energy vibrating in the ground beneath it.

She pressed her lips together before speaking. "When Frore attacked me through the king, I fought back. I planted something inside of him; I plan to wake it."

A noise sounded from the balcony, and they turned to see Odran, his green magic fading as he walked into the room. "It's too dangerous; you're not ready for this. Not yet."

"We have the Keys," Thomas said, warming up to Lucy's idea.

"There are three of them, and each one is deadly."

"I feel the power of the cup," Lucy said.

"That's the problem."

"Where were you?" Lucy asked.

"Distracting the enemy," Odran said, "but their strength is greater than any I've encountered—even greater than many of the elementals of the deep parts of this planet. I never knew humans could gain so much power. You're not ready to face them."

"Our magic has returned," Lucy said.

"You would struggle to beat the two lesser sorcerers. Frore would be impossible. They draw on great power. And I fear that the Emperor has reached out to a far greater and darker power. I fear he may be a puppet of something worse. But you have the potential to descend and take the Fire of Prometheus. They fear you; they fear what you may become and wish to fight you now, before you've reached your potential."

"The Fire of Prometheus is far away, and it's uncertain we'll ever reach it," Thomas said.

"You must believe," the gnome said. Chloris hissed at the sound of footsteps coming up the stairs. "Don't risk all by fighting before you're ready. You may kill one or two of these sorcerers, but that won't be enough. Take the Fire and finish it once and for all. To fight now is to hand great power to this sorcerer."

Lucy's eyes hardened, and when the doors opened and soldiers rushed in, she drew on her magic. Thomas felt the vibrations, and the men screamed, falling down holding their heads.

He raised an eyebrow.

"I did something with sound. This is different than before. I can use the magic in different ways." She turned to the gnome, her expression determined. "You speak well, but it's time to fight."

A horn blew from beyond the castle walls, and hounds bayed. Walking onto the balcony, Lucy and Thomas watched men running and shouting in the courtyard below. "They're welcoming him," Thomas said.

"The sorcerer influences their minds," Odran said.

"Let's change that," Lucy said.

Three dark figures rode through the gates at the head of a pack of giant hellhounds. Each hound was the size of a horse. Their red eyes glowed and fire frothed at their mouths as they watched terrified people run before them. One of the hounds ripped a man's head off. "They're things of magic imprinted into living hounds," Odran said.

"I know the riders from Frore's memories," Lucy said. "The grey skinned one is Xart, a goblin sorcerer." Odran hissed in distaste. "The other is a witch called Biddy Zo."

Lucy walked back into the king's room and lifted a crossbow from the wall. "Thomas. Help me load this. I've never used one before."

"This is a mistake," Odran said as Thomas showed her how to load the crossbow.

Grabbing one for himself, Thomas loaded it. "If what you say is true, then what better way to test it?" He hefted the crossbow. "We don't have to get too close." The magic warmed him and gave him confidence. "Just one bolt—in Frore's head," he said.

"Yes," Chloris said in approval.

From short fragments of conversation with Chloris, Thomas was aware that she resented the creators of her race, that she dreamt of freedom. He walked back onto the balcony. "It takes practice to hit your target the first time," he said to Lucy.

"Or magic." She aimed carefully, and Thomas felt her magic come alive. "This is for you." Frore looked up as Lucy's bolt flew the short distance down to the courtyard. It hit the sorcerer in his chest, and he tumbled from his hound. She smiled coldly. "That wasn't too hard."

Thomas watched Frore's prone body, expecting him to jump up, but it didn't move. "We should kill the other two, too," he said. But then it was too late. The remaining two riders rushed to the tower at the head of the pack of giant hounds.

"Let them come to us," Chloris said. "We wait."

"Where will you go if you live?" Odran asked.

Thomas felt uncomfortable with the gnome's question. "We'll search for deeper passages within the planet," Thomas said. He listened to the sounds of the hounds clattering on the floor of the reception room far below. "Will you join us?"

"No, my place is here. Gnomes stay with the earth we were born in."

"We could do with your help," Thomas said. "The plains will be dangerous."

"They'll be deadly. Even if you survive these sorcerers, the hounds will hunt and kill you."

"What do you suggest then?" Thomas asked. He was already having second thoughts about waiting for the sorcerers.

"You must seek a shortcut, as gnomes often do. You must travel through the elemental realm."

"How do we enter the elemental realm?"

"Seek the entrance in the swamps beyond the city. Ask for Lazolteotl."

"The Goddess of Filth?" Lucy asked. "She's real?"

"She's more than that," the gnome said, nodding. "And one more thing. You agreed to help me remove the basilisk."

"And we will," Lucy replied. She glanced towards the open doors. The hounds had caught their smell; their excited barks could be heard coming from the stairwell.

Thomas loaded the crossbows, putting Lucy's on the table before her. Magic was fine, but a pair of bolts would take out the first two hounds.

As soon as the hellhounds rushed through the open doors, bolts shot through their chests, but both continued to run towards them. Using a sword infused with the pentacle's magic, Thomas attacked the hounds. The sword hurt them more than the bolts, but they fought hard, snapping at him. Lucy had injured her own attacker but hadn't stopped it, and others pushed into the room.

Sweating heavily, Thomas managed to keep the hounds at bay, but he was beginning to regret his decision to fight. The gnome rushed along the ground as a green light; the hounds yelped and staggered as he cut their legs. Chloris fought hard and pushed the hounds back, but they were infused with magic and hard to kill.

An old woman cackled from the doors. The witch, Biddy Zo, chanted a spell, and Thomas felt a weakening in his resolve. "It's her spell," Odran said just before a tall dark figure pushed through the hounds, green magic crackling around him. Thomas's stomach sank. It was Frore.

Lucy stared at him openmouthed.

"You didn't kill me. Nor hurt me." He laughed. "What you saw was for show." He pointed at them, and Thomas felt a pull on the pentacle and a pressure on his throat. He started to choke.

When Chloris attacked Frore, the man slapped her with the back of his hand, and the ice demon flew onto the balcony and tumbled over the edge. "An ice demon as a friend?"

Lucy screamed as the cup was ripped from her hand and flew to Frore. She staggered forward, grabbing the table for support. Frore then pointed at Thomas, and he felt a strong tug on his pentacle.

Thomas attacked. His sword shone brightly with magic, but Frore countered with strands of energy. One whipped Thomas's wrist, and the sword fell to the floor. Frore stepped forward and ripped the pentacle from his neck.

The flow of magic stopped. He gasped in shock. This was not meant to happen.

Lord Frore smirked. "Not what you expected?"

Thomas felt dizzy, and he stepped back towards the table and Lucy. The pressure of magic pushed against him. He was choking. "What do you want?"

"To kill you, take the girl, and then make the Fire mine."

"You'll need to be able to use the Keys," Thomas said, choking. "Possessing them's not enough."

"You need them; I merely find them interesting."

Pain erupted all over his body, as if hundreds of fishhooks had been inserted into his skin and were being pulled hard. Pressure pushed and pulled his body at the same time. *"I'm dying,"* he said to Lucy.

"No!" she shouted.

A small green light ran along the floor towards Frore. *"Run!"* Odran said. Frore jumped back, but the gnome leapt onto his foot. Smoke began to rise. Frore cursed and stamped, releasing his grip on Thomas. He kicked Odran into the wall.

Lucy pulled him towards the balcony. *"Odran has given us a chance. We must escape."*

"He needs our help," Thomas said.

"Go!" Odran shouted. He tried to crawl away, but Biddy Zo bent down and screamed at him, and he burst into green flames. She crushed him under her boot.

A frown creased Lord Frore's forehead; one of the few expressions Thomas had seen in the man. "Why would a faerie creature do that? It doesn't make sense," he said, looking at the gnome's broken body.

Lucy tugged Thomas hard. *"I made a terrible mistake. Thomas, we have to go!"* Thomas stared at Odran's body, wishing him alive. *"He's dead, Thomas."* He didn't want to believe it, but he let Lucy pull him away. He was too weak to fight Frore, who was now walking towards them. The pressure increased, and his head throbbed. As Frore and Zo attacked, Lucy pulled harder and then slipped over the side.

"Lucy!" He fell from the balcony with her.

16

Thomas felt only relief as he fell—the headache had gone. "Thomas!" Lucy's shout roused him. She was several yards away, safely in Chloris's arms—the ice demon was clinging to the wall, blood dripping from her tail, sending the hellhounds into a frenzy in the courtyard below.

Twisting, Thomas reached for the stone wall with hands and feet, and he felt its pull. Away from Frore, his rock magic was freer. Like iron to a magnet, the pull slowed his descent, and he stopped about fifteen feet from the ground—close to a second-floor window.

Frore leant over and shouted, further enraging the hounds below. "I don't think we should be hanging about here," Lucy said as a giant dog leapt up. He felt the air brush beneath him. A second one jumped higher, and he climbed up a few feet.

Chloris had already climbed through the open window with Lucy; Thomas crawled along the wall after them. They were inside someone's living quarters. Footsteps were coming down the stairs, and Thomas ran to the door, locking and barring it. "Will that hold them?"

"It'll slow them." A hound smashed into the door, and the piece of wood he'd used cracked.

"Not for long," she said. Thomas ran into the bathroom. "You're not using that now, are you?" she asked.

Thomas laughed. "When you need to go, you need to go." She watched, reddening slightly when he opened the toilet.

"I'll leave," she said.

He grabbed her wrist. "We all use it," he said, grinning.

Chloris sniffed the hole. "To the sewers." He nodded, and she dived in.

"You came this way?" Lucy asked. He nodded. "I thought you smelt bad." The door to the room broke open, and Thomas squeezed into the toilet.

"Here." Lucy took his hand and lowered herself in. They slid down the shaft. He used rock magic to control their speed of descent. Chloris was below them.

"Coming down is easier than going up," he said.

"If you say so." She was staring up at the point of light above. "Someone's in the bathroom."

Thomas dropped faster. He looked up, but his senses extended in all directions. As a face looked down the shaft, he felt a lessening of pressure and prepared for the final drop to the pathway. Something was falling after them.

As soon as his feet touched the stone pathway, he pulled Lucy along it. "What?"

"Move!" Chloris hissed.

A dark substance poured from the shaft into the stream of sewage, releasing a toxic gas. They ran along the footpath at the side of the tunnel. Minutes later, they saw light at the end of the tunnel. At the entrance, he kicked the bars away.

"A boat's coming," she said. It was moving quickly in the current. Victor, Alain, and Frank were onboard.

They ran down the beach and jumped on. "You didn't replace the bars; they'll know someone entered," Alain said.

"They already know," Thomas said, watching black gas pouring out of the sewers.

Alain steered the sleek boat out into the dark centre of the river where the current took them. "Did you get what you wanted?"

"No," Lucy said.

Alain raised an eyebrow but didn't comment.

"What happened?" Victor asked.

"Lucy killed the king and burnt the basilisk. And we took the Keys," Thomas said. Victor grinned and began to speak, but Thomas interrupted him. "But Frore took them back."

Victor gave him an incredulous stare. "What?"

"We only just escaped with our lives." Thomas felt sick, and the words stuck in his throat.

"And Odran's dead," Lucy said. "One more thing," she continued, interrupting Victor. "The goblin sorcerer was absent. If he'd been there, we'd be dead."

"That's not good," Victor said. "Just when I thought I might get out of this alive." He shook his head. "Where do you think he went?"

The assassin pointed at a moving row of torches along the shore. "I'm not saying it's the goblin, but the subjects of Tartaros didn't decide to do that themselves—only the king could order that."

"And he's dead," Thomas said, hoping the goblin was dead, too, but doubting it.

"What now?" Victor asked.

"They'll keep trying to kill us," Thomas said. "We have

to leave the city, and you'd be better off without us. We won't be safe to be with." He noticed the assassin and his assistant exchange a meaningful glance.

"With you, I can fight the Empire; besides, where else would I go?" Victor said. "And I'm not sure this city is any safer." Thomas noticed him look at the assassin. The boat rocked violently as it joined the confluence of the two rivers. Chloris rowed frantically, trying to keep control. Thomas looked back towards the castle. Torches were burning from its walls, and in the river below, boats, also lit by burning torches, sailed towards them.

A horn blew downriver, and Chloris twisted round and hissed. She stopped rowing. "That's not good," Lucy said. The strong current pulled them towards a large barge. "It's coming for us."

"You can't know that," Alain said. "Although I admit it looks suspicious."

"I know it," she said quietly. She exchanged a look with Thomas, and his heart sank. He'd long since stopped questioning her intuition—it was second to none. The boats behind had fanned out across the river, and teams of rowers meant they were gaining on them, and the dark barge loomed closer.

"Surrender to King Val!" a sailor shouted from the deck of the barge.

"King?" Lucy said. "That didn't take him long."

"It's a punishment," Victor said.

"How do you know?" Thomas asked.

"It's the sort of thing imperial lords do; I spent enough time on Palace Moon to know. Being a king in a city like this is no reward."

"To the shore," Thomas said. Chloris tried to turn the boat, but the current carried them towards the dark barge.

And it was moving towards them, despite the current, rows of oars forcing it forward. Smaller boats were being lowered from the barge.

"You saved me to kill me later," Alain said. His eyes were hard as he looked at each of them. Thomas felt sure that if not for the ice demon, he would have already switched sides.

"We didn't plan this," Thomas said. He moved his hand away as brown water splashed over the side.

"You didn't plan anything. And tell that lizard to stop rowing. If we fall in this stinking sewer, we're dead." A purple fire burnt several feet from the boat. "Our best chance is to surrender."

"We can't surrender," Lucy said.

"That's your problem," Alain said. "I can bargain a better position."

Thomas waited as their boat drifted towards the barge. He'd climb onboard and fight once it was close enough. His choices were becoming more limited.

"Thomas," Lucy said. *"Something's wrong with Frank."*

Frank's face twitched. *"Is this what I think?"* He'd seen similar expressions in the caves when the gangers had been possessed.

"Yes. Frore's found a way in."

Thomas took out his knife, and Alain quickly drew his. "No need for that." Frank lunged at Lucy, grasping her neck with his large hands. She touched his chest and he gasped, slipping down against the side of the boat.

"What happened?" Thomas asked.

"I told his heart to stop," Lucy said quietly, her face pale. "I didn't think it'd really happen." She turned away, coughing at the toxic fumes rising from the river.

"You did well," Chloris said, looking back. She stood in the bows with an oar in her hand, ready to fight.

Without warning, the assassin dived towards Lucy. Thomas gasped at his speed as the knife touched Lucy's throat. Both he and Chloris were too far away to stop it. Victor moved forward, pushing the man away just in time. Alain slit his throat instead.

Fury and sorrow filled Thomas as he gripped his knife in hand—the assassin was going to die. Alain was fast, but for Thomas, with years of martial and magical training, the speed of a fast man appeared as if slow motion. The assassin gasped in surprise as Thomas dodged his dagger. Although it seemed longer, their fight only lasted seconds. Thomas was confident of winning, but time was scarce, and although he disliked sleight of hand, at this moment he didn't care. Distracting the assassin by mentally reaching out to a metal hinge in the simple seat he sat on and tightening it, he sent a splinter into the man's leg. Alain faltered for a second, and Thomas stabbed the assassin through his throat.

"Good," Chloris hissed, spitting out dirty water from her mouth. Their boat was now spinning around in the current between the boats following and the large barge ahead. "We swim."

"Victor saved my life," Lucy said. Her hands were covered in blood from trying to stop the bleeding; tears were in her eyes.

Thomas's vision blurred, and he blinked away a tear. "There's nothing we can do for him."

"Peg Leg died well," Chloris said.

The three of them were alone in the boat with three corpses. Chloris carefully sat them up. Thomas felt an emptiness. They'd lost everything.

"We leave now," Chloris said.

"Are you serious?" Thomas asked. He looked at the swirling grey water and the purple slick that floated towards them.

"It's the only way," Chloris said. "Use magic on these."

Thomas understood. He'd done this before: created illusions of life where there was none. "I can try."

"But why?" Lucy asked, wiping away tears.

"To give us time, Bright One," Chloris said.

"Don't call me that."

"It's who you are."

Thomas created a simple spell of animation around the corpses. It wasn't much, but at a distance they would look less dead than they were. The spell, like that of invisibility, didn't really create what it was called, just an impression of it.

"That's enough," Chloris hissed. "Use your magic to protect." She grabbed Lucy and dived into the churning grey water. Lucy's scream was cut short as she disappeared under the water. Thomas followed, leaving their boat turning slowly in circles above.

Thomas swam by second sight, and to him it was like following the vibrations on a web. Lucy and Chloris were ahead, and Lucy called to the fish of the river in the True Language. He doubted there were any, but she was persistent, and he swam behind them in silence.

Above them the boats had turned, and they followed. Frore had not been fooled by his simple deception, and Thomas felt almost embarrassed to have thought that he might. Chloris had slowed, allowing him to catch up—no human could swim at the speed of an ice demon, but it meant that Frore was getting closer, too. Again he heard Lucy speaking the True Language. He listened.

Two large white fish had answered her call, and she was

giving them careful instructions. He immediately understood, but was unsure her deception would work any better than his. They agreed to do what she asked; she had a way of persuading animals to help in many ways. Despite his sadness at the loss of his friend, he smiled as she told the fish to take no chances, and to dive deep at the first sign of trouble.

"We've lived for eighty years in this river. We can protect ourselves." The fish moved away from them, slowly rising closer to the surface but remaining beneath it. Chloris turned and took his arm; Lucy held the other. The ice demon swam powerfully downstream while the white fish swam towards the Old Port. Dark shadows passed overhead —they were chasing the fish.

Twenty minutes later, they rose for air. *"With your magic, you should last longer,"* Chloris said.

"Perhaps," Thomas said, looking back for the boats but only seeing shadows, *"but even with magic, it needs training."*

"Can you see them?" Lucy asked.

He shook his head. They seemed to be safe, but Chloris would take no chances. She dived again, pulling them quickly through the thick water. Thomas tried not to think what the soft objects they bumped into were. His eyes were closed, but his inner ears were open as he listened to the life of the river.

Rising to the surface every twenty minutes to breathe, they followed the powerful pull of the river. An hour later they passed beneath the wall bridge marking the outer limits of Tartaros. Half an hour later, Chloris led them into shallower water. Thomas stood and spat out filthy water, burning the magic within to kill the germs that covered him. Lucy stood by him and did the same; Chloris was exploring the shoreline.

After wiping her mouth for over a minute, she spoke. "I never want to do that again."

"Me neither." They walked from the river onto a grey sand beach. Many of the grains of sand glowed, and in the sky above, stars, as he'd begun to call them, glittered. But without his night vision, he'd have struggled to see. "Look." An old rowing boat lay at the top of the beach, surrounded by tall fungal weeds.

Minutes later, he'd pulled it onto the sand and was examining it—with his hands as much as his eyes. "It's starting to rot, but I think we can use it; as long as the marshes aren't too far. We just need some oars."

"I'll take a look," Lucy said. She disappeared into the tall growths of fungus at the top of the beach.

He examined the boat more carefully, and although he was sure it'd leak, it seemed usable. He had the sensation of being watched, and he turned and searched the misty river. A figure approached, coming over the water. He stood—hope filling him. *"Aina?"*

"Danger comes," she said.

"Aina."

The vision of Aina faded. "I'm not her," a girl said. A thin girl of about thirteen stood on the beach watching him. "And I wouldn't let Wilson see you looking at his old boat. He's bad to people."

Lucy emerged from the vegetation pulling two oars. "Can you use these?"

"I can."

"Is she Aina?" the girl asked, glancing at Lucy, who was now walking down the beach towards them.

"No." Thomas shook his head. The sadness of all his losses returned. "I just imagined."

A screech sounded about a hundred yards away. "Chloris," Lucy said.

The girl began to speak, but a shout turned their heads. "Get away from my boat!"

"Wilson," the girl whispered. She edged towards the tall vegetation.

"What are you doing with thieves?" the man said to the girl. Then turning to Thomas, he held up a short sword. "You're not welcome here." The man peered at them with one eye; the other was damaged. Chloris screeched again, then more men ran towards them.

"What's happening back there?" Thomas asked.

"Our village is being attacked."

The men surrounded them, but Thomas's attention was drawn to the water. A dark creature with bright red eyes crept from the river. "I think you should leave."

"You're the ones leaving." Wilson eyed Lucy more closely, then turned to Thomas. "She can stay, after we've washed her, but you're going."

"Thomas," Lucy said.

"I know."

The hellhound was the size of a horse. It stood behind the men. The girl watched by the tall vegetation. "Give me your sword," Thomas said. "Quickly!"

The hound attacked the startled men, killing one quickly, and Thomas picked up the fallen sword from its now dead owner. He stabbed the hound, and as he did so, he infused magic into the rusty blade. Yelping, the hound jumped back, and Thomas followed. He damaged the physical part of the dog, slashing its leg, but the magical part remained intact, and it attacked again.

Lucy stood by his side, and he felt her magic join his. It was not the same power they'd channelled when holding the Keys, but it was enough for Lucy to unravel the energy of the dog. Thomas maintained the physical attack while Lucy attacked psychically. A shadow ran along the beach towards them.

"Chloris," Lucy said.

The ice demon came up silently behind the hound and slashed its rear legs, then she jumped back to avoid its jaws. "Hard to kill," she said, "but you're draining its life. Leave it. We must go."

The girl had reemerged from the vegetation and stood by the only two men left alive. "More dogs will come," Thomas said. "And worse things. Don't go near them." He looked at the boat. "We're taking this."

"Wilson's dead. Take his boat," a man said.

"How far are the marshes?"

"It's all marshes," the man said. "But the wild part's half an hour downstream. No one . . ." He stopped speaking and stared at Chloris.

"They're special," the girl said.

Thomas dragged the boat down the grey beach to the river, and Lucy ran with the oars. Chloris was already wading into the water, searching for hounds. Minutes later, the current was pulling them towards what the man had called the wild part of the marshes.

17

Lucy watched a small yellow monkey in one of the giant fungi stare at them as their boat moved into the waterway. A constant drizzle fell over the swamp, and she wiped the water from her face; the tiny monkey copied her, and then they left it behind.

Thomas rowed while Chloris bailed out the water slowly gathering by her feet with her hands, and Lucy sat at the stern searching for any signs of intelligent life in the forested swamp.

"Need to eat," Chloris said. She leant over the side and tried to catch a fish from the channel. It slipped through her hand. The thought of eating fish from this turgid grey river made Lucy feel nauseous—and thankful she'd become vegetarian. But still, it was better Chloris eat fish than humans. The ice demon caught the next fish, a large yellow one, and swallowed it whole.

Thomas was rowing strongly, and they moved fast along one of the larger channels deeper into the swamp. Dark trees rose above them like giants with arm-like branches that reached over their heads; hundreds of aerial roots hung down into the waterway, like long beaded hair that shone in the dark. Many giant flowers grew on the banks and gave off their own light.

Lucy swatted a gnat as she continued to project her mind deeper into the forested swamp in search of larger forms of life, but it was only the smaller forms of life that found them. The giant fungal shapes that made up much of the forested swamp interested her, but as swarms of biting flies became bigger, focussing on anything but killing them was increasingly hard.

Thomas adjusted the course of the boat to the dead centre of the channel, and that slightly lessened the problem of biting insects, but not enough. He was already cursing them and slapping every exposed part of his body. "I think a little magic might be needed," Thomas said.

"What about Frore?" she asked. They'd already discussed the possibility of the three sorcerers sensing their use of magic.

Thomas spat out several mosquitos from his mouth. "I know, but this is ridiculous."

But she was still reluctant to attract the attention of the sorcerers any more than necessary; it was her magic that would have the greater effect on the insects, and her magic was more likely to attract Frore. The channel became narrower, and the tall plants enclosed them in a glowing tunnel. If it hadn't been for the insects, it would have been beautiful.

Then they passed fragrant varieties of the giant funnel fungi that glowed in reds, greens, and blues—it seemed that the gnats disliked them—and for several minutes they were left in peace, but as they moved further up the channel, the clouds of insects returned. Lucy swatted a charcoal-coloured fly the size of her thumb. They were beginning to hurt. She swiped frantically at the larger flies.

"Lucy?" Thomas asked. "Can you do anything? This is getting bad."

"Frore will know it's me immediately."

"We have to do something," Thomas said. "Didn't the gnome say something about it being harder to hear magic when it was further away?"

"Yes, but we're not that far away," she said. "And for someone like Frore, distance might not matter."

"But speaking to creatures is a softer use of magic," Thomas said.

"True," she said. "I'll try, but telling bloodthirsty flies to stop biting is unlikely to have any effect." She spoke telepathically to the biting insects, but they didn't listen. She shook her head. "Fresh blood has intoxicated them," she said.

"Great," he said, frantically slapping his face and arms. "I can't take this much longer." Chloris had curled up at the bottom of the boat and fallen asleep—Lucy doubted if the ice demon even noticed the insects.

Seeing some type of water horse swimming alongside the boat, Lucy called to it. It swam closer and watched her through eyes that protruded from the surface of the river. Thomas didn't appear to have noticed it. She showed it an image of the biting flies and a feeling of pain; it replied with an image of a long dark insect. Lucy called them.

Thomas spat more of the insects out of his mouth. "Lucy! We have to go back! Perhaps we can find another way —one with less insects. The riders might have gone further downstream anyway."

She doubted it and knew that Thomas did too. "A little longer; I'm calling more insects."

"I'd never have thought you had a sadistic sense of humour," Thomas said. "They're even biting my tongue."

"Come," she said. From across the swamp, a flight of dark creatures flew to her. Each had a body the size of her forearm. Thomas ducked as the dragonflies swooped on the swarm, and within seconds, the flies had disappeared. *"Thank you,"* she said to the dragonflies; they followed the boat deeper into the swamp.

"Thank you," Thomas said to Lucy. "I was about to turn back." He wiped some of the remaining flies from his face. "It seems we've picked up an escort." The flight of giant dragonflies followed, feeding on any flies that approached. "How did you think of calling the dragonflies?" Thomas asked.

"She told me." Lucy pointed into the river, and Thomas noticed the animal swimming beside them for the first time. It had a long head and a grey mane, but its body was covered in grey scales. As it swam closer, she saw that it was bigger than she'd thought.

"Some sort of reptile?" he said.

"She's a monotreme," Lucy said.

"A what?" Thomas asked.

"An egg-laying mammal." She reached out to the creature and it swam closer, allowing her to rub its neck. As she did so, she saw images of her eggs, which were close to being hatched. *"May your young be healthy and beautiful,"* she said with emotions and images. The water horse nickered in reply.

The animal continued to follow for the best part of an hour; she was a simple creature, but friendly and curious about a human who spoke the True Language.

"Ask her about Lazolteotl," Thomas said.

Lucy asked, but the water horse didn't seem interested.

Instead, the horse happily introduced Lucy to her life. She saw images of families of water horses and other creatures wading through the wooded channels, which ran some way from the river. She asked if there were any islands, and she saw some, then she asked if there were any inhabited islands, and the images stopped.

The animal was anxious. *"What?"* she asked gently. She saw an image of an old temple that appeared to grow from the ground. *"Take us there."*

As the water horse swam up the channel, she became more agitated. She seemed to be leading them away from the island. *"Why?"* Lucy asked. The creature showed her water horses frolicking in the river, and Lucy knew she was evading the question. *"Then show me where it is."* The water horse shared directions in a sort of mental map. Then the image disappeared, along with the peaceful creature who'd been their companion for the past hour.

"It got bored," Thomas surmised.

Lucy shook her head. "She wasn't bored. There's an island with an old temple deeper in the swamp—she showed me the way but was afraid."

"Of what?" he asked.

"Death."

"Can you elaborate?" Thomas asked with a grin.

She shook her head. "It was a feeling coming from her. Animals communicate intuitively with sensations, sounds, and images—not words as we know them." Lucy was also far from happy to sail to the isle, but the alternative was worse. She continued to navigate for Thomas as he rowed through the dark green channels to the misty isle she saw in her mind.

~

THE MIST-COVERED islet lay several yards ahead when their boat ran aground on a mudbank. It was impossible to move. They left it and waded through the swamp. All the time, Lucy was repelling the leeches that swam towards them. As soon as she stood on the muddy beach, she double-checked for any that had stuck to her.

"Leeches?" Chloris asked.

"Hundreds of them. I think I sent them away."

Chloris examined herself. "I'd never believed humans could speak to animals until I met you."

"Some people unwittingly speak to animals, but they seldom develop their listening ability, so they don't even know what they're capable of."

"Like Thomas?" Chloris asked. Thomas had wandered off into the forest.

"He prefers to speak to rocks." Chloris bared her teeth in an ice demon grin, and Thomas raised his eyebrows as he walked back onto the beach.

The trees on the island appeared older than in the rest of the swamp. Scores of aerial roots hung from the branches like strands of hair. Many of the trees were not true trees, but fungal varieties that sometimes looked similar. Lucy watched a series of weird ghostlike figures swaying slowly in the mist, and she had to blink to be sure they were only fungal growths.

"I think this is the only solid island here," Thomas said. "The rest seem to be floating masses of vegetation. Are you sure this is the island the animal showed you?"

Lucy nodded; she'd recognized it straight away. "Someone's coming," she said. They waited.

A few minutes later, three young women shambled out of the trees towards them. Lucy reached for them mentally but didn't find what she expected. She glanced at Thomas, who shrugged his shoulders.

"Hello!" Thomas said. The women's faces were concealed by their long white hair. None of them spoke.

"They're not human," Lucy said.

"What then?" he asked. She shrugged; she had no idea. They turned their heads towards Lucy, and their hair moved, showing their faces.

"What?" Thomas said, his hand reaching for his knife.

Lucy's eyes widened in surprise. They had white, perfectly shaped, smooth faces, but none of them possessed a single feature: neither nose, mouth, nor eyes.

"Perhaps this was a bad idea," Chloris said, seeming unnerved by the featureless women.

"We had no choice," Thomas said. "Our boat ran aground."

"True," she hissed quietly.

"Hello," Lucy said.

The three women together turned to face her. *"Who are you?"* They spoke in strange puffy images.

She showed them selected mental images of their journey and then waited while they seemed to converse amongst themselves. They answered with an image of the temple.

"A temple," Thomas said.

Lucy nodded. "They want us to follow them there. It seems the water horse's memory was true." The young women slowly turned and shambled back into the trees. As they followed, Lucy studied their slow and strange motion.

"What are they?" Chloris asked.

"I don't know," Lucy said. "Their minds appear blank."

"But they spoke to you telepathically?" Chloris said.

"Sort of. It's almost as if they're drugged. I think they're servants of the temple. I hope that when we get there, we can meet the high priest or priestess."

The forest path twisted through a tangled mass of vegetation. One of the trees they passed had scores of shining white fruit. Lucy made a simple request to the tree, and a glowing papaya-shaped fruit dropped into her hands.

"Was that some strange chance?" Thomas asked.

"Of course not. I asked it." She smiled at his expression and took a bite. "It's good." She grinned with a mouthful of white light and caught a second one. She offered it to Chloris.

She turned her head away. "Normal fruit doesn't glow in the dark."

Thomas laughed. "Not much is normal here." He took the fruit Lucy offered.

After only about twenty minutes, the women walked into a wild garden of dark and bright plants. The garden itself was surrounded by a low wall and beyond that, the forest of pale giant fungi. A single giant fungus grew inside the garden; it looked like a wild man with a single eye and a strange hairstyle. "The hair's moving," she said. Then she noticed that its eye was moving, too.

"I saw that," Thomas said quietly.

"Is it alive?" Chloris asked. The ice demon seemed anxious on entering the garden.

"All plants are alive." She paused. "Unless they're dead." Thomas grinned.

"Its movements are stranger than these blank-faced women," Chloris hissed.

She was right. Lucy watched more carefully, then she projected her mind into the tree and laughed aloud. "It's not an eye at all, it's a nest of wasps—big ones." One landed on a short flower nearby.

The faceless women waited by the temple in the middle of the garden; it appeared to grow from the ground. It was made from fungus: some was dead, but much still seemed to be growing. Lucy wondered whether it came from a single fungus, and how it'd been possible to grow the temple in such an ornate way.

One of the young women pointed at the temple entrance. *"Enter."* The three women then walked along a path by the side of the building. Thomas and Chloris climbed the gnarled steps ahead of Lucy. She followed and entered what she was now sure was a living temple.

The inside was lit by candle-like red fruits growing from the temple itself. Smells of earth and spice mixed together; the fragrance came from the hardened wood of the giant fungus. She stood in the outer hall while her eyes adjusted to the dim light; there were further halls deeper in the complex, and a set of uneven twisting stairs to a higher level. A figure stood in the centre by the trunk of a tree. She was an ancient woman, apparently naked apart from her long white hair, which hung low, covering her face and much of her pale body, until it touched the dirty ground. Lucy stared at the woman's dirty feet and the dirt around them; hygiene was not important here. Then she looked more carefully at the detritus surrounding the woman. "Thomas!"

"What?" She pointed at the woman's flat, round feet with dozens of octopus toes. "I know. She's pretty strange."

"No." Lucy shook her head. "Look at what she's standing on." The ancient woman stood on the decomposing body of a young man, and dozens of toes moved around inside the body like the legs of an octopus. Dried blood covered her feet. "I feel sick." The woman looked up; she had a perfectly formed, featureless face.

18

Lucy couldn't bring herself to speak; she just stared at the remains of the body. The man's head was mostly intact. He must have been in his late twenties. The woman wiggled her long toes in his oozing gut. Not much shocked her, but this...

"What are you?" Lucy managed. When nothing happened, she repeated the question in the True Language.

"We are what you see."

"I'm not sure what I see," Lucy said. *"You eat people?"*

"We consume organic matter."

That sounded the same to Lucy. *"All life consumes organic matter."*

"We feed on decaying organic matter."

Lucy felt her jaw drop. *"You're a fungus!"*

"We're saprophytes."

"So you didn't kill him?"

"He was already dead." The ancient fungal woman waved a strand of hair that wasn't hair, but a tendril of some sort, at an old man sitting quietly on a bench by the wall. Lucy hadn't noticed him before. She looked at his worn face; he

smiled at her. He sat with a doglike animal that looked as old as himself. *"We take care of the old,"* the woman said.

"*By eating them,*" Lucy said.

"*We remove their pain, and in exchange, we consume their bodies when they die.*"

"*He was too young to die,*" she said, pointing at the young man's body.

"*Accidents happen. If you wish to stay . . .*"

"No!" Lucy said aloud, unsure if this was some sort of fungal humour.

"Why have I never heard of your people before?" Thomas asked.

"*This planet is large, and many species live here. We saprofolk used to occupy much of the interior, but now we only inhabit a few places. Our work is continued by simpler species.*"

"Is your work breaking down dead organic matter?" Lucy asked.

"*We purify the world.*"

Lucy wondered what kind of accident the man had had. Perhaps they weren't killers, but she wasn't sure. And Thomas was far from convinced. He glanced at her and shook his head. She looked away when the old woman wiggled her toes again inside the man's body.

"*How well do you know this land?*" Thomas asked.

"*We know this isle and the swamp around.*"

"Who are you?" Lucy asked.

"*I am the Keeper of the Temple of Lazolteotl,*" the woman answered.

Lucy remembered the temple they'd passed in Tartoros. "*The Goddess of Filth?*" she asked.

"*The Goddess of Purification,*" the keeper corrected.

The former seemed a better name to Lucy. She'd discovered other remains in the shadows around the room. *"We seek her realm,"* Lucy said.

"No one enters the goddess's realm uninvited. And certainly not a monster like that." The keeper had no eyes to look, but it was clear to Lucy that she spoke of Chloris.

The ice demon hissed her displeasure. *"She's our friend,"* Lucy said, *"and she comes with us."* She felt the white snake come alive in her pocket. She took it out, and it stood up on her palm.

The saprofolk cried out in unison, and Lucy cringed at the high-pitched telepathic cry. *"Who gave you that?"* the keeper asked.

"It came along uninvited," Lucy said.

The keeper held out a hand. *"I'll return it to its owner."*

Lucy shook her head. *"We go too,"* but the snake had its own mind, and it dropped to the floor of the temple and wriggled towards the keeper.

"What's happening?" Thomas asked.

"I'm not sure."

The white snake bit the keeper's foot, but the strange keeper didn't move. *"I understand your journey,"* she said.

Before he could speak again, the woman became distracted; her long hair moved around as if searching for something. *"Others come—the dogs and riders that pursue you."*

Lucy heard nothing, but she imagined that Frore would follow their trail. *"I'm sorry, we've brought danger to your temple,"* Lucy said.

"We've faced countless threats during the long centuries we've lived in these swamps," the keeper said. *"We were here long before humanity appeared. We're unafraid."*

"Perhaps you should be," Thomas said.

"The temple may be destroyed, but the doorways to

Lazolteotl's realm cannot. The temple can be regrown. As can we. Death only changes our form."

"What about us?" Thomas asked. "We don't change form so easily."

Dogs barked in the distance. *"All life changes form."* The white snake had detached itself from the keeper and was crawling back to Lucy.

"Nice philosophy," Chloris hissed, "but we have unpleasant company." The ice demon cracked her tail on the hardwood floor and walked to the temple entrance, from where she watched the forest beyond the temple garden.

"Can you help us?" Lucy asked.

"The saprofolk must speak." She became silent and still.

"These doorways to other worlds better be more than a metaphor," Thomas said.

Then the keeper spoke. *"Our goddess does not welcome these riders or their hounds."*

"Not many people do," Thomas said.

"Within the temple there's a door to her realm, but beware, not all of the realm's inhabitants will welcome you."

"We're used to that," Lucy said. "Where exactly is the door?"

"The knowledge is hidden, but if you are what you say, then you'll find it."

The keeper exploded with a loud pop. All that remained of her body was the cloud of white dust that slowly settled over the remains of the corpse.

A HORN BLEW from the forest and the hellhounds bayed. They were much closer than Thomas expected. "They're here! Everyone search for the door!" If they didn't find the door within minutes, they were dead.

"Where?" Chloris asked.

"Anywhere in the temple." Thomas left them and ran up the stairs that twisted up. He heard Chloris's tail periodically cracking like a whip as she walked through the inner rooms.

The upper hall was similar to the lower one. Several white fungal people rocked backwards and forwards over piles of something he didn't care to examine. Nothing in the otherwise empty room resembled a door. He climbed the final set of stairs to the top floor. The small area was open to the elements and was empty apart from the large fungal growths by the walls. He glanced down at the forest surrounding the temple garden, but nothing was there yet.

"Thomas!" Running down the winding wooden stairs, he found Lucy in the centre of one of the inner halls, next to a standing stone the size of a man.

"Have you found it?"

"Perhaps," she said.

He rubbed its surface, feeling an electric tingling in his fingers. "This is it."

"Open it!" Chloris walked into the room, acid dripping from her half-open mouth. "The dogs are moving through the trees beyond the garden."

Thomas continued to run his hands up and down the standing stone. "I need time to understand it." He felt a lattice of energy running backwards and forwards across the stone; he searched for the key.

"No time!" Chloris said.

"Make me time," Thomas said. "And don't talk to me."

"I have an idea," Lucy said, running out to the garden. Thomas focussed his attention on the stone. It possessed its own power, and if he could access that power, then he might be able to open it.

Chloris settled by one of the open spaces in the vast

fungal tree that served as a window to the garden. From there, she watched Lucy and the forest beyond her.

Thomas projected his mind into the stone, and it was almost as if his pentacle was still with him—the rock became alive with energy. The magic expanded around him, encompassing the area around the standing stone, too. As the stone softened under his touch, he called on more magic —aware but unconcerned that the sorcerers would hear. He plunged his hands and arms into the rock that for him was now more like warm clay, and he sweated as he stroked the bands of energy within the stones.

His hands hurt as he pulled and twisted the threads within which made up the larger bands of energy. Then he threaded them together into new patterns with a power he'd not known he'd possessed. When the threads rested in the position he wanted them, he rested, too. All he needed to do was give a final twist, like turning a key in a normal door, but before he could turn the lock of magical energy, pain started shooting along his arms—the rock was solidifying around him. He fell back with a scream and his world went dark.

Chloris slapped him. "Wake up!"

Thomas opened his eyes, feeling groggy. "I'm almost there." He was covered in cold sweat.

"What happened?" she asked.

"I got overconfident and almost got trapped inside the stone. It's been a long time." He breathed heavily.

"They're running through the trees around the garden," Chloris whispered. "I've heard them."

"The riders?"

"Hounds."

"Where's Lucy?"

"She'd doing something in the garden." Chloris paused. "She's acting a little strange."

"And you didn't stop her?"

"She's the Bright One—she ordered me to remain with you."

Thomas hoped that Lucy knew what she was doing; he had no time to think about anything else. "I need to finish this." He couldn't risk the threads within the rock unravelling before he made the final twist to open the door.

"She's rushing about the garden with armfuls of rotten fruit," Chloris said. "She's making a doll with it."

Chloris must be exaggerating. "What's that smell?"

"She said it's an offering to the goddess. She said the goddess likes rotten fruit and vegetables."

"I don't have time for this. I'm almost ready. *Lucy?*"

"I'm making a doll," she said. He saw an image of her adjusting the dress of an ugly doll of rotten fruit, which leant against an old looking funnel fungus in the garden.

"Lucy, I don't know what you're doing, but I need you here now."

"Is the door open?" she asked.

"I need a few minutes."

"Then I'm helping more by being here!" she said. *"Call me when you're ready!"* Then she vanished from his mind.

"Lucy?" He heard a laugh, and then no more.

"Look," Chloris said.

Thomas stood by the ice demon. Dark shapes moved through the fungal forest. The hellhounds watched the temple with burning eyes. "They're waiting for their masters," he said.

Chloris stretched through the window. "Lucy!" she hissed.

But Thomas had left the room in the temple behind and had reentered the world of the stone. He twisted the threads, but as he'd feared, the rocks had solidified, and his work had started to be undone. He worked the rock magic again, and again the stone warmed and its threads and bands of energy opened up for him. This time he was faster. He was lost in his work when Chloris shook him.

Spaces had appeared in the temple walls; the living temple seemed to be rearranging itself, and this had resulted in open windows to the garden being formed.

Lucy was wandering about the wild garden, tending the plants as red-eyed hellhounds watched from the trees. "Lucy!" Pain shot through his hands and along his arms; he turned back to his work. He was concerned about Lucy, but he had to open the door if he was to be of any help to anyone.

Energy again flowed freely though him, coming from the stone and drawn strongly into his body. He pushed the door, but it remained locked.

"What's wrong?" Chloris asked.

"I don't know." Everything seemed correct; he couldn't understand why it didn't open.

"Door bolts?" Chloris asked. Thomas stared at her large head. "I know nothing about magical doors," she said defensively.

Thomas probed deeper, looking for bolts. He found two bolt-like energetic blocks. "Good idea."

"But it's too late," Chloris said.

Thomas turned to see a tall goblin sitting on the back of a hellhound. Xart stared at Lucy's back—a sick grin on his face. "What's she doing?" Thomas asked. She was pottering around a flower bed.

"I help her?" Chloris said.

"She asked you to remain here," Thomas said. "Perhaps you should ask her again. I can't help her without closing the door. And I won't be able to open it again quickly."

"It's open?"

"It's slightly ajar."

Lord Frore sat on the largest of the black hounds at the top of the garden. He too was watching Lucy, who seemed completely oblivious to her danger. The hounds left the forest and crept through the flowers towards her. There was nothing he could do to help her without releasing the stones. *"Lucy!"*

"Thomas! Stay where you are! And tell Chloris, too." Her voice was strong and took him aback; in the garden she was humming a childish ditty.

A large hellhound leapt over the hard lichen-covered ground; sparks jumped from its feet. Its red eyes shone, and its magic was visible as a blue flickering light that rippled around it. It leapt on Lucy, and Thomas felt his stomach drop. The stress of Frore's attack on her had overwhelmed her. He closed his eyes in shock and sadness, wishing he'd done more to help her, but he couldn't see how. He'd kill the riders for this.

"Look!" Chloris said. Thomas opened his eyes to see the hound sniffing the ground in confusion.

"What happened?"

"She vanished."

Three dark figures rode hellhounds the size of horses around the wild garden. Blue fire danced within the sleeves of Frore's cloak and from the dark space beneath his cowl. The witch was still chanting her spells.

"I'm ready—but Lucy?" Thomas felt as if he'd been kicked in the stomach. To lose Lucy was too much. He debated whether he should stay and fight as he began pushing back the final energetic bolt.

"Surrender yourselves!" The voice of Frore came from the garden, but vibrated with power throughout the temple, and Thomas understood what the gnome had tried to tell him about the power of his opponent. Without any feeling of ego or emotion, Thomas knew he'd lose a straight fight against this man. Waves of magic radiated from the sorcerer. Thomas leant against the door, feeling light-headed. Chloris leant against the standing stone with her eyes closed.

"Wake up!" Thomas said. Chloris opened her eyes. "He's using magic to disorient us."

"It's working." She was breathing deeply.

Frore turned to the goblin. "Find them."

Thomas gasped as he felt the goblin's pressure. A headache like none he'd ever had throbbed painfully. The goblin's magic began to unravel the work he'd done. The door closed, and Xart and Biddy Zo laughed from the open windows. Then something distracted them, and they turned back to the garden.

The goblin pointed. "The girl!"

Thomas felt hopeful, but when he looked, Lucy was not in the place Xart had indicated.

"There she is," Chloris said. "And there."

Several Lucys appeared in the wild garden: some were talking to insects, some picking flowers, and others staring into space. One danced through the garden. At first, Thomas thought the fungal people had disguised themselves to help, but the figures moved naturally, as Lucy would, not in the awkward manner of the fungal people.

"She's alive. She's created images of herself," Thomas said. Relief and hope lifted his spirit. Again he opened the door.

The three riders watched the moving images of Lucy. Then, Frore raised his hand and green energy leapt forward and struck one of them. It vanished.

The old witch cackled. "Not that one." Frore struck

again, but again it was an illusion. One by one, Frore and Xart struck the images of Lucy with their magic, and one by one, they vanished. Soon only one remained: it sat quietly beneath the giant fungal tree—it looked different to the others.

"Leave Prometheus!" Lucy said. It was her. She leant back against the funnel fungus. She struck Frore with a thread of white energy. Even Thomas saw that it lacked power.

Yet Frore's head snapped back as if someone had slapped him. "Foolish girl," he said. She struck again, but he brushed aside the attempt. "I'd hoped for more from my little witch." She struck him again—harder.

This time Frore responded with anger. His magic ripped into her body, and a putrescent smell drifted towards them. Thomas felt sick as he watched Lucy's body slump forward. It didn't vanish as the illusions had. Instead, Lucy crawled along the ground in a grotesque way: one of her hands seemed to separate from the rest of her body and moved by itself.

"That can't be happening," Thomas said.

"She's seriously hurt," Chloris whispered.

A loud buzzing came from her body. Frore struck her again with green lightning. Her body completely fell apart, and tiny lights rose.

"Her spirit?" Chloris whispered.

"I don't think so," Thomas said. Hundreds of lights flew towards the riders.

"What's this?" Biddy Zo asked. The buzzing lights struck the riders and the riders screamed, frantically trying to knock the lights away.

"Wasps," Thomas said. He laughed aloud. Lord Frore had destroyed a pile of rotten food dressed as a doll, and the wasps, probably directed by Lucy, had been feeding on it. But where was she? Despite their attempts to knock them away with magic, the wasps continued to sting the riders. The hounds panicked and ran into the darkness of the forest, followed by the riders and hundreds of enraged wasps.

"Good trick?" a voice said from behind them.

Thomas lost his balance and fell against the standing stone. "Lucy!" He took a deep breath. "I thought you were dead—twice. Sometimes you really surprise me. Actually, quite often."

Lucy watched them with a big grin on her face. "Is the door open?"

"Almost." Thomas twisted the final bolt, but it was stiff.

"They're coming back," Chloris said.

The riders emerged from the forest again. This time their magic was fully activated; they all shone with dark light. The hellhounds rushed through the garden.

"Can you control the dogs?" Chloris asked.

She shook her head. "They're not animals, but spirits bound by magic. The animal part is mostly dead, and I don't think they'd recognize anything other than their masters."

Chloris stood, ready to fight, and Lucy stood by her side. "Do something." Thomas pulled harder, and the bolt began to move just as part of the ceiling fell into the room. The temple was on fire.

She looked at the ceiling above a hound that had entered. A burning piece of wood fell on it, and the hound leapt back with a yelp, but then it crept towards them again. When more of the ceiling dropped onto its head and the hound was covered in white dust, it ran in circles, temporarily blinded. "Thomas?" she asked. "We could really do with an exit right now."

Thomas stepped back. "It's open." They looked at the shimmering lattice of energy that had appeared around the standing stone.

"That looks promising," Lucy said.

He nodded and quietly thanked the long-dead troll who'd been his teacher on all related to rock magic. "I hope whatever we find's no worse than this."

"If it's worse, we die fighting it," Chloris said. "Death is honourable."

"But let's save it until later," Thomas said.

"Something's watching us," Lucy said while peering through the door.

"What?" Thomas asked.

"A pair of turquoise eyes."

"Human?"

"No, definitely not human." Lucy stepped through the door and vanished.

Chloris screeched as part of the burning ceiling fell on her. Her tail caught fire. Pulling her towards the standing stone, Thomas pushed her through the doorway. The temple was burning all around him as she disappeared. More parts of the ceiling fell; soon there'd be little left. A burning rafter glanced off his arm, knocking him to the floor. He crawled towards the door.

The three sorcerers walked through the flames with a hellhound at their heels. It leapt at him, and Thomas thrust his hand into its throat, using magic to cut its flesh. He ripped out its windpipe. The hound shrieked, but he kept a steady grip and used the dying hound as a shield against a blast of goblin magic. Lord Frore shouted, and a stronger magic hit him, catapulting him backwards through the door. Thomas saw flashing lights, and within the light he sensed Aina's presence; then all was darkness.

19

Lucy splashed into brown water that reached her waist. Her feet sank into the mud, stopping when it touched her ankles. Something swam into her, and she kept very still —a water snake, and it was as shocked as she was. She sent it feelings of peace, and it swam deeper into the swamp.

The tropical swamp looked similar to the previous one, with islands dotted around, but the light had a tint of blue, and the smells and sounds were different. It stank of decay, and insect sounds permeated the forest: buzzing, clicking, and sawing.

It was also hotter and more humid. The turquoise eyes had disappeared, but the doorway between realms was still there, suspended about three feet above the surface. She pushed away a raft of decaying matter that floated towards her and waded back to the shimmering door. A lattice of blue and grey energy stretched across it. She stepped back as the lattice cracked, and a burning demon flew through the door and dropped into the swamp. "Chloris!" The water hissed around her tail. Chloris stood in the swamp and shook her head, sending sprays of water over Lucy.

"Where's Thomas?"

"Fighting."

Lucy's eyes widened. "All of them?"

"They came suddenly." The frills around Chloris's neck were expanded, showing her unease.

Lucy waded back to the doorway, which had lines of flashing light crisscrossing it, and touched the bottom—its energy made her hair stand on end. She let go as Thomas flew through the door. He reached back, trying to close it, before splashing into the swamp. Chloris pulled him up. "He's unconscious."

"Thomas." There was no answer.

The dark silhouette of the goblin looked through the crack in the doorway.

"Close the door!" Chloris yelled. Three dark figures moved on the other side; they came closer and peered through. "If you can do something, do it quickly," Chloris said. Lucy heard the fear in her voice. She felt it herself.

"I know."

The three shapes studied the door, and then one pushed its hand forward, and the light around the door brightened. Lucy searched for a lock. She knew from Thomas that these were invisible to the naked eye. But to her, the stone's energy was strange and different from her magic. A pale grey hand reached through—the goblin. Its long, pointed fingers were reaching for something.

She looked closer and saw the bolt of hard energy only inches from its fingertips. She needed to turn and push it in place, but knowing and doing were not the same, and she struggled to move it. Then the goblin grasped the bolt; it seemed unsure of which way to move it. Lucy pulled its wrist, hoping it would react against her and bolt the door. If it followed her pull, the door would fly open. But the goblin reacted—it fought her. The door was closing, and the lattice of energy dimmed, but the door was still ajar.

The head of a hellhound squeezed through the crack. Its red eyes regarded her as it growled. Calling magical energy to augment her strength, she drove the bolt in place. The door slammed shut, and the hellhound's head vanished in flames.

"Let's move to the island," Chloris said, picking up Thomas.

They waded towards the nearest forested island. Chloris pushed through the dense vegetation and placed Thomas on the ground, knocking a large spider away with the back of her hand.

Lucy knelt next to him. He was stirring. "Thomas!" His eyes fluttered open, then closed again. *"Thomas. Can you hear me?"*

He muttered something, then opened his eyes. He tried to sit up but fell back to the ground. "Rest for a moment," she said as Chloris disappeared.

He opened his eyes again, but didn't attempt to sit up. "Where are we?"

"In some type of alternative swamp."

"Aina was with me; she protected me from the magical attack."

Lucy looked away and breathed deeply. She didn't want to destroy his hope, but she also didn't want this distraction. "She's in a better place, Thomas."

"I know, but I think she may be alive."

"Thomas?" He wasn't making a lot of sense, but neither would she if she'd been blasted with the sort of magic the riders used.

"She's waiting for me."

Lucy carefully guarded her thoughts; she didn't want to

hurt him. As strong as he was, he was sensitive too. "You've been hurt by the magic. You're disoriented. Just relax for a few moments." She hoped they had enough moments before the sorcerers appeared.

Chloris crashed from the trees, interrupting them. The frill around her neck was opening and closing. Lucy waited for her to speak. "They're coming."

From the forest, several grey shadows emerged. They sniffed the ground and slowly moved backwards and forwards, but with each step they came closer.

"Thomas, we must go." She helped him sit up. He stared at the shadow dogs sniffing their way to the water.

"They've found another way in," Chloris said.

"They're not completely in this world," Lucy said. She had no sense that the sorcerers had entered.

Thomas stood and walked unsteadily towards them. He looked up at one of the shadow dogs.

"Thomas?" Lucy said.

"It's okay."

"I don't think it is."

He touched the nearest one anyway, and then he pushed his hand inside its body. "You see, there's no problem. They're not really here." It snapped, and he pulled away just in time. For a second, its eyes glowed red.

"It grew more solid when you touched it," she said.

More shadow dogs surrounded him, sniffing frantically. "Perhaps that wasn't such a good idea." He stepped away, being careful not to touch any of the shadows. They continued to search for his scent with their heads to the ground. "Where are we that we can see their shadows? And that they can smell us?"

"A world between worlds," Lucy said. "Or perhaps

Frore's using magic. He might be halfway here already. We should go."

"No argument," Thomas said. "But where? These shadows are everywhere."

She watched the hounds sniffing their way through the trees; they avoided the water, but otherwise they were getting closer. "If nothing happens to stop them, they'll soon be in the swamp." She watched something very long moving slowly beneath the surface.

Then she felt a presence in the forest. Thomas nodded at her. At least he was recovering from the attack. She scanned the edge of the forest carefully. Chloris followed Lucy's gaze and bared her teeth at a line of insectoids, walking and crawling from the trees. They appeared to be searching the ground for something. Their thoraxes bent upwards, with four legs for movement and two upper ones as arms. The tallest were several inches shorter than Lucy. They stopped when they saw the humans.

"Walking cockroaches," Thomas said. Their shining black eyes stared blankly. "Lucy?" Thomas said.

"I'll try." They were completely different from anything she'd communicated with before. And she only heard the sound of silence. "If they speak, they're not answering." Although their heads only reached her chest, their antennae waved several feet above her head. One moved very close, but she didn't move, unsure whether they'd take it as fear. Its red face looked like a demon mask melted onto its head. Several proboscises poured from its mouth—she froze, feeling sickened by its bad breath. Thomas's eyes widened. He felt it too. A scratching in her mind. Then they clicked aloud together.

Images of decay appeared in her mind. "They're trying to communicate."

"What are they saying?" Chloris asked.

"I wish I knew." Antennae brushed her head and neck; she shivered in disgust.

"I don't like this," Chloris said as one of them rubbed a collection of proboscises against her face.

"I don't think we should react," Lucy said.

When one did the same to Thomas, his magic surged, and the insectoid's mouth caught fire.

"That might not be a good idea," Lucy said.

Thomas's magic acted like the pouring of a flammable liquid on a fire; flames burst from the insectoids, and they retreated several yards, thrashing about to put out the fire. For several seconds they rolled on the wet ground to put out the flames. Then they clicked together, and the sound rose like a great chorus. They charged, and Thomas fought them with punches and kicks.

Lucy tried to send a message of peace to the creatures, but it was too late. One of them jumped on Chloris, and she immediately sliced it in half with her razor claws. Another approached, opened its mouth, and vomited dozens of proboscises onto her burnt tail. The ice demon shrieked and attacked the creatures, slashing wildly.

Thomas's natural magic was alive, and dozens of the creatures smoked when he touched them. But as he drew magic, the chorus of clicks spread throughout the swamp; scores of the creatures flew from other islands.

"Thomas!" she shouted.

Chloris leapt into the air, slashing at the incoming insects. Lucy ducked when a dark shape flew towards them. It hit Thomas in his back, knocking him to the ground. The cockroach poured proboscises from its mouth, and they pressed against his skin but didn't puncture it. More flying roaches landed on top of him and licked or sucked as if he were a giant ice cream. Soon he disappeared beneath their weight.

"They're feeding on your energy." She tried to pull them off him. "Stop using magic; they're like moths to light."

She felt his magic lessen and then extinguish, but the roaches continued to suck. And then they appeared to anger. One punctured his skin and drank blood. Without any use of magic, Thomas swung it away, kicked another into the swamp, and then used his knife to chop at another—Chloris killed several, too. They backed off a few feet, but more were swimming towards the island.

Then they stopped and turned to the forest. Others from the swamp, and those in the air, joined them. They gathered around a darkening grey nimbus of energy. Lucy stared in horror at the pack of ghostly dogs forming in its centre.

The hellhounds attacked the roaches viciously, but for every one they killed, scores more landed on them. The insectoids were in a feeding frenzy—more flew across the swamp, attracted by the chance of food. They dived onto the giant hounds, stabbing them with sharp proboscises and sucking hard. The hellhounds cried and yelped, shrivelling into empty husks as they fell dead to the ground. Then the walking cockroaches stopped feeding and stood on their four legs.

There was a movement in the centre of the nimbus. Three shadows walked amongst the dying dogs. The head of Biddy Zo appeared, and she looked around at the dead hounds and the standing roaches. One of them flew onto her face and she screamed, but the creature quickly dropped dead to the ground.

"We have to go," Lucy whispered as a second shadow began to form more clearly next to Biddy Zo.

"Where?" Chloris asked, looking around at the other islands.

Lucy felt something watching her and turned. A large grey cat sat on the beach of a nearby island, looking at them. "That's what I saw before."

Thomas crouched and pushed his hand into the grey sand. Lucy felt his rock magic quietly probing the ground. A few seconds later, he stood up. "The water's shallow, and the islands are joined by a submerged sandbank." He walked towards it. "Come. We have to go; the cat's island is as good as any."

The witch's head had fully materialized and the proboscises of the standing roaches stroked her as she hummed a spell. "She's mesmerizing them," Lucy said. She shivered as she realized her own attraction and repulsion to the witch's song.

"Don't listen to her," Thomas said. "If we listen too long, it'll weaken us, too."

Nodding, Lucy shook herself free from the seductive spell and looked to the second dark figure. Lucy recognized the grey skin of the goblin.

"In the middle," Thomas said.

She'd already seen and recognized the third presence. A pair of eyes glowed in the centre of the slowly organizing mass. As it saw them, more hellhounds appeared. They barked as they smelt their prey.

"Lucy!" Thomas squeezed her arm, snapping her awake. "Cut the connection and shield yourself."

Shivering as she realized what the witch had been doing, Lucy raised her shield. When Thomas gently tugged her arm, she followed. Chloris was already leading the way through the water.

Through Thomas's eyes, she saw the submerged path to the other island. *"Thank you."*

"The witch is more dangerous than she appears," he said, echoing her feelings exactly.

Lucy felt him reaching out mentally into the sandbank as he navigated their way across the water. She looked into the water itself. "Faster!"

"What?"

She pointed to a group of dark lines, wriggling in unison as they swam towards them. "A sucker of leeches."

"Is that what they're called?"

"I don't know. I just made it up, but that's what they are." She wanted to call them something ruder but resisted the temptation. She'd tried speaking to them, but the sucker swam faster after them.

"Watch out for the channel," Thomas said.

She'd already noticed and swam across it. She was close to the island now, and Lucy chose to swim the rest of the way, rather than step on the moving mass of vegetation growing from the swamp bed. She'd already felt the first of the leeches biting her legs.

As soon as she stepped on the shore, Lucy burnt the leeches with her magic. She shook them out of her clothing, apart from a particularly long one, almost a foot long, which she pulled out. She held it up and grinned.

Chloris spat one onto the grey beach. "I hate the things." She stared down at the six-inch leeches squirming around her feet.

Thomas stood still, and she felt a faint burst of magic. The leeches fell from his body en masse. "How did you do that?" she asked. He just grinned back.

Feeling the cat's presence, Lucy looked up into the dark forest at the top of the grey beach, but she couldn't see it.

Then, like lights shining, she saw a pair of bright turquoise eyes. "There it is." The grey cat sat on a branch watching them.

"It's big," Thomas said. "It could be dangerous."

He was male, and the size of a large dog. "Perhaps, but I don't think he means us harm."

They walked up to the cat, but before they reached him, he jumped to a lower branch and waited. Lucy resisted her urge to stroke him and spoke instead. He turned his bright saucer eyes to her. He was unlike any cat she'd spoken to before: dignified, in a way. "There's something about him," she said.

"Magic?" Thomas said.

"Possibly." The cat stretched, then walked along the branch before jumping onto another, and then moving deeper in the trees, disappearing from sight. "I think we should follow," Lucy said.

"Why?" Chloris asked.

"Because there's no better option," Thomas said. Lucy knew he'd picked up on some of her feelings.

She went first, pushing through the branches into the forest. Chloris and Thomas followed close behind. The cat waited ahead of her on a narrow path. "At least there's a path."

"A path means that bigger things than cats live here," Thomas said.

She sensed the life of the forest but only felt small animals and insects. The cat increased his pace and barked. "He's impatient and wants us to hurry." She felt the white snake coming to life again. It was moving slowly around her wrist.

As they followed the cat along the path, she heard the sounds of the hellhounds crashing through the forest. Lucy wanted to stop and look around—this island felt far bigger than the previous one, and they passed a black tree with hundreds of dancing flowers of red flame that intrigued her—but there was no time to stop. When the path narrowed even more and then disappeared, the cat didn't slow. He pushed through the undergrowth; Lucy struggled through after him.

The forest had become misty, and it was hard to see the cat running ahead. Chloris crashed through the undergrowth with Thomas. "Strange weather," he said.

"If that's what it is," Lucy said. She suspected there was more to the mist than weather.

The sounds of the hounds were fading behind them as the mist became thicker. "They're lost," Chloris said.

"We might be, too," Lucy said. "The cat's disappeared."

20

If there was magic here, it was a kind that Thomas didn't recognize. The forest smelt of rotten vegetation, and the smell became more intense the deeper they walked along the path. A red-faced creature appeared in the mist; its face was almost human, but antlers rose two feet above its head. It clicked in what might have been a language.

"Who are you?" Thomas asked.

"A servant of Lazolteotl. The goddess awaits you." The red-faced creature's antlers bent back. *"Come."* It walked along the path ahead of them.

Thomas gently pushed a skull aside with his foot. Thoughts of Victor returned, and he felt Lucy take hold of his hand. "It was all my fault," she said quietly. "If it wasn't for me, Victor would still be alive. And Odran, too."

"You shouldn't blame yourself for their deaths."

"But I do," Lucy said. She was crying. "He saved my life."

Thomas nodded. He was also sad to lose a friend. "We mustn't allow his death to be for nothing," he said.

Lucy nodded. "Nothing must stop us. Two people have sacrificed their lives for us. For a faerie creature like Odran to sacrifice himself is unusual; it was important for him, too." Thomas had been thinking the same thing. She squeezed his hand tighter. "Thomas, I don't feel worthy of their sacrifice."

Thomas felt a lump in this throat, and he struggled to contain his emotion. "Neither do I, but we must move forward." She nodded and let go of his hand. Chloris walked silently beside them.

The vegetation became shorter and sparser, and the smell became more intense. "We're walking over a dump," Lucy said. All around them was rotting matter, and all of it was organic. Not a single piece of metal or plastic.

They climbed over an old stone wall and then walked through a decaying urban area with a very rural feel: trees and plants grew through dilapidated houses, some of which had residents. More red-faced, antlered creatures appeared, and some blue- and green-faced ones, too. Other devilish-faced creatures watched them through open-air windows in the stone buildings. A larger, more ornate building rose above the others, and it looked as if they were heading there. The red-faced creature turned and pointed with one of his antlers. *"The Palace of Lazolteotl."*

The palace was a ruin: most of the roof had gone, and trees grew inside. They walked through what once might have been a large reception room. "It's more like an orchard," Lucy said, touching one of the exotically coloured fruits. They passed through a stone arch into the remains of a great hall.

A woman with deep black eyes watched them. A golden scarab crawled slowly up the back of the ornate wooden throne the woman sat on. One of her legs was casually thrown over the arm of the throne, exposing her brown skin. Her presence filled the room. Around her throne grew tall wild flowers, but in front was a muddy puddle in which she dipped a toe.

"Come," Lazolteotl commanded in a rich voice. The red-faced creature led them forward. Several similar but smaller creatures attended her.

"The Goddess Lazolteotl, Goddess of Purification," the red-faced creature announced. It then stood by its mistress, displacing the lesser creatures. She looked neither young nor old. Her legs and feet were splashed with mud, and she smelt of fresh earth. She was beautiful. Her magic permeated his being, and for the first time since he'd met Aina, he felt drawn to another woman. But then his thoughts of Aina returned.

She smiled as the grey cat jumped onto her lap, and more warm magic emanated from the goddess, washing over them and filling the chamber. The woman wore a purple tunic that reached the middle of her thighs. Lazily, she reached out to stroke the cat. "Tu!" The cat purred loudly.

"Hello," Lucy said.

"Hello." Her voice was rich, clear, and vibrant.

"Why did you bring us here?" Thomas asked.

"One reason I brought you here was because what you're doing is similar to what I do. And I was curious." She reached out, and Lucy cried out in surprise when the white snake dropped from her wrist and crawled towards the goddess. "This is the other reason." The cat pounced on it, then taking the wriggling snake in its mouth, jumped back up and deposited it on the lap of the goddess. Lazolteotl picked up the white snake by its tail and swallowed it—for a second her eyes grew brighter.

Lucy glanced at Thomas with wide eyes. *"Being here*

might not be a good idea," she whispered in the True Language.

"A little late to decide that," Thomas replied. The goddess grinned at them. *"She can hear us."*

"Thank you for bringing me breakfast. An interesting item, full of flavour and significance."

"Are we your waiters?" Thomas asked.

"Much more than that. You're workers for something bigger, and like me, you remove blockage from life."

"Frore?" Lucy asked. "He's dangerous."

"Many of us are dangerous." And for a moment, the energy of the room changed into something menacing. The grey cat jumped to the ground and watched them. "But you needn't fear him while you're in my realm. If he were foolish enough to enter, he'd be purified."

"You'd kill him?" Thomas asked.

"That's one way of saying it; his kind are blockages to be flushed away, and I'm a cleaner." Again she grinned—and the atmosphere relaxed. The cat purred loudly. "Tu is sensitive to my moods."

"Does Tu belong to you?" Lucy asked.

"He belongs to himself and wanders where he will, but he chooses to spend time with me."

The goddess clapped her hands, and several tall, blue-faced insectoids rushed around a moss-covered table that stood by an opening in the wall. And like ants in reverse, they filled the table with food. "You brought me my breakfast, and I offer you lunch." The goddess joined them at the table, and like Tu, had a good appetite. Chloris, too, ate large dishes of meat contentedly.

"Why did you eat the white snake?" Thomas asked.

"To absorb its knowledge," Lazolteotl said.

"Do you have many creatures like this helping you?" he

asked.

"I do." But she didn't elaborate. "In a sense, you are my helpers, too. At least we share some similar concerns."

"Killing Frore?"

The goddess grinned and drank more red wine. "You're direct, but yes, that's a part of it."

"And if he comes here, you can kill him?"

She looked at him coolly. "I can."

"So, we're the bait." Thomas resisted another glass of wine.

"They won't enter my realm whatever the bait; they'll wait for you to leave and then attack." Thomas noticed she didn't answer the question directly.

"That's not good," Lucy said.

"She's hiding things," Thomas said.

"I know."

The goddess grinned, and her charm washed over him again. "It's death for him to come here, but I have other workers. And others seek him, too."

"Do we have your protection?" Chloris asked.

"Within my realm, yes. Beyond it, you only have my good wishes, but our interests may coincide."

Chloris's tail flicked once; she didn't look impressed.

"But I can give you information. I know of your task, and I can show you a shortcut deeper into the planet." The air above Thomas's skin vibrated as the woman spoke. Her magic was unlike any he'd encountered before. She returned to her throne and indicated they should follow as her servants rushed to clear the table.

"Where are we?" Thomas asked, standing again before her throne.

"The Plane of Purification." Thomas had no idea what she was talking about. "Between your world and others."

She turned her gaze to Lucy. "You've met some of my helpers. The white powder and mushrooms are part of my realm—transformers."

Lucy's brow furrowed. "What do you mean?"

"My work is purifying and transforming the world—and that's your work, too."

"Cleaning it of dirt like Frore," Chloris said.

The goddess smiled at the ice demon. "Much more. We share a purpose, and more is at stake than it appears." She looked at Thomas. "You think of the dead."

Thomas's heartbeat raced. "She lives?"

"Death is another state of being; we move between death and life for many ages." She raised her hand to prevent his next question. "Aina will tell you more." She dug her big toe deeper into the mud in front of her and watched a flower grow quickly from the puddle. "You know something of creation, too," she said to Lucy. A flush crept up Lucy's neck, and Thomas wondered how much the goddess's energy attracted her, too. Lazolteotl was almost magnetic in her pull.

"Enough of philosophy. I have some gifts. Things to help on the way. For Thomas, my gift is the hope that Aina lives." Thomas smiled as he listened; for several seconds, his hope overpowered his natural disbelief, and he felt a warmth inside.

"Thomas." Aina stood in front of him—insubstantial in form. She put a finger to his lips. *"Come to me."* And then she was gone, and again he looked at the goddess on her throne.

"What happened?"

"Do you need words?" Lazolteotl asked, raising her eyebrows. She turned to Lucy, and taking a deck of cards from her clothing, gave it to her. "An oracle deck. It has special qualities and remains hidden from prying eyes."

"Thank you." Lucy's eyes widened as she studied it more closely. "An animal oracle!"

Chloris stood behind Thomas and Lucy, staring through the opening in the wall, and her tail flicked in surprise when the goddess spoke to her. "Come closer."

Thomas stood back for Chloris to pass. Even this hardened ice demon softened under the gaze of the goddess. "I have a gift for you." Chloris's tail flicked again—a sign of discomfort. Lazolteotl handed her a silver knife. Chloris took the knife. "It's infused with its own magic, and there's little it won't cut." Lucy pointed to the guard of the knife: a snake eating its tail. "An ouroboros," Lazolteotl said. "To give your dreams hope."

Thomas was familiar with the symbol of rebirth. To his surprise, Chloris clicked several times—a sound Lucy had insisted indicated happiness. Chloris bowed before the goddess. "Thank you."

"Your dreams?" Lucy asked.

"To free my people," Chloris said.

Thomas had never even imagined an ice demon dreamt, and felt shamed by his assumption.

"Come," Lazolteotl said. They followed her deeper into the old palace and entered what might once have been a royal drawing room. Lazolteotl sat in an empty window space overlooking the misty forest. Near her was an arch with steps leading down to what might once have been gardens.

"It's time for you to leave this world and return to your own. I've thought about your journey; like me, you seek to purify a world, whether you know it or not. If you succeed in raising the Fire, you would do more than you could imagine to aid my work. But if you fail, you'll be killed or worse."

"What's worse than that?" Lucy asked.

She smiled. "There are worse things than dying, but I hope you'll never find out." Before Lucy could ask her meaning, the goddess continued. "The dark sorcerers wait at the edges of my realm."

"Can you help us?" Thomas asked.

"I already have," the goddess said. And again he felt her power. "Now I give you information. It's up to you to use it. There are doors, and a tangle of paths, between the planes. Shortcuts to many places. One of these leads to the deepest inhabitable part of your world." She turned to Chloris. "You can go no deeper." Turning back to Lucy and Thomas, she said, "To go deeper, you need to retake the Keys."

"What is this place?" Thomas asked.

"Its inhabitants call it Copper. It's a rough town at the end of the world. You can find the entrance at the end of the path." They looked at the path through the old gardens and back into the misty forest.

The grey cat had reappeared, and he brushed against Lucy. "Tu wishes to travel with you." As Lazolteotl spoke, the cat purred loudly.

Thomas shook his head. "We can't take an animal with us. We're going places he can't enter."

"I'm not sure," Lucy said. Thomas caught a little of the communication between her and the cat.

Lazolteotl shrugged. "He can go to many places, just as he's lived many lives. He's a mao and special. There are few like him left in any universe, and like others of his kind, he possesses magic of his own." The cat barked. "He's curious about you."

"He told me he can follow us," Lucy said to Thomas. "Is he from this world?" she asked Lazolteotl. "I asked, but the answer wasn't clear."

The goddess shook her head. "I found him floating on

an old wooden map in an ocean on another world. He's stayed with me for half a lifetime, but he misses the sea. He's been a ship's cat several times."

"There's no sea where we are going," Thomas said, but all three—the cat, the goddess, and Lucy—just stared at him impatiently. Thomas sighed. "I still don't understand why you're helping us."

"I've already explained. You, like me, purify the world, and what you do is important beyond your world—even beyond your universe. All life is connected, even the lives of those in distant galaxies in other universes."

"A multiverse," Thomas said. "What do you know of that?"

"Millions of universes exist in the same space, each containing countless worlds." She raised her hand to stop Thomas from asking another question. "It's enough to know they exist in the same space and are connected. By helping you, I help myself and many others."

"Can you purify Frore?" Chloris asked.

She laughed. "He's toxic and dangerous. After he dies, the Universe will purify him—or dissolve him back into basic elements. But that's not my job."

"What's he doing now?" Lucy asked.

"Waiting with his friends, but as soon as you leave, they'll follow you. Tu will lead you to the edge of my domain—perhaps further. Beyond is a valley. The doorway is at the deepest point."

The mao barked from the archway. Lucy turned back to ask a question, but Lazolteotl was gone. Thomas raised his eyebrows and shrugged. "We'll have to find our own way," he said.

They followed the large grey cat along the misty path.

21

As they followed the cat, Lucy touched a long-leaved plant, feeling its energy. She was now sure that magic was stronger here than on her version of Prometheus. Reaching out with her magic, she felt a web spreading through the forest and beyond. She listened to threads vibrate with a meaning she didn't fully understand.

"I can feel it, too," Thomas said. *"More vibrant than our plane."* She nodded absently, just realizing that they'd been walking in silence for several minutes. *"My magic's more alive, but that might mean theirs is, too."* She had no need to ask who he referred to.

The mist ended, and the mao stopped several yards ahead, waiting for them to reach its outer margin. Images of speed came to Lucy. "He's telling us we have to sprint," she said.

Tu ran from the misty part of the forest, and all three of them sprinted after him. Seconds later, the hounds bayed. *"They're on our trail,"* she said. Thomas just grunted. The others were already a little ahead of her. Lucy followed through the forest, speaking to the trees to ensure a smooth passage—until a branch snapped behind her. She projected her mind into the forest, and she felt Thomas doing the same through the ground. "A hound," she whispered, feeling its life force. Chloris's ears twitched as she listened.

"It's creeping towards us," Thomas said. "Its magic is vibrating through the earth."

"No magic," Chloris said. "There's only one."

Short sword drawn, Thomas moved quickly towards the sound. Chloris was right behind. The hound bounded from the trees, knocking Thomas and Chloris aside before spinning round to face them. Thomas rolled over backwards and came up on his feet, advancing on the hound.

But the hound had moved away, towards Chloris. It attacked suddenly, pulling at her leg and ignoring the cat swiping at it. Chloris slashed wildly, but claws could only hurt a creature half-made of magic so much. Lucy cringed as the hound bit deep into the ice demon's leg.

Lucy ran to Chloris and helped staunch some of the bleeding with her magic as Thomas charged the hellhound. Without the cup, Lucy could only do so much. And Chloris wouldn't wait—she attacked again, slashing from one side, while Thomas cut deeply with his sword. He managed to sever a front leg; Chloris slashed the tendons behind its rear knee. The hound fell to the ground, still growling fiercely, but blood gushed from its mouth—it was weakening.

"All that to disable a dog," Thomas said. When Chloris attacked again, Thomas called her off. "It's a better use of time to find the portal to our world."

But Chloris took out her knife, and before anyone could speak, had stabbed the hound. The knife glowed as it entered its body—it died quickly. Chloris wiped the blade clean, looking very pleased with herself.

They ran from the dead hound without another word.

The pack had heard the fight and ran towards their dead companion.

Hearing the cat ahead of them, Lucy led the way. The path soon descended into a valley. At a fork in the path, they stopped. They could hear the hounds barking as they followed their scent.

"This way," Thomas said, starting to run down the left-hand path.

Lucy hesitated, sensing Tu's presence. "I think it's this way."

Thomas stopped. "Lucy! Lazolteotl told us to descend."

"She told us to go to the bottom of the valley, but she didn't tell us which path to take. This one descends, too."

"Not much."

Chloris looked at the two of them. "Quickly!"

Thomas had turned back to look at her. She felt him reaching into the earth. "They both descend," he said. "Are you sure it's not Frore, interfering in your mind again?"

Her eyes narrowed in annoyance. "Tu went this way." Lucy ran down the right-hand path. Thomas cursed and went after her. The hounds were crashing through the vegetation behind and around them. "They're trying to cut us off!" he shouted. As they turned a corner, they came upon a dog the size of a horse.

Lucy held up her knife and Tu hissed at the hound. She was ready to fight, but looking at Thomas's expression, she stepped aside. He laughed a little manically, and without stopping, he charged the dog. It backed off slightly. Thomas's rock magic was hard, and he punctured the hound's body, while Chloris hit the hound with force. Its legs gave way, and despite having some magic protection, it struggled to fight back. Thomas and Chloris stabbed the creature. It soon lay dead on the ground. Sweat ran down his face when he looked back at Lucy.

"Thank you both," she said, considering her friends, at that moment, to be more like forces of nature than people. "But Frore would have heard us."

Thomas nodded at her, and the three of them ran after the wild-looking cat. The forest had a feral nature, too, and feelers from the brambles reached for them as they passed; Thomas was hacking them back as he ran. "This forest is too alive." Another bramble head rose before her, and two more tried to entangle her. In the rush, there was little chance to communicate with the forest, but at least most of them let go after touching her. When a bramble head reared before Lucy, she caught it and it withered as her magic burnt its way along its stem. She hated using her power like this, but she had little choice. The plants seemed to learn and pulled back; the path widened a little. She turned a corner and stopped in a small clearing. Her heart sank; her intuition had failed her.

"Not good," Chloris said.

They were surrounded by wild forest. A tightly knit patch of white mushrooms, about seven foot tall, grew on one side of the dark forest, with protruding feelers waving towards them on the other sides.

"I'm sorry." She'd led them to a dead end.

Hounds ran along the path towards them. "We have to fight somewhere," Thomas said. "We have about a minute before they arrive, and there's only one way they can come." He walked around the small clearing, slapping away the creepers that reached towards him. "Where's Tu?"

She shook her head. She'd tried to sense the cat, but couldn't feel him anywhere. "I don't know."

Thomas reached towards the gently swaying mushrooms; they tightened together when he touched them. "Are these the same plants that helped you before?"

She nodded. They whispered as she walked to them and reached out towards her. Lucy shivered. They were similar enough, though these had specks of grey along their bodies. They seemed to recognize her. "Almost the same." Although the others didn't have flat caps.

"They seem to recognize you," Thomas said. "Perhaps your intuition was right."

"Perhaps. I don't know." She didn't like the feeling of the fungus and had no wish to be smothered inside their flesh.

"Maybe they'll help us again."

She shrugged. The mushrooms' whispers were unclear, and they were not speaking to her. She pushed at the tall mushrooms, but they refused to move. She felt Tu's presence inside the patch. He really did seem to go wherever he wanted. She heard Thomas and Chloris preparing for the hounds.

The slender stems rose above her and were capped with large, white, disc-like heads. As they moved from side to side, they crackled with energy. She rubbed one of the smooth pale stalks and spoke quickly to them, explaining how they'd helped her before. A fibrous snakelike strand wrapped around her neck and pressed against her cheek. She slapped it, and it loosened, pulling away. She heard Chloris hiss as hounds ran into the clearing, but she still spoke to the plants. *"Let us through—make a passage for us."*

She glanced back to see Thomas and Chloris facing a pack of hounds. If she couldn't find a way soon, they'd be facing Frore and the other sorcerers—and this time without the Keys. Thomas and Chloris were nervous, too; both were eyeing possible escapes through the dense and aggressive vegetation, and both were breathing rapidly.

The patch of mushrooms swayed more violently. *"Help us!"* Then she looked down at the ground. *"They've answered."* Tiny mushrooms appeared from the ground and grew fast around her feet.

"I hope so." Thomas glanced back and then at the hounds.

Chloris held her silver knife and waited. "Why don't they attack?" she asked. Yet more hounds pushed into the clearing.

"They're waiting for their master," Lucy said.

22

Lord Frore rode into the clearing on a large hellhound, the witch beside him on her own hound, still humming her sickening spell. Xart stopped at the entrance to the path.

"At last," Frore said. His lips cracked into a smirk when he saw Lucy. "You're trapped and alone." Thomas and Chloris backed up towards her. Lord Frore rode forward, holding a whip loosely in one hand.

Lucy felt Thomas pulling a little of the pentacle's power. She could feel the call of the cup, but Frore held it securely on his hound.

Picking up a stone, Thomas threw it hard at Frore's hound. The hellhound yelped but didn't move. She knew they had a serious problem. Frore laughed and, without warning, lashed out with his whip. A shimmering cord coiled violently around Thomas's neck and jerked him forward.

All the while, the witch never stopped humming. Lucy could feel the effects of the spell sapping her energy. She threw her knife at the witch's chest, but the blade bounced off without disturbing the spell. Now she was unarmed, and the plants behind her were doing no more than whisper and sway.

Chloris protected her, slashing with her silver knife and claws and spitting acid, as Lucy tried to pull the tightening whip from Thomas's neck. Chloris'd killed one of the hounds, but they were strong and fast and ignored the open wounds she'd given them. She was still being pushed back.

Thomas had fallen to the ground near the creepers while Lucy tried to help him. When one of the creepers twisted around his ankle and pulled him towards the forest, Frore loosened his whip and watched with interest. *"He's playing with us,"* Lucy said.

Thomas rolled over, and a feeler from a tree touched his hand—she noticed it was a black flame tree; she'd seen them before. Lucy felt a moment's contact between Thomas and the tree. A single flame rose from his fingertip. Frore frowned and lashed out again. The whip wrapped itself around Thomas's wrist, but this time he didn't resist, but hummed to the flame. It responded and flames danced, and as he grasped the whip, fire burnt along its length, and the coils fell away. Frore screamed in rage and released a dark, inky magic that reached towards them.

Chloris cried out as fibre fingers from the white patch grasped her ankles. More white tendrils had wrapped themselves around her thighs. *"What are you doing?"* Lucy asked, but they didn't answer. Chloris slashed the tendrils, but each time she cut them, more appeared. Another of the hounds lay dead in front of her, and the others waited warily beyond their reach. The tendrils from the white fungus pulled Chloris into the patch.

"Why bother with this stuff?" Lucy shouted at Frore past

the wall of flames that separated them. "Why not just attack?"

Frore smirked. "This stuff makes minds pliable—even stiff ones like his."

Lucy cursed. He wanted confirmation of what he'd found in her memories, or perhaps he wanted a clue to accessing the power of the Keys.

"The flames are harder to break through than he admits," Thomas said.

"But he is breaking through."

Thomas didn't answer as the hounds pushed closer. Only a single line of flames stopped them from reaching him. A black flower of fire floated over Thomas, and he touched it. As he did, the row of flames on the forest floor blazed high into the air, blocking the darkness that touched them.

Frore no longer looked so confident, and he spoke to the goblin and the witch. The goblin moved forwards, stopping at the line of flames. Energy swelled outwards from him, and a few of the flames were extinguished. The witch's chanting changed its rhythm, speeding up, and the black stuff began to writhe as it pushed into the remaining fire.

The dancing flames moved in a chaotic fashion, leaping from one place to another, as if an unseen wind blew against them. Lucy guessed it was real; a psychic wind the goblin and witch sent out, spreading them across the clearing. Xart's and Biddy Zo's plan didn't appear to be working exactly as they'd wished.

"What are they?" Lucy asked.

"Elemental creatures of this plane, I think." Thomas picked himself up off the ground. The creepers had released their grip on his ankle. He looked exhausted. "Highly organized energy," he said.

The leaping spirits of flame altered their dance, and as Thomas hummed, the organized energy responded to the vibrations of his voice. His music magnetized the spirits of flame, and they danced towards the hounds. A hound sniffed the swaying flames and caught fire. Wailing desperately, it ran into the dark forest, where the cold fibrous feelers wrapped around it. It yelped wildly as they pulled it apart.

Biddy Zo's rhythmic chanting continued. It was unwholesome and sickening, and each time her voice deepened, the flames flickered. Then they vanished, and the hellhounds attacked.

Staggering under the force of magic, both she and Thomas fell back against the vibrating bodies of the white mushrooms. *"Help us,"* she called again, not expecting these cold plants to care unless threatened themselves.

Xart rushed Thomas, sending out a strand of black energy that breached his defence, knocking him to his knees. Thomas's face reddened where the black fleck of magic burnt him. Now, only a single flame was between him and the goblin.

Lucy was covered in sweat, and she began to feel dizzy as Frore and the hounds pushed forward. "We're losing," she said quietly.

"We can't win this fight," Thomas said. *"But we can make it hard."*

Frore stared with intense, cold eyes, and he opened his mouth wide, vomiting a toxic black cloud that drifted towards them. But from the swirling fungi, a mushroom of white dust arose, covering them and easing their pain. Lucy breathed in relief. The mushrooms' powdery cloud had lessened the power of the black magic, but it still pushed them back against the fungi. And when a strand of black energy struck Lucy's face, she vomited on the ground.

Lucy struggled with the darkness around her and could hardly move. Lord Frore stepped forward. This was the first time she'd seen him so close. His skin was grey; his irises a similar metallic colour. "I've been gentle, hoping to speak to you. If killing you had been my objective, you'd already be dead." His breath sickened her. She turned away, trying to avoid breathing in any of the wisps of inky stuff that still trickled from the sides of his mouth. His words vibrated and weakened her further, but she heard partial truth in them. He still hoped to learn from her: the ways to Earth and knowledge of the Keys that despite his power, he still lacked. He reached for her, and she felt herself fading.

But before Frore touched her, a white shape flew from the fungi patch and smashed into his face. He screamed and stepped back.

"What did you do?" Thomas asked weakly.

"Nothing," she answered.

More white shapes flew from the fungi patch, smashing into Frore, Xart, and Biddy Zo. Each time the white discs hit, they exploded into clouds of white powder. Belatedly, Frore formed an energetic barrier that blocked the dust and the discs, but the mushroom caps were detaching themselves faster and still pounding his defence.

Frore attacked the patch of fungi with fire, but the fungi did little more than smoulder. Lord Frore shouted. He was now furious. Still he attacked, sending another wave of fire into the plants.

Glancing at Thomas, Lucy doubted he could take another attack. His head was dropping down; it was obvious he'd lost his strength. As she watched, he fell back towards the plants.

She tried to reach him, but the chanting had sickened her, and she felt as if she were walking through water. Looking up, she saw a grey thing fly from the fungal forest—its movements a blur.

"What?" Thomas asked. He was losing his focus.

She blinked, trying to see what it was. Whatever it was, it penetrated the sorcerer's magical defence and hit him in his face.

"From the fungi?" Thomas said.

She couldn't see clearly but shook her head. *"It's moving."*

Frore screamed and clutched his face, thrashing from side to side, but it stuck to him and howled as he screamed. When he pulled it off and threw it to the ground, one of Frore's eyes hung from its socket. The witch's humming faltered, and Xart's eyes widened as Frore fell to the forest floor, staring through one eye. The cat's bloody body lay still on the ground.

Lucy knew that it was partly the shock of the attack that had stopped Frore, but he would recover soon. She was shocked by the death of Tu—another sadenning loss—but there was nothing she could do. As she looked around, she realized Thomas had vanished into the fungi. Lucy desperately crawled to the fungal patch, and this time they opened a path for her. The smell was pleasant as she crawled inside, but as the plants tightened and vibrated around her, she felt sick again. They vibrated faster, then they silently exploded in a white cloud and were gone.

She lay on damp ground. Struggling to remain conscious, she noticed the quality of light was different. Then the world around faded into darkness.

23

Thomas lay on a stone floor. He could neither open his eyes nor speak, but he could smell the sweat in the room. And he felt the kick in his ribs. Several men spoke Dnassian, but with an accent he didn't recognize. They compared him with someone else who must have been lying on the floor nearby—he prayed it wasn't Lucy. He'd been drugged, and later the men's comments confirmed it.

Thomas waited, but he learnt little, except that they were all captives, and that they trained for the Games. Even as he felt control returning to his body, he kept his eyes closed and reached out, listening to the language of the rocks. He was about twenty feet underground, and he sensed a warren of tunnels around him.

A thud, followed by a groan and then laughter, told him the other person was awake. It was clearly a man. The boot connected with the body again, and the man cried out.

"The other," someone whispered.

Thomas felt the footsteps vibrating through the ground—it was the same man who'd kicked him before. Thomas let him approach. His eyes were still closed, but he saw clearly enough with his rock sense, and when the kick came, Thomas twisted and caught it, striking the man in the knee and using the back of his knee to push up. The man dropped to the ground, and Thomas kicked him hard in the ribs.

He looked around the room and counted nineteen men, including the one by his feet; the other newcomer was a scared boy. A large hulking man and a thin wiry one stood at the front. Thomas took them to be leaders, of a sort. "Where am I?"

"The House of the One Fist," the thin man said.

"Copper?"

"He's a fast one," the thin man said.

Thomas's thoughts turned to bigger problems. He hoped that Frore would follow. The sorcerer now had revenge as a motive, as well as his dark attraction to Lucy.

The man struggled to his feet and Thomas stepped back. He didn't want to fight, but when the man threw a punch, Thomas turned a fraction, guiding his arm past with a hand. He shook his finger at the man, but he wanted more, swinging wildly at Thomas's head. Thomas caught his arm and threw him to the ground. The man fell awkwardly, cracking his elbow, and he backed off, rubbing his hurt arm and scowling.

"You might survive a day of the Games," the thin man said. He glanced at the boy. "But not this one."

Thomas noticed he was wearing a grey T-shirt and shorts; the same as everyone else. And he smelt the same, too. He walked towards an empty bunk.

"That's mine," the big man said.

Ignoring the man, Thomas sat on the bed. Either he'd attack, in which case Thomas would fight, or not, in which case he'd sleep. He leant back and closed his eyes, but his rock sense was alert, and the man rushed at him—surprising him with his speed. Although the drugs had dulled Thomas's speed and magic, they hadn't completely taken them away, and he still had his natural strength and martial training. He stood, opening his eyes and sinking his energy into the ground. The man was big, but Thomas had once trained against a troll. Thomas pushed him with open palms, sending him several inches into the air. The big man staggered backwards to laughter. But then he charged again.

They fought for several minutes—the men watched, appraising his moves. Thomas was faster, but his opponent was strong. Thomas attacked hard and felt a drug-induced headache start. Annoyed by the increasing pain in his head, he attacked even harder. When the big man landed a punch, Thomas shook his head. "You fight like a troll."

The man grinned, and at that moment one of their jailers opened the door and looked around the room. He'd handed Thomas a stalemate, which was preferable to an enemy.

"What's happening?" the jailer said.

"Bedbugs!" Thomas said, slapping the bed. The man stared at him for several seconds, then left. The others looked at him, apparently unsure what to think. Thomas looked up at the big man who was still deciding what to do. "One-punch hangover," he said, rubbing his head. This brought another grin from his opponent and a relaxation in the room. He'd passed the test—now his test was to escape and retake his key.

Over the next few hours, as he forced himself to stay awake, he heard some of their stories. Some were like him, strangers and in the wrong place at the wrong time, others were sold by their family, some were debtors and thieves. The man he'd just fought, Big Tom, had killed a man.

"Why not escape?" Thomas asked.

"Where to?" the thin man, called Jones, asked.

Thomas realized that he didn't know the geography of the bottom of the world. "I was drugged before I came here, and then drugged after I arrived," he lied. "I've not seen any cities since Tartaros."

"There aren't any—some small towns is all," Jones said. "I heard that Tartaros is a myth."

All eyes were on Thomas when he shared stories from the city. They were eager listeners but also eager sharers. Thomas learnt that the slavers lived together in a white house in the centre of the city.

Copper was a hard place, harder, perhaps, than Tartaros, though smaller; its economy depended on metal and slaves. The dream of most of these men was to win their freedom and work as bodyguards or swords for hire for the local lords. Some simply dreamt of drinking their way to oblivion.

The afternoon was spent in the training yard. They fought with wooden swords and knives, staffs, sticks, and nets. He noticed that most of the other fighters avoided Big Tom, but he liked working out with the man. Perhaps because Thomas had once trained with a troll, and this tough man reminded him of those days.

During the second day training, Thomas felt his power returning to its natural level. Thugs with bronze swords watched over them. While killing them, even with wooden swords, might be possible, there were many of them throughout the underground complex. He decided to wait.

A few times he felt Lucy's presence, but her voice was distant—she may also have been drugged. He'd found out from the men that the sedating of new domestic slaves often continued for up to a week, as a precaution to stop them escaping. He decided to make a move on the third day. He'd find Lucy, whether she was drugged or not.

THE GAMES WERE HELD in the Copper Pit—an open copper mine, long since exhausted of the metal. Steps carved out of the side of the pit led down to the stands, where the holders of the cheapest tickets stood, forming a horseshoe shape around the arena. Manual lifts, pulled by slaves, lowered the fighters into the cages at the open end of the horseshoe.

More money bought a seat in the stalls, also carved from the side of the pit. These were above the stands and reached by safer stairs. Lord Copper sat in the Lord's Box with about twenty minor lords and ladies, who were attended by slaves. The box was served by its own stairs and a special lift.

Copper had several stables of fighters: the Coppers and the Eight Hands were the most respected and had their own cages. Thomas had been bought by the One Fist, a newer stable, fighting to gain respect. He waited, chained to a post with Big Tom, in the common cages and had a clear view of the jagged and uneven combat area.

He already knew the order of events: first the oldest, poorest, or sickest were killed by trained fighters; second, fighters killed exotic animals, if any could be found; and finally, the fighters fought fighters—this was where the serious bets were placed. Thomas had no intention to kill for the entertainment of the people—now was the time to leave.

A cart raced into the middle of the arena, and eleven people were pushed or thrown to the ground before the cart span round and raced back out of the arena. The audience was in high spirits as they jeered, shouted, and talked in the stands. Two fighters walked casually to either side of the confused group and drew their swords. When a bell rang, they ran at the oldest and sickest first. They died quickly and added up the score. Only then did the men turn to the able-bodied poor. One of the men disarmed the shorter fighter but lost a hand in the process. The audience cheered when the other fighter killed him with a sword in his back.

The fighters were even with five kills each. The last man ran to the rock face beneath the box. The elite of Copper leant over the edge, staring down at the man who was desperately climbing towards them. He climbed well, pulling himself up by his hands.

One of the minor lords appeared to be instructing his son. Giving the boy his sword, he pointed down at the man and made stabbing gestures. The boy waited, and when the man was close enough, he leant over and stabbed his head. The Lord of Copper nodded his approval as the man tumbled to the ground. Both fighters stabbed him, and both claimed the kill.

Anger rose in Thomas towards both the lords and the crowd. But as he was planning how he might end this practice, the hairs on his body stood on end—magic was being used in the pit. He searched the stadium but saw no likely source for his feeling. The fighters exited the stadium. "What's next? Exotic animals?" he asked.

Big Tom shook his head. "We killed most of them years ago. It's fighters against fighters now."

The fighters fought matches on the rough surface. Thomas watched more men die, then a giant man strode into the ring and roared. "Hammon of the Eight," Big Tom said. The audience screamed in excitement. "No one's ever defeated him."

"Are all fights to the death?" Thomas asked.

"Since the new lord decided to make his mark."

"How do you get to be the Lord of Copper?"

"By killing the old one," Big Tom said.

"Brand!" a slaver shouted. "You're next!"

"Thomas, beware!"

Thomas eyes widened in shock. *"Aina?"* It couldn't be her; he looked around but only saw the fighters staring at him. Some laughed—misunderstanding his expression for fear. But he had no time to think about what had happened, as men dragged him out into the arena. Something was shimmering in the air to one side of Hammon.

Thomas strained to see what was materializing next to the man. *"Aina?"* But the red eyes of a hellhound stared back at him. When Hammon stepped towards him, Thomas ran to the vague form of the hellhound and stabbed it. The crowd roared with laughter as they misunderstood his actions, and fresh bets were placed.

Hammon charged, and Thomas cursed. He had no wish to engage this man. Even if he beat him, it would risk the unopposed entry of the hounds. Instead, he jumped to one side and telepathically taunted the emerging dogs.

But the giant fighter was intent on killing him. Thomas turned away his opponent's thrust and slapped the man's studded wristband with his sword. The man jabbed a few times, testing him, and each time Thomas easily evaded them. When Hammon attacked more forcefully, Thomas chose a beginner's move and struck his sword directly. The man's eyes widened in surprise and anticipation of an easy kill, but the connection of metal to metal allowed Thomas to send a shot of magic along the sword, snapping at the man's hand. Hammon leapt back in surprise but managed to keep hold of his sword. The next time their swords touched, he repeated, but this time the shock was stronger. Hammon cried out and almost dropped the sword. Thomas attacked aggressively. Another shot of magic numbed the giant's hand, and he dropped the blade, clutching his hand in pain. The crowd turned on him.

Thomas picked up Hammon's sword. The giant was rubbing his forehead, trying to understand what had happened. Thomas raised his swords. "Do you want death?"

The crowd roared, "Death!"

"Then I'll give it you," he said quietly. He approached Hammon. "I have no fight with you." Thomas threw the man's sword to the ground.

The man's eyes widened in surprise.

"Leave the pit before the dogs kill you." Hammon blinked when he saw a dog appearing in one of the depressions at the pit floor.

Putting his sword in the scabbard given to fighters, and ignoring the jeers of the crowd, Thomas walked to the rock face beneath the Lord's Box and rested his hands on it. He called his magic, and it drew the hounds as he'd intended. They materialized around the pit; the crowd became excited, thinking them part of the show.

Thomas felt the welcoming energy of the rocks, and ignoring the hoots of men and howls of hounds, he ran up the rock face with the rocks pulling him in like a magnet. Once he reached the top, he used a skill he'd rarely attempted, and flipping the rock magic like a switch, he reversed the energy, using the repulsive power of the rocks. He flew into the Lord's Box, drawing his sword at the same time. A guard went for his sword, but Thomas pushed him away.

Through his rock sense, Thomas felt the pursuit. The crowd was standing and staring at the strange pack of hounds that crawled up the rock face to the Lord's Box.

The Lord of Copper, unable to see what the crowds saw or what Thomas felt, stood and glared at him. "Who are you?" he demanded.

Thomas decapitated him. Holding up his head, he spoke to the crowds, and his voice, assisted by rock magic, carried throughout the pit. "The last Lord of Copper is dead. Your city has been invaded by forces of the Empire. Run!"

Without waiting for their reaction, he tossed the head over the side and ran up the steps and out of the arena.

24

Lucy dreamt of dirt and animals and things moving around her. She tried to wake up when she heard shouts and laughter and cries of disgust. She was roughly moved and dropped. They left her, but something remained. Something guarded her while she lay in an unnatural sleep.

Much later, she woke up in a dirty bed. Her body itched, and she smelt bad, but otherwise she felt all right apart from the headache. *"Drugged."* Trying to sit up to see who spoke, she felt dizzy and fell back onto the bed. *"Gather your strength. Kill them later."*

"Who are you?"

"Rest now."

She passed in and out of sleep for several hours, aware of a presence nearby, but unsure what it was. She wasn't even sure where she was; this was all so unfamiliar. However, she remembered the fight with Frore and the death of the cat.

The next time she woke, she felt slightly better. She got

up, but staggered forward, and almost fell into the opening door. A man pushed her back onto the bed, and she looked around for signs of the speaker but couldn't find any. A man and woman, both aged around forty, walked into the room.

"Feeling better?" the woman asked in a flat voice. "The sedatives are for your own good. You'll feel fine soon, but you stink, and you've got fleas. You need a bath and then we can sort you out."

"No," the voice whispered. *"Better stink."*

"No," Lucy repeated.

"You'll do what you're told here, but you'll get used to it. It's not so bad, just relax and enjoy."

"Where am I?"

"The Copper Flower," the woman said. "A pleasure house."

"A brothel?"

"What else did you think? Get your clothes off and follow him to the bathroom." The woman turned her nose away and glanced at the man. "You really do smell bad; even Dirty Del wouldn't go near you. He normally does all the girls when they come in."

Lucy fell back on her bed. "I don't feel well. I need to rest."

The woman looked into her eyes. "You won't get out of it that way, but you do look a bit off. I'll be back soon. You can clean the room later, too."

"You're leaving her?" the man asked.

"She's going nowhere. Idiot Larry can't control the doses—he kills half of them, but this one's strong." With that, they locked her in the room again.

She automatically felt for her cup before remembering she no longer had it. She tried to call Thomas, but the drugs they'd given her had dulled her mind. However, she noticed something in her pocket. Reaching in, she took out the oracle deck, remembering that the goddess had said something about it remaining hidden from prying eyes. As she turned the deck over, a card jumped out. Turning over the card, she saw a wolf staring at her.

"Were you speaking to me earlier?"

"Who else? And I lent you my fleas, too." She involuntarily scratched herself. *"They've gone now. Mostly."*

"Who are you?" Lucy had used oracle cards before but had never imagined cards like this.

"Your significator."

"And what do you represent in me?"

"The will to fight and survive. Shuffle the deck and ask to be shown a way out. Help is in the cards." Lucy wanted to hug the animal in gratitude. The wolf's head seemed to reach out from the card and nuzzle her hand; his nose was wet. Then he was gone, and again he stared out at her from the forest on the oracle card. She smelt the back of her hand where his nose had touched; there was a faint smell of wolf.

"What type of magic does this oracle possess?" she asked herself quietly.

"Shuffle," the wolf whispered in her mind.

The man and woman were talking outside her door, and this time they were going to force her to do what they wanted. She quickly shuffled, and as she did, she repeated the question out loud: "How can I escape this place? Show me a way out." As she shuffled, she was drawn to one of the cards. She pulled it out. A brightly coloured monkey stared at her. *"What are you telling me?"*

The picture moved, and the monkey swam in a forest pool. Other monkeys were sitting on a log. The monkey grabbed the tails of two of the other monkeys and pulled them into the water. Jumping out, it raced up the tree and threw fruit down at the others. Then it sat back on the branch and howled, and it was loud. Keys jangled outside. Lucy quickly put the card facedown on the top of the deck, and the sound stopped. What was the message? To play? It didn't make sense. She was about to put the deck away when the card moved.

"What?" she asked, nervously turning it over.

"Let's play."

"I don't want to play," Lucy said frantically as the door started to open.

"Monkeys know the value of play." Lucy jumped as the brightly coloured monkey reached out of the card and pulled her nose. The door was opening, and she had no idea what to do. She didn't want them taking her oracle deck.

"*Hide*," she whispered. The monkey just stared at her. *"What kind of oracle card are you?"*

"One that helps you release your natural magic more easily." Then the monkey howled with strange laughter and leapt from the card, climbing the door as it opened. *"Are you real or a part of me?"* she asked.

"What's the difference?"

Lucy had no idea. She put the cards away, and they seemed to melt into her pocket, almost as if they weren't there. But the bright red and orange monkey remained.

"What's the noise?" the man said.

The monkey leapt onto his head and screeched. The man cried out and fell to the floor, hitting his head against the wall. It stole his knife. "Give me that back." The man chased the monkey down the corridor.

"How did an animal get in here?" the woman asked.

"Through the window," Lucy said.

"There is no window."

"Oh, I hadn't noticed," she said. The woman slammed the door shut, locked it, and ran after the man.

"Nice," the wolf whispered.

"I thought oracles were supposed to answer questions."

"We show answers and lend a little assistance." In the distance, the monkey whooped and howled. She heard things smashing.

"He's having a party," she said. The noises got closer, and a key was inserted into the lock.

"Take out the two cards," the wolf said.

Lucy didn't have to ask which ones. The wolf stared out from one, but the monkey card was empty. The door opened and the monkey walked in, grinning wildly. It leapt at Lucy, then disappeared into the card. The wolf walked out. *"We go."*

She had no objection, and they walked along the corridor. A man blocked their way, but when he saw the wolf, he disappeared into a room. Lucy's magic was slowly returning; she had the feeling that the wolf was helping her find it. She could now hear the locations of the people in the building. She led the way. *"There's a man by the entrance."*

"I know."

The man took out a long knife, but Lucy sent him feelings of drowsiness, the same as those they'd given her with the sedative. It was fresh in her mind. He appeared unsteady on his feet, and when the wolf growled, he staggered back. "Open the door," she said. The man obeyed, and they left the building.

"That was easier than I thought," she said.

"These humans are simple creatures, the easiest to influence.

It's your magic, not mine, that placed the suggestions in their minds."

"Can you kill the sorcerers for me?"

"The power must come from within you. We can only advise."

The true purpose of oracle decks, she thought as they walked down the street.

25

The shadow wolf followed Lucy down the street, although passersby only sensed his presence, unconsciously moving aside as they passed.

"I can smell the rock man," the wolf said.

Lucy smiled at the description of Thomas. *"Where is he?"*

"Close."

They were walking close to the city wall, which was lit by torches and fires at regular distances. She studied the figures that moved along the top.

"Be careful."

"What?" A group of young men walked towards her.

"Not them."

Then she saw a flickering about ten feet ahead, and the dark muzzle of a hellhound poked through. She was vaguely aware of the boys approaching her.

"What's she doing?" a boy said.

"She's lost," another said.

"We can show you around," one of them said to her.

Lucy ignored them and approached the nose of the hellhound that pushed through the rupture between

Lazolteotl's realm and her world. *"Hit it,"* the shadow wolf hissed. She slapped its nose, and the boys whooped with laughter, thinking the empty slap was for them. They imitated her, but she hardly noticed. She did notice that the hellhound had withdrawn its head slightly.

"What happened?" Lucy asked.

"Do you remember the feeling you had when you reentered this world?"

"It hurt." That gave her an idea. *"If we could find Frore when he reentered, then we might have a chance of getting the Keys."*

"Yes," the wolf said. Again, Lucy wondered how much the wolf was a part of her. *"We're all connected,"* he whispered in her mind. She smiled at the wolf.

"She likes you."

Lucy turned and slapped the boy who'd touched her shoulder. "Grow up!" she said, raising her voice.

They stepped back but continued discussing her. She was more concerned about the reemerging hounds and how to find Thomas and Chloris. She touched the air where the hound's muzzle had appeared. It was still shimmering. She sensed movement beyond it. "Do you want me to get rid of the young men?" the wolf asked.

She looked at the boys again, but they were the least of her concerns. *"No, I can deal with them."* She spoke to the boys. "You're in danger here. Go home." Their laughter stopped when a hound nipped one of them. She pushed its head back, using a small amount of magic to do so. "I can't hold these things out much longer."

"You don't need to." The wolf's form brightened for a moment.

"What?"

"I sense a disturbance."

She listened, but her concentration was disturbed when one of the boys touched her again. "I warned you." A hound's head emerged from a shimmering break in the air. Its breath stank, and this time they noticed.

"What's that?" The hound grabbed the speaker in its mouth, then tossed him aside.

"Come!" the wolf said.

The boys completely forgotten, she followed the shadow wolf along the street, listening to the sounds of the city with the True Language.

"Lucy?"

"Thomas. Where are you?"

"I was drugged and detained, but I'm moving towards you now. What's happening?"

"The hounds are breaking through, but there's a bigger disturbance. I'm moving towards it now. I think it's Chloris."

Soon Lucy heard screeches, confirming her thoughts, and she ran faster, stopping in surprise upon entering a crowded square. Hundreds of people gathered around a stone stage—cages lined the back of half the stage, and in one of them Chloris was screeching at two men who were poking her with staves. She snapped one in half to a roar of approval from the crowd. She'd walked into a slave market.

A man was watching her, and she didn't like the look in his eyes. She pushed past him, but he quickly stepped in front of her, grasping her wrist. In sudden anger, she sent a short shock of magic up his arm. He let go, his eyes widening. "Who's in charge here?" she asked.

He nodded at a group of men sitting to the right of the cages, separated by a short wall. "But they won't help you," he said, rubbing his wrist. "What did you do to me?" She tried to force her way past the man, who sniggered at her attempts.

"Move!"

The wolf jumped at the man, and he fell to the ground in shock, but she didn't have time to enjoy his expression; she rushed after the wolf as he disappeared into the crowd. People moved aside in surprise or indignation, and she received several unfriendly comments, but she soon left them behind.

As she reached the front of the stage, Chloris noticed her. The ice demon was trying to speak to her, but she noticed the hackles along the wolf's back raising. Turning, she saw shimmering patches of light around the square.

"We have company," Chloris said.

"We do," she said aloud. She climbed onto the stage to quiet gasps from some in the crowd. "How did they catch you?"

"Drugged me while I was unconscious; otherwise, I'd have killed them all," she hissed. The men in front of her cage took several steps back. One glanced at the master's section, his mouth slack.

"What's the matter with you?" a slave master shouted.

"It spoke, sir."

"Nonsense, you idiot. And what's that girl doing on my stage?"

Men strode towards her. She sensed Thomas entering the square. *"I could do with some help here."*

"I'm with you." Thomas ran through the crowd, elbowing people aside, and she could sense him using a little magic to make his path easier.

Two men took hold of her; she looked for the wolf, but he was gone. She felt the pack of cards settle in her pocket. *"You don't need my help for now."*

She wasn't at all sure about that, but Thomas was halfway across the square and would be with her soon. The men dragged her in front of the masters. "Who are you?" one asked.

"Lucy Thomson."

"What sort of name is that?"

She admitted to herself that it was unusual for a Dnassian name, but not so much for a Silvan one. "Free the ice demon immediately!"

The masters laughed. "Who are you to order us?"

"You're all in great danger here." The forms of the hounds were becoming more solid. One howled.

"What was that?"

"Hellhounds." The men shook her, and she felt her cards moving in her pocket; they were restless. "I think you should let go of me," she said. When one of the men tried to slap her, she reached out and drew a random card. She smiled at the forest scene but couldn't see the wolf—then she realized it was a tropical forest. A large cicada flew from the card, followed by what looked like a brown tornado that rose above her, before landing. The cicadas sang together, and the men let her go, instead staring at the insects that had covered the cages. She ran back to Chloris's cage and fumbled with the lock.

Thomas had reached the stage, and he ran straight into one of the men, knocking him down; the other, he pushed away. Lucy looked at him. "Thomas, a bit of rock magic . . ." He grinned as the lock fell away. "I wish I could do that."

Chloris burst out of the door and knocked one of her tormentors from the stage; the other leapt into the crowd. Chloris stood tall beside them. "Thankz, but maybe magic is not good now. The demon dogs are coming," she hissed.

"Worse," Lucy said. A familiar dark nimbus was forming on the stage, and within were the shapes of the sorcerers. "Chloris. It's time for us to go our own way." Chloris tilted her head at Lucy. "We're going to retake the Keys, and if we succeed, we'll disappear from this world. You must go. Wait for our return."

"I will wait," Chloris said. Lucy touched the ice demon on her arm, then Chloris leapt from the stage before disappearing along a dark alley.

Giant dogs materialized around the square and were attacking people indiscriminately. The slave masters turned from the loud cicadas and stared at the hounds in confusion before rushing from their seats.

Thomas began pulling power from the pentacle, and Lucy felt the cup calling her; she accepted its power. The hounds seemed to have sensed a danger to their emerging master. Several giant hounds leapt onto the stage, but the magic forming around them seemed to confuse the dogs. They hesitated.

"Kill them!" Frore's voice boomed from the dark cloud.

A hound leapt at Thomas. Turning slightly, he slashed its neck with his magic-infused sword—a line of blood appeared, but it barely slowed the creature down. It bit his hand, taking the sword in its mouth and throwing it to the ground. Moving with incredible speed, it attacked Thomas again, and as it did, it breathed a red misty substance towards him, burning the back of his hand where it touched him, but he stabbed it with his other hand, which was now bright with magic. The hound yelped as his knife hand entered its body. Force rushed from Thomas into the creature and it burst into flames. Gasping for breath, Thomas pulled his hand back. Lines of red energy crackled over the hound's body before it fell to the ground, burning and sending off a toxic smoke.

"Well done," Lucy said. "Now the Keys." She reached out and drew energy to herself, and the cup responded, wrenching itself from Frore's clothing and flying into Lucy's open hand. She burst into golden light.

"Thomas!"

Biddy Zo was chanting her sickening song. "I know." He reached out and ripped the pentacle from the half-formed body of Frore. The sorcerer screamed, but Thomas was now shining with silver light. A dozen red-eyed hellhounds edged towards them.

Despite the deafening song of the cicadas, she heard Thomas clearly. *"From here—together."* He showed her his plan in a single image. She grimaced but nodded, and taking out the empty card, she held it up. The cicadas swarmed around her and then into the card. *"Lucy."*

Three dark figures stood before them; their magic made Lucy's skin creep. She stepped forward and took hold of Thomas's hand, and as soon as she did, Lucy felt the stage soften beneath her feet. Their magic flared, joining together and brightening the square.

"No!" Lord Frore screamed.

Thomas and Lucy blazed with bright energy as the sorcerers rushed forward. She raised an eyebrow at the enraged Frore as she and Thomas dropped like bright molten lead through the planet's crust.

26

They fell through the hot and sticky liquid rock, their combined magic lighting them up like a rocket shooting into the depths of the planet. Rock magic like this was relatively simple, unlike combat; the toll was in the energy it used, but with the Keys, they were accessing the power of the planet.

Their magic blended, and Thomas felt Lucy's nauseousness and her need for rest. She cried out in pain.

"Keep focus."

"What was that? It hurt."

"Diamonds," Thomas said. *"We're passing through the final part of the crust now; the part where all cavities have been squashed flat."*

"Don't say that."

He saw the rocks around them as patterns of energy, and he watched these patterns change as they descended. As he studied the rocks, he saw a space beneath them. *"I spoke too soon."*

"What?"

"A cave." He changed the direction of their descent. Then

they fell into a space and dropped onto the floor of a very flat cave. They sat in a cavity no more than five feet high and eighteen feet across at the widest place. Stopping to breathe air was a relief—even the stale air of this cave.

"There's not much air," she said.

"Enough for a few hours, perhaps longer. I'm surprised to find a cave so deep."

"I want to sleep," Lucy said. Thomas walked around the small space. "Exploring?"

"Checking for ventilation." He touched the roof. "There are cracks here; some air's coming in from somewhere."

"Do you think we're safe?"

He shrugged. "There's enough air for a short break."

"I didn't mean that."

"It'll be hard for them to track us." He lay on the cavern floor and closed his eyes.

Lucy did the same and fell asleep immediately.

THOMAS OPENED HIS EYES—HE realized he'd been asleep for hours. Something was moving through the rocks towards them. Cursing, he rolled to his feet and placed his palms against the wall of the cave. The vibrations were clear, but he wasn't sure what it was.

He shook Lucy. "Wake up!"

She opened her eyes. "I've only been asleep a few minutes."

"A few hours. Something's here with us."

She sat up. Her cup cast a golden light around the cave. He felt her probing the dark corners of the cave. "There's nothing here, apart from us."

"Try looking in the rocks."

She touched the rocks and shook her head. "Are you sure?"

"I'm sure. It's very close. I think it's watching us."

"There's nothing here. Only rocks." But Thomas's large hands were flat against the rock wall again as he listened to the rocks. "There's nothing," she said again, leaning back against the cave wall. "I need to sleep for a whole day—I feel like I've got a hangover from the rock walking." Lucy screamed and scrambled away from the wall, wiping saliva from her face as a large snout pushed out of the rocks. Bright red eyes stared and then vanished back into the rocks.

"I didn't even sense it there," she said.

Thomas touched the wall where the snout had disappeared. "It's a skilled hunter; I only felt the slightest vibration."

Lucy looked around the cave. "We should leave."

"We can't," Thomas said. "It's waiting for us to reenter the rock. For a few seconds, we'd be vulnerable."

"But if we wait here, then more of them will come."

"I know." They waited in silence for several seconds. Thomas walked around the hollow space, following its invisible movements as it circled them. "If we reenter the rock at different points..."

"Then it'll pick off the first person," Lucy said as he felt the rock. "Thomas, be careful."

"I'm okay. I know its exact position."

"Which is?"

"It's stalking you." She moved away from the wall. "I don't think it'll come through. If it did, it'd be as vulnerable as we would be entering the rock."

"I think Frore's used magic to alter it," she said. "It doesn't feel the same as the ones we've met before."

Thomas's face crinkled. "That's not good." He continued to walk around the small cave.

"No one could have expected Frore to have altered them."

He shook his head. "Not that. There are six or seven . . . We're surrounded." A dog's head burst out of the floor next to Lucy's feet; she stamped on it and it withdrew. Another head appeared, close to Thomas. He struck it hard, and it yelped and disappeared back into the rocks. From several places in the cave walls, red eyes glowed and watched them. Some of them growled. "They're calling their master."

"Thomas!"

"Use rocks." Heads snapped all around them, but none of the dogs risked exposing themselves completely—yet. Lucy threw rocks at them, but it didn't stop them, and gradually they were pushing more of their bodies into the cave. One jumped up from the floor again and snapped at her ankle. She kicked it in its head.

"Thomas! Use your rock magic!"

He knelt on the ground, examining his fingernails. Again he'd noticed tiny crystals. "Thomas?" He didn't want to explain; he was unsure how much Frore could hear through the hounds. The red eyes had moved closer to him, which was what he wanted; Lucy had succeeded in making them wary. If they thought him weak, then he'd succeeded. A hound rushed from the floor of the cave directly under his knees, and he plunged his fingers into its eyes. The creature howled but couldn't pull away. A blue lattice formed around its sockets and spread over its head. The red flickering sparks were replaced by blue crystals. The hound howled. Then there was silence when the half-emerged creature fell dead at his feet.

"One down, six to go," he said as the other hounds retreated back into the rocks.

Lucy shook her head. "How can you joke?"

Motioning around the cave, he said, "At least they're gone." He sat on a small boulder and rested his head in his hands. An idea began to form.

"What're you thinking about?"

"The secret life of rocks."

She raised her eyebrows. "Another joke?"

He shook his head. "There's life here." He touched the cave wall. "Crystals have feelings you know."

"And?"

"And rock spirits," he said, deliberately misunderstanding her question. "I can feel them. Do you remember the fire spirits in Lazolteotl's realm?"

"Of course."

"They're here too. Or something like them."

"Then use them."

"I can't order them; they're living creatures. I have to ask or charm them."

Thomas calmed his mind and slowly drew power into himself, not wanting the hounds to hear. He sensed them slinking closer to the cave again, and he called in the True Language. A wave of thought passed through the rock, and lines of light—organized units of energy—moved in response. Hundreds of dancing flames, small and blue, leapt towards the hounds. They moved towards the cave like lines of fiery blue ants, twisting as they followed the bending path of least resistance through the rocks.

Snarling dogs' heads were pushing through again; several red-eyed hounds stared at Thomas, but they hadn't noticed the lines of bright blue light advancing on them. He felt magnetism as he pulled the dancing energy towards him. The tiny blue lights swarmed around him and then rushed out into the emerging hounds. The hounds were puzzled at first as they snapped at the blue lights, but when lines of the blue lights entered their bodies, they screamed and frantically tried to escape. But it was too late.

Their red lights went out, replaced by blue. The rock spirits were feeding on the magical energy of the hounds. And then all was silent. Blue crystal heads stuck out of the walls—replicas of the hellhounds—glowing in the dark.

Lucy backed away from them. "Frore will be angry," she said with a smile.

"He will. He's just lost a lot of helpers. We should go." Stepping closer to Lucy, he held out his hand.

She took it, and their magic combined, the huge concentration of energy making their hair stand on end. The molten rock bubbled around their ankles and legs as they sank into the rock floor. They descended rapidly. Lucy fell asleep, but her power still flowed. Thomas searched for life but found none so deep. He did notice that the rock had become more viscous. The softer rock was a relief at first, but it had its own difficulty.

"It's sticky," Lucy said, waking up.

"We're in the mantle." He also struggled with the stickiness of the rock. He changed direction.

"What is it?" Lucy asked.

"A river. It's a few miles away, but I think it'll be easier if we swim."

"In rock?"

"No stranger than walking through it. And I need a break from this." Thomas moved steadily through the rock, and then he felt a lightness. And it was brighter. He stood on the shore of a river of molten rock that descended deeper,

almost vertically, through the mantle; the river flowed slowly down.

"This is the strangest place I've been," Lucy said. She watched the changing patterns and flows of rocks around her. The elasticity and warmth felt different from the solid rock of the crust.

"I can see something," he said, looking at a dark outline near the river. *"A nest of some sort."*

He sensed her nervousness. *"Thomas, I think we should keep away from anything like that."* She strained to see it. *"I can see a dark shape by the riverbank."* He moved closer, leaving her standing by the orange river. *"What?"* she asked from a distance.

"It is a nest."

"What could live here?" She nervously scanned her surroundings for life.

"We're here," he said. *"Perhaps something else has found a way to live here, too."* He stood very still and listened to the gentle waves that flowed around him. Something moved. He pointed at a jewelled snake, about a foot long, slithering through the soft rock towards the river. They kept very still until it'd gone.

"That was beautiful," she said. *"But I don't think I want to meet it again."*

Thomas returned to the river, and they stepped into the hot flowing rock and were pulled along by the current. *"This is easier than rock walking."* She closed her eyes and fell asleep again. They drifted down the river for hours. Fascinated by the geology of the planet, Thomas watched everything. Then he saw something on the shore that wasn't quite right, but even with his acute sense of vibration, he couldn't see it clearly.

"*Lucy. Can you see anything there?*" Her eyes opened but didn't focus. "*You're not looking.*"

"*I've already seen her in a dream that wasn't a dream. I can sense her, that's enough.*"

At her words, Thomas looked back to the shore. Then he recognized the spectral figure of the witch sitting on a hound and watching them. He waded towards the figure on the shore.

"*Thomas?*"

"*They've overextended themselves,*" Thomas said.

"*What do you mean? That might be an apparition, but it's still dangerous.*"

"*It is an apparition, and it is dangerous. But she's come alone and given us an opportunity.*" The closer he got to the shore, the faster he moved. Biddy Zo watched him placidly, apparently confident in her abilities. He wanted to teach her a lesson. He took some of the blue crystals he'd saved and threw them at the witch. She now appeared uncertain.

A line of blue crystals moved towards the witch like a bright blue arrow. At first she did nothing, but soon realizing her danger, she edged her hound away. She was too slow, and the blue crystals swarmed over her and her hound. The woman and hound flickered as the blue crystals sucked energy from them. The hound solidified and turned to crystal; Biddy Zo vanished.

"*I'm impressed,*" Lucy said. "*Your rock magic's improving.*"

Thomas grinned. "*I'd like to leave a gift for Frore.*" His eyes shone as he spoke.

"*Tell me.*"

"*I'm tired of them dictating our movements; we need to take control. I have an idea of how to delay them, and perhaps lose them for good.*"

She grinned as he described his plan. *"Do you really think that could work?"*

"Let's find out, but I'll need to give it all of my attention."

"I'll keep watch," Lucy said. She walked towards the river, and Thomas worked his rock magic. His energy glowed as he worked, moulding the elements into the shapes he wished. He'd almost forgotten where he was when Lucy called him. He felt the ripples in the rock before she could explain. Something was moving towards them.

27

When she moved, the hound sensed her movement and changed direction. It was a strange and misshapen creature. She could stand and fight, but she lacked Thomas's skill in moving through rock, and his martial magic. She ran instead. *"I'm coming back! Something's chasing me."*

"I can see it. Just keep coming towards me."

She was scared as she ran and almost breathed in the rock. Thomas grabbed her, and his energy cleared the sticky rock from her mouth. He strode towards the hound, and it hesitated.

"There's something strange about it," she said. *"It's not quite right."* When Thomas showed it some of the blue crystals, it fled.

"Thank you!" Then she saw what he'd done, hardly believing it. *"You've built a house!"*

Thomas grinned. *"Come inside."*

They walked inside a small inn, and she breathed the air in relief. There were lights and a fire burning in the grate. Several people stood around drinking, but none paid any attention to them. "What have you done?" Then she saw herself talking to Thomas at the bar.

She was fascinated. They seemed to be alive, but when she probed them, she found only the simplest forms of life. "The blue flames?" she asked.

"They were too basic. I fashioned these replicas with more complex life, things with more mind, and things I can influence."

"Like the crystal forest you created in the prison?" Lucy asked.

"Similar, but more advanced than that."

Lucy now sensed the organized units of intelligent energy that moved around her, and she felt a little uncomfortable. "Thomas? Isn't this a type of black magic?"

"I asked their permission, and they were willing. There's an equal exchange of energy." She was about to ask, and then she remembered the blue arrow absorbing the energy of the hound.

"So when the sorcerers touch our images, the energy will feed on their magic?"

Thomas nodded. He was shining; she'd seldom seen him so bright, and she knew the three riders would see him too. He grinned. "I want them to." She didn't even complain that he eavesdropped on her thoughts; she watched the replicas of her and Thomas as they sat at the bar and talked.

"Mine's wrong," she said. She walked over and touched her strange twin, changing details on its face and in its voice. "That's better." She laughed to see herself sitting in a one-room bar deep within the planet, but also felt unnerved. "How much can they say?" Lucy asked.

"Not much. They'll repeat two basic conversations. When the riders arrive, they'll throw a few insults too."

"But this will only delay them if they physically touch

our images," she said. "They might understand they've been tricked and leave."

"I've added a surprise." He pointed to four blue flames dancing in a hearth. "When they enter, I'll call the flames, which will spread to the powder." A substance surrounded the four flames. "And when they do, the inn will burn. The sorcerers' magic will attract more of the creatures." Lucy nodded, still finding it hard to think of flames as creatures.

"And then?"

"The creatures will swarm over them. If we're lucky, the fire might attract some snakes, too."

"What if they don't use magic?"

"Then they'll burn in the fire. Either way we win."

"Unless their magic is enough to combat the trick."

"Frore might not be affected, but it should slow the other two, and make them more wary of us. And one more touch." Thomas placed a small crystal on the fireplace and another behind the bar. "Our eyes." He showed her another crystal. She saw herself and her clone through the crystal on the mantelpiece. They left the artificial inn as the red eyes of the hounds were appearing around the building. The three riders stopped and studied the structure before dismounting and approaching the inn. As they stepped inside, she and Thomas waded back into the great river of rock, the viewing crystals in hand, and floated away, watching the scene inside the inn.

The door of the inn opened. A hellhound sniffed, then saw the apparitions. It growled. Thomas, through his clone, called one of the blue flames from the hearth. It came on his command, and then he pointed at the hound. The flame obediently rushed to the startled dog. The dog yelped and ran from the room as the flame ignited the powder.

Lucy felt as if she watched a thriller. She held her breath

and started when the door burst open. Frore, Zo, and Xart walked into the inn. The artificial Thomas and Lucy sat and talked, apparently oblivious to the three standing behind them.

"Something's wrong," the goblin said.

The artificial Thomas turned. "Get out!"

The Lucy clone stood and spoke. "Your evil plans are doomed!"

"Hey!" Thomas said after the real Lucy punched him in his side.

"Is that really the best thing you could think of for me to say?" She grinned despite herself.

"I was in a hurry."

Lord Frore strode towards the replica of Thomas and pulled him forward. The artificial Thomas disintegrated into the smaller energies he'd coaxed to play the game. "What's this?"

"It's a trap," Biddy Zo said. She turned to the door but was engulfed in the flames that flared around them. The whole habitation was on fire, and the three used their magic to protect themselves. The witch laughed. "But not much of a trap."

"Wait for part two, dear," Lucy said. Thomas grinned, and together they watched scores of shining jewelled snakes, attracted by the magic, crawling into the remains of the structure. The scene became chaotic as the snakes attacked, coiling around the legs and repeatedly biting to suck out the magical energy the three were generating. Lord Frore was alight with energy that vapourised the snakes that touched him. Xart was almost as fast; they watched the goblin run through a wall, dozens of snakes following him.

The witch sang her song, but the jewelled snakes were not creatures of flesh and blood, and they did not respond to her spells. A snake drew blood, and, attracted by the scent, more snakes returned to attack the witch. She struggled by herself; neither Frore nor Xart returned to help. And the more she called her magic, the more the snakes gorged. She died alone—Xart and Frore were already running to the river.

Lucy watched the changing colours of the mantle as they descended. Thomas slept; he'd depleted his energy and needed rest. She made sure he didn't drift too far away, and she tried not to worry that Frore and Xart hunted them, but she was not succeeding and felt a sense of dread. Hours passed, and then the sensation she'd been dreading came. The coldness inside alerted her that they were not alone. She shook Thomas. *"They're here!"*

He was awake in seconds. *"Where?"*

"Close." She watched him feeling for vibrations in the soft rock.

"They're in the river. Swim to the shore. They'll be washed past us." Then someone dropped past Thomas, hitting him as he passed. He cried out as a pair of grey hands pulled on his legs. Frore was sending electric shocks through the molten rock, striking them both.

Burning pain wrapped around her leg. Desperately, she cried out in the True Language. She turned to see Xart holding a whip of flames. The pain was intense, and tears came to her eyes. He whipped her again, and she began to materialize inside the soft rocks, bringing more pain. She coughed soft rock from her throat.

The current was powerful, but uneven, and when they passed through rapids with larger, harder rocks, the sorcerers' attacks wavered. Lucy and Thomas swam to the shore, ignoring whips on their legs, and they crawled up onto a beach of soft rock.

She was exhausted and felt like crying when she saw hounds swimming towards them. Pushing her fear aside, she erected a magical defense. Hellhounds leapt at her, but bounced off the barrier. They were on their feet in seconds, scrambling over the barrier.

An animal howled in the distance, and the hellhounds stopped their attack and barked. The goblin glared at her. *"What did you do, fool?"*

"She's called a hunter," Frore said quietly.

Lucy heard but didn't understand. The fighting slowed, mostly because everyone was tired. Fighting in the soft rock river was hard. Thomas moved to her side and waited. He was covered in blood.

"What did you do?" Thomas whispered.

"I don't know. I just cried out in the True Language. I didn't think anything would answer. Frore called it a hunter."

"You've upset them."

"Things like that demand payment!" Xart yelled. *"What can you give it?"* he asked.

"You!" she shouted. Despite her bravado, she was nervous and had no idea what she'd called.

A black dog the size of a hellhound ran towards them. Like the hellhounds, it had red burning eyes. But the magic it possessed was something more elemental. Frore and Xart backed away as the hounds attacked it. The black dog ripped their throats without any apparent effort. Soon the nearest ones were dead. It rippled with energy, and the more Lucy looked, the more it appeared to be a creature of electricity, not matter.

Lucy studied its magic: it was simple yet complex. And

she sensed intelligence. The dog growled, and magic and vibrations rippled through the mantle. Frore was shaking.

Lucy's eyes widened. Wondering if he was scared, she remembered what Lazolteotl had said about others hunting him. Was the huge dog one of those? But its mind was opaque—this made her nervous. Then she understood what Frore was doing; he was simply calling a sort of magic she hadn't previously seen. She stretched her arms out, trying to keep balance. He was inducing tremors in the rocks.

The mantle around Frore vibrated, and an abyss, thousands of feet deep, opened up between her and Frore. Thomas and the dog stood just in front of her; the goblin sorcerer by his master. Lucy breathed out in relief. *"He can't reach us here."*

"We're safe," Thomas said. *"Unless the black dog . . ."* A jet of lava flew out of the abyss on top of Thomas.

"Thomas!" But he was gone—pulled into the deep chasm.

The black dog towered over her; its hackles raised, and a deep growl rumbled in its throat. She backed away, but it was facing the pair of sorcerers. She started as it leapt across the gap, sending the sorcerers flying into the hole. The chasm snapped shut and they were gone. She stood alone in darkness.

28

Molten rock rained on Thomas as he fell, his rock magic burning brightly, protecting him, and even when the rocks snapped shut, he continued to fall. He'd seen Frore and Xart fall with him. He wished them dead, but like him, they had their own ways to protect themselves. At least Lucy didn't have to face them, and he was confident she'd find the river again and continue her descent.

He followed lines of relative weakness in the rock down to the core, and as he found better paths, he moved faster. Faster than Frore, he was proud enough to hope. He ran down the interlacing paths for hours; then the pressure altered.

He tumbled into a scalding orange sea. The outer liquid core of Prometheus. His protective magic bubbled out like a strange jellyfish, then just as fast, it flattened against his skin. Screaming in pain, he pushed again, and the pentacle shone like a small sun. He swam through the sea with a translucent outer body protecting him.

But even with the magic of the pentacle, the heat was

still intense. He doubted he could spend more than half an hour submerged in a molten metal sea. For several minutes he swam through the sea of bright colours, with shades of red, orange, and yellow. A school of fish, each the size of a horse cart, swam past, and to his relief, paid him no attention. He swam along the bottom. Above him, in the orange sky, a bright sun shone. And that was his final destination—the inner core of the planet. As he tired, his feet touched the seabed, which was actually the outer rim of the mantle. He walked along the bottom of the inner ocean feeling disoriented.

Bright and shining tropical creatures swam or crawled around him. A sea anemone wrapped its stinging tentacles around his protective shield, and he was forced to punch it. It swam away to find easier prey. Streams of different shades flowed around him. Some were dangerous, and he used his rock magic to stick to the rocks, avoiding being swept away.

A dark shape loomed ahead, and he moved towards it. A mountain rose from the seabed. As he got closer to the mountain, the ocean cooled, and he breathed more freely. The mountain had a presence of its own, affecting the ocean around it, which moved more slowly here.

Desperate to escape the intense heat of the sea, Thomas swam quickly. The sea surged around him, and he found himself falling. He hit the surface of the mountain and groaned. He was more shocked than hurt, but the sudden drop had winded him. Looking up, he noticed that the mountain had a protective bubble. He'd just fallen through it. Next, he saw the path that twisted up the mountain, and with nothing better to do, he followed it for half an hour, until he came to a set of steps. They led to a long tunnel. It was almost half an hour before he even saw a light at the end, and it felt like hours before he reached the far side of the mountain.

His eyes widened as he stared across a valley to the next mountain. A brightly coloured city rose from its peak. It was surrounded by a great wall, and a long bridge joined it to the mountain he was standing on. Tomorrow he'd enter the city.

THOMAS HARDLY SLEPT during the bright night, and several times he'd awoken to strange sounds, but he'd seen nothing. Feeling stiff and hungry, he resumed his journey along the path to the shining city. Hours passed, and eventually the path became a stone road. The heat had increased, and above him, the hot sea swirled around the mountain like a red sky. He hoped that the inhabitants of the city drank water.

Something approached along the road, and he walked on to meet it. Sooner or later he'd have to make contact with the inhabitants of the city, and it might as well be sooner.

The troll stared down at him. He was bigger than Orange had been, but not by much. *"Hello,"* Thomas said.

The troll looked surprised. His thick eyebrows drew together as he considered Thomas. *"What type of troll are you?"*

Thomas was puzzled. Was he joking? *"A human one."* The troll laughed and moved on down the road, leaving Thomas looking down at himself. Did he really look like a troll, or was it trollish humour?

Later he passed four dwarfs on the road. He saw them glance at him, but no words were passed. When he saw the five grey-skinned men whispering together and glancing at him as they rode towards him on horse-like animals, he could almost read their minds, and he rested his hands on his two knives. Though they were shorter than Xart, they were otherwise similar in looks. Their eyes were sunken in bony skulls, and their ears were triangular. He wasn't surprised when they surrounded him. They made no attempt to speak the True Language. "What are you doing here?" They spoke a language similar to Silvan.

"I go to the city."

Laughing, they mimicked his words. The nearest one jumped to the ground, his head inches from Thomas's face. His breath was foul. "Humans are not allowed in Ben Doors."

Thomas was familiar with this type of confrontation. When the grey man stood on his foot, Thomas punched him. He was taken by surprise and fell, sprawling, to the dusty ground. His three friends laughed aloud, but the man sprang to his feet and attacked with a knife.

As he slashed at Thomas's face, Thomas ducked and stuck his sharp knife into the man's thigh, then standing, he threw a handful of dirt in his face. When the man jabbed, he slashed his wrist. The man's knife dropped to the ground, and Thomas scooped it up.

"How dare you! Do you know who I am?"

It was then that Thomas realized how little was different between his world and this—apart from magic. A slight smile came to his face, which enraged the man, and Thomas felt magic building in his opponent; his bleeding had already stopped. His friends encouraged him, and the man's emotions overflowed. His arms thrust forward in something like a punch, but instead, a grey shadowy substance came from his hands.

Thomas sidestepped the slow-moving substance and punched—a vibrating fist. The man's eyes opened wide, and he tried to speak, but couldn't. Thomas's punch had stopped inches from the man's skin, but its energy vibrated through him and knocked him to the ground. The grey substance rushed back into his body. His friends looked worried and backed off; their friend lay unconscious on the ground, his body twitching unnaturally. "Take him!" Thomas said, noticing a look of relief on their faces as he continued his walk to the city, adding the third knife to his collection.

He passed few others on the road: only a male and female goblin, each riding dark horses. They glared at him insolently, but he paid them no attention, and they rode on. The road led to a distant bridge that reflected the light of the inner sun as if it were glass. As he walked, his rock magic hummed smoothly, and he reached out into the environment around him, noticing several eyes watching him; but when he looked, they vanished.

Later that morning, as he decided to think of it, he reached the black obsidian bridge that spanned the deep and rugged gorge to the city. The city walls were made of the same glassy rock as the bridge, and from the tops of the walls, figures watched him as he walked across the bridge. On reaching the city gate, Thomas's attention turned to the gatekeeper, a toad-like creature, shorter but broader than Thomas, watching him from a platform on one side of the open gate. Two of its eyes followed him, a third, located in the middle of his forehead, gazed elsewhere. The creature raised a webbed hand. Thomas spoke in the True Language; its third eye turned to him while the other two returned to the road. *"What's your business in Ben Doors?"*

Thomas considered lying, but as he knew nothing of the customs or abilities of the inhabitants here, he decided honesty would serve him better. *"I seek the Fire of Prometheus."*

All three eyes focussed on him, and he waited, sweating with anticipation. Eventually, the creature spoke. *"Enter."* The creature's eyes turned back to the bridge, and Thomas entered the city.

29

Despite the stares he received, Thomas kept his eyes forward as he walked up the street. He saw no other humans. Goblins, the shorter half-goblins he'd met on the road, and trolls made up the majority, but there were shorter creatures, too. Dwarfs that reached his waist, and gnomes, the tallest only reaching his knees. A few of the gnomes widened their eyes on seeing him; a couple smiled, but not many. And there were others he didn't recognize, including flying heads, nebulous beings that emitted light, and cloudy ones that seemed to suck light into themselves.

He wandered through the streets with no intention but to explore. The mountain city was beautiful, and he felt like a tourist in the centre of the planet. The buildings gracefully blended into the mountain, and sometimes it was hard to distinguish between the two.

Shops, workshops, taverns, private houses, beer houses, large communal halls full of life, and peaceful doorways to wild gardens of colour lined the streets. Each doorway promised another world.

A tall green and blue humanoid vendor tried to sell him

an object he didn't recognize. He moved on, wondering which unit of exchange they'd accept here. Ahead was an empty square.

Strangely, there was only one road in and out of the square, and most of the buildings had turned their backs on it: there were no doors or windows, except one very large door. In the middle of the square lay a large boulder of obsidian. Thomas walked up to it and rubbed his hands along its glassy surface. *"Beautiful,"* he said quietly. As he rubbed it more, he sensed its magic—the magic of another form of life, one he didn't recognize, and one that had been working shaping it.

The hair on his arms stood, and he looked up to see someone watching him. His eyes widened. A giant leant against an enormous building. Thomas wasn't sure how he'd not noticed the giant man before. He was about eighteen foot tall, half-naked with a shaved head, and magic radiated from him. His body was covered in tattoos of battle scenes, fights, and faces of heroes or gods. This giant made even the biggest troll look small, and although he could read the face of a troll, this creature's face was hard to interpret; his eyes glinted like the black obsidian in front of him.

"Hello," Thomas said.

The giant growled and the air vibrated. Thomas realized why the square was empty. Perhaps it would be a good idea to leave. He slowly backed away, glancing around for escape routes, but the only one he could see was the way he'd come, and that was too far if the giant decided to chase him. Stepping closer, the giant blocked the way to the exit. Thomas wondered if he'd made a fatal mistake—each of the giant's flexed fists was bigger than his head.

"Hie!"

Thomas looked around for the speaker. The giant raised

his fist, and Thomas leapt away as it fell. A wave of magic rippled around the square, and he felt a sharp pain in his leg. Twisting round, he pulled out a shard of black obsidian shaped like a dagger. The giant roared.

"Knucklehead!" Again he searched for the speaker. "Hither!" Then he saw her. A girl of about fourteen stood in a tiny gap between two buildings about fifteen yards away. He limped towards her while the giant watched. "Make haste, knucklehead." She seemed to be speaking an archaic form of Silvan.

He was still holding the fragment of obsidian. "Return it!"

"What?"

"The rock you stole from the giant!"

"I didn't steal it!" All the time the giant watched. Thomas wanted no more trouble with a giant and held out the bloody fragment, but the giant bellowed and smashed the boulder again, sending more slivers of rock-like arrows around the square.

The girl pulled him into the gap between the buildings, saving him from more cuts. "He says you can keep it as a reminder." She looked at him with disapproval as he struggled into the gap. She was slim and looked almost human apart from her eyes, which glittered as if they were tiny mirrors, her pointed ears, and her brown skin, which was flecked with green.

"Have you ne'er seen an elf before?" He began to answer in Silvan, but she silenced him. "What kind of blockhead walks into a giant home?"

"A foolish one."

She grinned. "I can see that. Lucky he liked you."

"Liked me?"

"Otherwise you'd be dead. And he gave you a gift."

Thomas almost smiled. He wiped the sliver of rock clean, almost dropping it again as he cut himself. It was a dagger. The girl shook her head. He carefully put his new knife away. He looked at his leg. "I'm bleeding."

The girl's eyes widened. "So fix it!"

Then he remembered he could, and his magic stopped the flow of blood and closed the wound. The girl obviously considered him an idiot, but at least he had someone to ask questions. "I'm new here."

"That's obvious."

Before he could ask his question, the giant growled. The girl shrank deeper into the gap, a blue magic sparking from her skin. She looked into the square, sensing something he couldn't. Then he recognized a familiar magic.

Two riders wearing dark robes rode into the square on large red-eyed hellhounds.

"They have an evil aspect. The giant won't like them entering his home." Thomas watched with hope as the giant stared at them.

Magic danced around Lord Frore. "Out of my way!" He glared at the giant.

"Another blockhead," the girl whispered. "A worse one than you." Thomas wasn't sure what to think about the girl; instead, he turned to watch the two riders face the giant.

The hounds ran around the giant's legs. When Xart's hound tried to bite, he stamped on it. The goblin fell from the hound and rolled on the ground. The flattened hound twitched, and its magic buzzed as it died.

Magic flickered from Frore's fingers and rushed to meet the giant. Where the energy touched the giant's skin, red blisters appeared, then vanished. The giant roared and ran at Frore, killing more of the pack as he moved. And he moved with incredible speed.

Xart leapt onto another hound, and he and Frore attacked from different directions, but neither attack did more than enrage the giant. Again, he stamped on Xart's hound, killing it instantly and trapping the goblin underneath. Xart screamed as the giant pulled him from under the hound and threw him at the wall near the entrance to the square. The injured goblin crawled along the ground, dragging his disjointed legs through the dust. The giant watched him and roared as he crawled out of the square.

The giant's eyes glowed as he turned back to Frore and the remaining hellhound. Thomas felt the elemental magic coming from the giant like a scalding heat. Frore and his hound ran wildly out of the square.

"I'm going and so should you," the young elf said. Before he could ask a question, she was halfway along the gap between the buildings.

"Wait!"

"What, Knucklehead?"

"Don't call me that." The elf grinned insolently. "I'm looking for directions."

"Then look." She turned to go.

"To the centre of the planet."

She stopped and looked back. "Nobody goes there."

"I must."

She shook her head. "I don't know why I'm helping such a knucklehead, but ask in the Tangle." Before he could ask more, she'd disappeared.

Thomas squeezed along the narrow gap and into the street at the end. He moved quickly through the crowds in the hope of catching her up, but she was gone. The buildings in this district looked old and were made of wood and stones; some had lightstones embedded in their walls. The influence of nature was strong in the city. Glowing flowers grew from walls, and trees grew wherever they wanted. He walked past a house with a tree growing in the middle. Insects and birds flew around it. Turning a corner, Thomas entered a street where people sat outside, talking, eating, and drinking. In a few shops, people crafted tools and sold their wares.

A procession of musicians and dancers the size of sparrows weaved along a nearby branch and waved at him as he passed. "What are you?" Thomas asked.

One of them, a woman half the size of his hand, looked at him as if startled. "Hobs," she said. She laughed at his expression and put her trumpet to her mouth again, and as she blew, a dwarf drinking nearby hummed along.

Thomas waited for her to pause for breath, and then he spoke again. "I'm looking for information."

The hob nodded her approval. "Not many are wise enough to ask a hob for information. What do you want to know and how much will you pay?" The hobs laughed.

"I've just arrived and have no money."

The hobs spoke amongst themselves in whispers. Then a young male called up to Thomas. "You can pay us later. What do you wish to know?"

"I'm travelling to the centre of the world, but I don't know how to get there."

"Of course you don't; nobody does," the woman said. They spoke together again, and Thomas's hopes faded a little.

"I was told to ask in the Tangle."

"Who told you that?" she asked.

"An elf."

The hob's eyes raised slightly. "An elf?"

"She thought I was a harmless fool."

The hob nodded in apparent understanding. "The Tangle is a place where somebody may know."

"How do I get there?" But the procession of hobs was already disappearing into a hole in the wall. "How do I pay for things here?"

"With metal and music," one of the hobs said. And then they were gone.

He felt his clothes. He had his knives: three of them were made of metal and the new one of obsidian, but he was reluctant to part with any. The only other things he had were two pieces of copper currency he'd picked up in Copper; perhaps they'd be worth something.

Both hungry and thirsty, Thomas walked into the next inn he saw. The doorway was low, forcing him to crouch, and he hit his head on a wooden beam, causing laughter inside. He stopped in shock. The chairs and tables were child-size, and dozens of hobs and gnomes stared up at him. At the far end of the common room a band of hobs played music. "I'm sorry," he said, slowly backing out of the door, but a gnome that Thomas guessed was the landlord rushed towards him.

"We have a special seat for big folk." Reluctantly, Thomas followed him to a stool designed for a dwarf. "What do you want?" Thomas hesitated. "Pies and porter are our finest!" the gnome said.

"I hear you take payment in metal or music." Another round of laughter at his expense.

"Are you a hob?" the landlord asked. "Only a hob would say that."

That makes sense then, Thomas thought. "Would you accept these?" He held out the pair of copper coins.

The landlord took them and tossed them in the air, catching them quickly and studying them again. His expression was serious, and the room went quiet; everybody was following what was happening. The gnome flicked a coin back at him and pocketed the other. "One will do." And again the patrons laughed at him.

"Pay no attention to them!" a voice said from his ankle. He looked down at a tiny boy. "It's our way—we mean no harm."

"Are you a hob?" Thomas was unsure.

"You're not from here, are you?" The boy studied him while the landlord placed a pie and a porter besides him. Thomas was relieved that the pie was actually what he'd consider a normal size, and the dark ale was a half-pint pot —it would have to do for now.

"Sorry, no."

"I'm a gnome. When I grow, I'll be as tall as other gnomes."

Thomas relaxed as he ate the pie and drank the dark ale. A small crowd gathered around him, and he found himself telling his tale. About half an hour later he found a second pie and another pot of porter beside him. He finished with the tale of the giant, and many of them nodded in sympathy with him.

"Do you understand the nature of Ben Doors?" a gnome called Sunne asked. Realizing there was no point in lying, he shook his head. "We're on the threshold of the Tangle."

"That's where I've been told to ask for information."

Sunne shook his head. "Not the inn, the real Tangle." Thomas had no idea what he was talking about.

"He talks of the world between worlds," another gnome said. "This is a mountain city of doors to other realms. Most travellers enter that way; you're unusual."

"And most of them want to access other worlds," a hob said. "No one goes to the inner sun."

"Goblin bargemen do!" the boy said.

Sunne's eyes narrowed at the boy. "Who knows what the bargemen do."

"I've heard people talking."

Sunne shook his head and looked up at Thomas. Thomas had the feeling he was being judged. "Take him to the Tangle," he said to the boy.

"Do you think his tale's true?" a hob said.

"We'll see!"

Thomas found himself following a throng of tiny men and women, and he gained raised eyebrows and startled looks from some of the taller people on the street, but he enjoyed the company of the hobs and gnomes. Their positive attitude was a relief. They took him around the first corner and gathered close to him, forcing a procession of elves to walk around them. "Here?"

"He can't do it," a hob said. "He can't even see the door."

Then Thomas understood. "I'll try." He turned his attention to the bare stone wall. And as his old friend, Orange, had once taught him, he both touched and mentally connected with the stone. He felt its coolness, and as his mind entered the rock, he saw a different picture. The rock was laced with ribbons of energy; the lattice of energy concealed something. He scanned the wall up and down, feeling impressed. Whoever had made this understood rock magic at a very high level. He searched the lattice for any irregularity, but there was none. Then he changed his approach: he asked for entry and then he saw a door handle—a circular spiral of energy. Drawing on his own magic, he turned the handle; a doorway shimmered before him. Some of the gnomes gasped and one of the hobs laughed and gave him a small push.

30

Thomas walked into the Tangle. Trolls, dwarves, elves, gnomes, and others stood and sat at tables. Many turned from where they stood or sat to watch the only human in the large room. Above him, the arched ceiling showed scenes from stories, but his eyes were immediately drawn to a large well which lay within an ornate cage in the centre of the room. An old female troll sat watching him from inside the cage.

Curious, he walked towards it, but an albino troll, red-eyed with long white hair, blocked his way. Tattoos of mythical scenes covered his half-naked muscular body. And Thomas sensed more than physical power. "Who are you?" the troll asked. He spoke in the same archaic Silvan the girl had spoken.

"Thomas Brand."

The troll gave a brief nod of acknowledgement. Minutes passed before he spoke again. Used to troll ways, Thomas waited, staring right back. "Who taught you how to enter?"

"No one."

"Those who can enter can enter," another troll said.

The albino troll grunted.

Thomas studied the occupants of the room. He didn't recognize what all of them were, but each one exuded magic. And they were dangerous. He tried to pass the troll and touch the well. Something about it called him.

"No!" the albino troll said. "It's forbidden to touch the Well of the Dead."

But Thomas felt the urge again, and for a second, he thought of Orange. "Tell me about it."

"It's forbidden."

"It's calling me."

The old female troll stood. She was also naked above the waist and covered in even more tattoos than the albino. "I am the Keeper of the Well. Let him approach."

Two more trolls stood by the albino: a female with light brown skin and a shaven head, and a green-skinned male with milky white eyes and a ridge of hair growing from his spine. Thomas felt the threat from the trolls, but he was still drawn to the well.

"Approach," the keeper said. This time the albino troll let him pass. The old woman opened the cage door, and he walked inside.

"Why would the Well of the Dead speak to a human?" the female troll asked.

"We will find out." The keeper faced Thomas. "Touch it if you dare, but bear in mind that not all who touch it live."

"There's something familiar about it," Thomas said. He heard a distant voice. "Did you hear?" He touched the well and then leant over the edge and looked inside. A deep sound reverberated from the well.

The keeper's eyes widened, and she said, "Stop!" The albino troll came forward and took hold of him, but drawing his magic, Thomas stuck to the stone well. Murmurs, and then voices raised in anger, came from the Tangle, but familiar magic was rising from the depths of the rocks, and he smiled in recognition. Other trolls grasped him, but flames roared from the well, and they were forced to let go.

"What have you done?" the keeper said. "I've never seen this happen." Thomas had no idea, but it felt right. Watching the orange flames, he waited. A murmur came from those watching as a bright orange troll flickered in the flames.

"Orange!" Thomas said. He felt warmth radiate through his body, and he couldn't contain his smile. "You're here." The other trolls now stared at Thomas with wide eyes.

"Thomas. It's been a long time since we walked together. You've done well to come so far, but there's more to do."

"Are you alive?" Thomas asked.

"My spirit lives."

Thomas was unsure of the troll's meaning. "Aina?"

"She waits for you, Thomas. Go to her—go to the core."

His desire to see Aina was so strong that Thomas no longer cared about whether he believed if it was possible for a dead person to live. He'd reach her by any means possible. The ghost of Orange turned to the trolls. "Do you know me?"

The albino nodded. "We do."

Words passed that Thomas could hardly hear, let alone understand. Then Orange spoke to the trolls for all to hear. "Help this man and his friend."

"Who are they?" the albino asked.

"The Fire Bearers, some call them the Bright Ones." The flames vanished and with them the image of Orange.

Thomas turned to see the three trolls bow before him. They then stood straight. The albino placed his clenched right fist over his heart. "I am Tusk Bas."

"Green Rock," the green-skinned troll said, making the same gesture. At least his name would be easy to remember, Thomas thought.

"Pebble of the Heart." The shaven female troll repeated the gesture.

"The story of the Fire Bearers signifies change," Tusk Bas said. Thomas knew the prophecy, but he'd never been sure how he felt about being a part of an old legend about something yet to happen.

"You knew Orange?" Thomas asked.

"All trolls know of Orange," Pebble said. The other two nodded. "We will help you in order to honour a great troll." More trolls grunted their agreement. "And because the prophecy has meaning to trolls."

Relaxing for the first time since he entered the inn, Thomas said, "Thank you." The help of a troll was significant—and he had the help of three. "I'm came here in search of information."

"Then you came to the right place," Green Rock said. "What do you want to know?"

"I need passage to the centre of the planet."

"The inner sun?" Green Rock asked.

Thomas nodded. The trolls spoke in a language he didn't recognize, then Tusk Bas gestured for him to follow. Thomas and the three trolls walked to the back of the room. The patrons of the Tangle had returned to their drinks.

Thomas followed them into a second room deeper in the inn. Seeing the huge glasses of ale, he remembered the hangover he'd had the first time he'd got drunk with a troll. He decided moderation was best.

Tusk Bas chose a large stone table and shouted at the barkeeper. Within minutes, mugs of ale were slammed down in front of them. Thomas sipped the huge tankard slowly. Several plates of food arrived, and it looked good. Thomas reached for a loaf of bread, but it rolled away from him. Pebble grinned. He reached again, but again it moved.

"Magic?" Thomas asked.

A tiny figure looked up from behind the loaf. "Not magic! Get your own food!"

"I'm sorry."

He'd not even noticed the gnome. She was smaller than Odran: no more than seven inches tall. She took some cheese, a grape, and pulled a piece of bread from the loaf, then sat in the middle of the table with her food around her. Noticing Thomas staring at her, she bowed from a seated position. "Nest Deep."

As they ate, Thomas recounted his story, from his arrival in the world above, to the death of Aina, his imprisonment and escape, and his journey to the centre of the planet. The trolls listened silently, but Nest Deep was talkative, asking several questions, particularly about Odran, and she explained more about Ben Doors to Thomas. "You were right to listen to the hobs," she said. "Few do, but they're the most good-natured creatures of the city." Even Pebble of the Heart nodded her agreement.

When the food was taken away, Tusk Bas spoke. "The inner sun burns wildly. It's an impossible voyage—even for the goblin traders."

"Does anyone travel there?" Thomas asked.

Tusk shook his head, and Thomas's heart sank. "The inner sea might appear calm from our shores, but it's wild the further you travel from the coast, and even magic can't completely protect you from the heat."

"There are stories of travellers reaching its shores and returning," Green said.

Tusk made a sound, then continued. "Only the ferryman can sail there, and he's not been seen in my lifetime."

"He's a myth; if he ever did exist, he doesn't now," Nest Deep said. "The only boats to navigate the inner sea are the goblin barges, and they hug the coast."

"Who is this ferryman?" Thomas asked.

"No one knows," Nest said, "but they say the ferryman follows different rules. And that he asks for a life in exchange for a passage."

"What do you mean?" Thomas asked.

She shrugged. "Ask the ferryman."

31

Lucy's travel through the mantle had been easier than climbing this mountain. At least on her legs. The higher Lucy climbed up the twisting mountain path, the more magical creatures she encountered. She realized that she was now a magical creature, too. Nevertheless, when goblins and other creatures with a bad feeling approached, she hid by the side of the road, often becoming invisible until the creatures had passed. She wanted to take no chances.

She sensed that Thomas had already passed this way, and when she'd asked her oracle cards, the wolf had appeared and confirmed her suspicions. Eventually, she crossed the narrow bridge to the city. A three-eyed, toad-like guardian stopped her.

"What's your business in Ben Doors?"

"I'm looking for my friend, Thomas Brand. Has he passed this way?"

All three eyes watched her. *"And what is his business here?"*

"We seek the Fire of Prometheus."

It turned its head to face her directly. *"One human passed

these gates. Like you, he spoke the truth. He, too, seeks the Fire. Another human, or something close, stole into the city with a goblin."

Lucy's eyes widened. *"Frore and Xart."* She knew that Frore had altered himself with science and magic and might not be considered fully human.

"You know them?"

"I do, but they're no friends of ours."

"You may enter."

Ben Doors was bigger than she'd expected, and she wondered how to find Thomas while avoiding Frore. From the stares she received, she guessed that she appeared strange to them. She asked the gnomes she saw about Thomas, but they shook their heads without stopping. She thought about asking some of the other creatures, but many of them intimidated her.

Deciding to explore some of the side streets instead, she turned off the main street and found herself in a small square. A boy watched her from an alley while a gang of children played nearby. She smiled at the boy, but when she turned to go back to the street, a scream made her stop. The gang of children had surrounded the boy and were pushing him into a corner. "Leave him!" she said. But they continued to beat him.

The boy looked at her with blood and tears running down his face. There seemed something about the boy that was wrong. She felt like walking away, but she couldn't leave him alone. That seemed selfish to her. She couldn't believe her intuition would tell her to leave a small boy to be beaten.

She walked up to the gang, and all but one stopped and stared at her. She was sweating and had a strange feeling in her stomach. She was sure she felt her oracle cards moving in her pocket. "Stop it!" she said to a boy who was still hitting him. The others stepped back to watch. She pulled the attacker away, realizing that they might not be human; their skin was too grey.

Ignoring her dislike of the bullies, she looked at the boy's cuts. "Are you all right?" The boy was crying, and she hugged him while the five bullies taunted them both.

"Hobgoblins," the boy said. "They hurt me." He held a bleeding hand up.

It was a scratch, and the healing power of the cup would fix it in seconds. She opened her jacket to expose the cup hanging from her neck. Its golden light lit the dark corner of the square. "Touch it." When the boy touched it, his bleeding stopped.

One of the hobgoblins kicked her from behind, and she turned to knock him away. But he'd jumped back. "What?"

"Hobgoblins are fast," the boy said. Someone tugged her jacket, but when she turned the girl was out of reach.

"You can let go of the cup now. Your hand's better." She smiled at the boy, but he didn't let go. Energy rushed from the cup, and she suddenly felt chilled. Her smile disappeared.

As the hobgoblins pushed closer, the boy bit her hand and pulled at the cup. Even if he snatched it, she knew the cup would come to her call, but something was wrong here. The boy tugged her jacket. "Get off me!" He spat in her face, and a heavy feeling settled in her stomach. He was a hobgoblin, too. Magic began forming around him, and suddenly he snatched the cup from her neck and moved deeper into the corner, searching for a way past her.

She called the cup, but her emotions were too disturbed for her to access her magic—she tried to calm down, but she didn't know how to. The cup's light dimmed; neither of them could access its magic. When one of them tugged her jacket again, the oracle cards spilled out onto the ground. She felt dizzy, and her legs suddenly felt weak. The hobgoblins laughed. "Circus magic," one said.

The hobgoblins rushed at the oracle cards that lay on the ground, but the cards moved and one turned over. The wolf leapt out, knocking into the nearest hobgoblin.

Bright magic sparked around them as they fought, but other hobgoblins attacked from behind. The wolf cried out as fire burnt his back—his need calmed her. She called again for the cup, and this time golden light poured from it. At first the hobgoblin grinned, but when the cup ripped itself from his grip and flew back into her hands, his grin turned into a squeal.

Power came to her. Her anger had found a way to use the magic of the cup in direct attack; something she'd never been able to do before. With flashes of golden light, she drove the hobgoblins away, leaving her alone with the injured wolf.

Despite its objections, she poured her healing energy into the wolf. She wasn't really sure what this creature was; whether it was alive in the human sense or whether it was wholly magical. Its body faded into a blue grey mist, which then poured back into the damaged card. And then it was gone. She picked up the oracle cards and put the wolf at the top. The card was singed around the edges, and the wolf's bright eyes watched her. "Are you all right?"

"You should have killed the goblin."

She was startled when he spoke in her mind. *"But what about you?"*

"Sacrifice."

But Lucy didn't want to sacrifice the wolf. She sensed gratitude and warmth in its eyes. The card had now returned to its original perfect condition. She held the cards close to her chest and silently thanked them before putting them back into the inner pocket of her jacket. She stood still, breathing heavily. The attack had shocked her, and she promised herself that in the future, she'd listen to her intuition. And if she was attacked again, she'd remain calm enough to use her magic.

"Lucy!"

"Thomas, where are you?"

"Nearby. Don't move. We're coming to get you now."

"How did you know where I was?"

He laughed in her mind. *"Very easy with all the energy you were giving off. And, by the way, a very large group of hobgoblins is approaching you right now."*

"I hope you're joking."

"No, I'm not. We're almost there!"

How big was this group of hobgoblins, and how close was Thomas? He'd said *we*. Who was he with? She waited alone in the square, studying each entrance. Then she saw a movement in the shadows. The hobgoblins were returning, and there were far more of them.

This time she called on her magic with a coolness that surprised her, and a golden aura projected from her. Shadows were moving on the far side of the square, and she stepped into the alley to hide from them. But they'd seen her and soon stood at the entrance to the alley. Another larger group of hobgoblins had emerged from the shadows at the other end of the alley. She was trapped.

Despite her magic, her heart pounded as she waited because there were so many of them—she counted over a hundred. Behind the bigger gang of hobgoblins, a tall shadow moved, and her heart sank. It wasn't Frore, but it could be a goblin. But as she watched it, she realized that its movement was wrong for a goblin.

The troll roared and smashed into the hobgoblins, sending them flying into the alley walls. A second figure, just as big, joined him. From the other side, Thomas ran with a female troll. She waited, her magic vibrating in readiness, as the four figures wreaked havoc on the gangs of hobgoblins. Then peace came to the alleys, and the hobgoblins either lay dead or were gone.

"Thomas."

"We came as fast as we could," Thomas said. "That was crazy magic you were throwing about earlier."

"They took me by surprise."

"That's how it happens," the female troll said.

"This is Pebble of the Heart," Thomas said. "And Tusk Bas and Green Rock."

"I'm glad to meet you." And she meant it. "You give me confidence as Orange once did." All three trolls bowed to her. Thomas grinned. She must have said something right.

"You did well to fight so many," Pebble of the Heart said. "We sensed what happened at a distance. Through your connection with Thomas," she said, apparently reading her expression or thoughts; she wasn't sure which.

"Was this planned?" Lucy asked. "Or just an opportunistic attempt at robbery?"

"Planned," Tusk Bas said. "A goblin sorcerer has been hiring hobgoblins. It's time we paid him a visit."

She felt concerned. "I'm assuming this goblin sorcerer is Xart." He nodded. "Thomas, this might not be a good idea."

"Something's happened recently."

"What?"

"Lord Frore and Xart are no longer working together." He told her the story as they ran into the goblin quarter.

"So Frore left Xart because he was crippled and no longer useful?"

"Apparently," Thomas said.

She almost laughed aloud. Suddenly, she realized that the neighourhood had changed. "Where are we?"

"The Goblin Quarter," Pebble of the Heart said.

"Is it safe?" Lucy asked.

"For who?" the troll asked.

Lucy smiled as she glanced at the three trolls. Thomas was half like a troll with his magic. And they called her the Orange Witch. She grinned at the impression they must be making.

She was in the centre of a square formation, with Thomas and Pebble running ahead of her, and Tusk Bas and Green Rock behind. The sounds of their footsteps reverberated down the street. People were watching, but no one challenged them; she doubted if it'd be the same if she were by herself. The streets brightened when they ran into the commercial section of the Goblin Quarter. Here the streets were busier, and goblins, hobgoblins, and others moved aside as they ran. Lucy noticed nervousness in their eyes.

Tusk Bas stopped by a stone arch that spanned one of the alleys. On the top of it was a carved demon head. "They were here."

"Back into the Goblin Quarter?" Green said.

"Scared?" Tusk asked.

Lucy glanced at Green. He grinned as they walked down the path, which soon became dark. There were no lights, and roofs arched over them, mostly blocking the distant red glow of the inner sea that flowed above them.

Thomas and the trolls tracked the goblin's magic. Lucy felt as if she were a passenger, except that she had to run everywhere. She felt fitter than she had for some time, but she was still out of breath after running up the steep streets for forty minutes or more, until the trolls were happy they were close enough to the goblin's house. From there on, they walked in the shadows. The area had a strange fishy smell.

"We're close to the old port," Pebble said quietly, watching Lucy sniff the air.

Lucy noticed a red glow at the end of the street, and as they got closer, it increased in intensity. "What's that?"

"The inner sea," Pebble of the Heart said. A red wall of hot liquid rose above them, lapping gently against the invisible energetic barrier surrounding Ben Doors. Dark shadows swam on the far side. Old towers rose from the port, with spires that penetrated the protective wall and projected into the red and orange sea.

Tusk Bas raised his hand, silencing them. He pointed. Lucy's eyes adjusted; she saw several dark shadows creeping along by a derelict stone building further up the road. "Goblins," the troll whispered. A bent figure opened the door—they'd found Xart.

32

"I must get closer; I need to know their plans," Thomas said. He'd lost the excess of confidence he'd had on his first meeting with the goblin. This time it'd be enough to listen and learn.

"Green Rock is good at this," Tusk Bas said.

"Without your rock magic," Lucy said, "I'd be in the way."

"We can wait nearby, in case they need help," Pebble of the Heart said.

Tusk Bas nodded. "If anything happens, I'll break the door in seconds. Magic lock or not."

Thomas wasn't sure whether this was truth or bombast, but the albino troll was clearly dangerous. The five of them approached the windowless house. When they got close, Lucy, Pebble, and Tusk Bas concealed themselves opposite the door, and Thomas and Green disappeared up the narrow alley next to the building.

Thomas moved his hands inches from the wall, feeling for any magical traps—he felt none. Both he and Green Rock listened to the vibrations through the stone. He heard hobgoblins; the goblins were deeper in the house, and the sounds were muffled. Thomas stepped into the thick wall, followed by the troll. It was about two feet thick, enough for them to move unnoticed. He waded right up to the interior wall and waited. Eventually, the goblins' voices reached him. He counted four of them.

"I'll leave him standing on the docks," Xart said.

"The sorcerer's dangerous," a goblin said.

Xart hissed his displeasure, but it didn't intimidate the other goblin. "You didn't even get the human girl."

"Hobgoblins! But it doesn't matter. The humans don't know about the ferryman." Thomas held his breath.

"Strange that this ferryman's not been seen in a lifetime, and then he suddenly appears in the old port the same time as you," the goblin said.

"He appears when there's a passenger," Xart said. "And that passenger is me. When I return with the Fire, the sorcerer will be irrelevant. The magic belongs to the goblins. Help me now, and I'll help you when I return."

"*If* you return," another goblin said. The tension in the room was clear from the vibrations he felt.

"Are you fit for this?" the second goblin said. A crash sounded, and then a moan.

The first goblin laughed. "You're still sneaky enough, but can you pay this ferryman?"

"Let's find out." The hobgoblins started talking. "One of you wait here, and you four follow behind us. Keep a watch for anyone following. You know what to do."

Thomas heard the goblins moving about the room. Minutes later, Xart limped out using a stick to help him walk. Two goblins and several hobgoblins accompanied him. Thomas listened to the remaining hobgoblins.

"What's happening?" Tusk Bas asked from outside.

"We have business here," Green Rock said. "You follow them."

Thomas and Rock waited for Xart to get far enough away. Then they walked through the wall. Five hobgoblins were drinking coffee around the body of a goblin. Green clubbed two heads at once, sending them to the ground. Thomas's black blade cut through the neck of another. The fourth managed to stand as Green's punch broke his ribs; the club finished him. The final hobgoblin ran to the door but fell with Thomas's dagger in his back.

They left the building and ran towards the old port, soon catching up with the others. Once the five were together, Thomas told them what had happened. The trolls considered it good work. "How big are the old docks?" he asked.

"Not so big that the arrival of the ferryman will go unnoticed," Pebble said.

The old port was busy with goblin bargees, sea elves, and those seeking work or passage. Many of the doors to other worlds were in the coastal waters, and that accounted for over half the traffic, according to Pebble. Four towers pushed through the invisible barrier keeping back the inner sea. The nearest tower was blue; the others were black, grey, and silver. From the tips of each, metal quays extended further into the sea, and boats were moored from them.

They walked in the shadows by the sides of the buildings, keeping out of sight of the goblins and hobgoblins who were walking towards the silver tower. A black barge was moored from the upper quay, floating gently in the orange sea.

Frore rode a hound towards the tower. He leapt from the hound and entered the tower. It was the first time Thomas had seen him run. Meanwhile, Xart limped along the docks as fast as he could, his walking stick beating the stone paving, but Frore would reach the ferryman first.

When they neared the silver tower, the hound jumped at the nearest hobgoblin, biting him hard. Xart killed it with a quick strike; he'd hardly seemed to touch it. "You pick powerful enemies," Tusk Bas said.

Thomas nodded. He knew, and he held his breath as he watched and prayed the sorcerers would kill each other, or that the ferryman would turn them away.

"What now?" Lucy asked.

"If the ferryman takes them onto his boat, I'll sprint. I can be there in half a minute. I doubt the sorcerers would attack me while on his boat." He knew how desperate it sounded.

The ferryman and Frore faced each other. Both wore black cloaks, and they matched each other in height. It was impossible to know what they were saying. Neither turned as Xart, in his dark grey cloak, limped onto the platform.

"We'll kill the goblins at the base of the tower," Tusk said. Thomas nodded, at least partially relieved, but also concerned. The trolls were tough, but they lacked the extreme magic of the sorcerers.

"I'm with you," Lucy said. Her face was pale with fear, but he knew that wouldn't stop her.

Pebble of the Heart whistled quietly. "Look at his face."

Frore's face was red, and his empty socket appeared to burn. "I think the ferryman isn't giving him the answers he'd hoped for." Frore raised his hands and flames shot into the air, disappearing just as quickly as they appeared. Frore pointed to the city, then attempted to push past the ferryman and board the boat, but the ferryman raised his hand, and Frore slipped, almost falling to the floor.

"I've never seen him so agitated," Lucy said.

The goblin spoke to the ferryman, but nothing seemed to happen. The two sorcerers left the extending quay. Seconds later, they raced from the silver tower. Xart stopped to speak to his followers. The hobgoblins scattered, perhaps on different missions, the goblins guarded the base of the tower, and Xart hobbled back to the port.

"This is our chance," Thomas said. "We must speak to the ferryman before they return." The five of them ran across the docks to the silver tower. The goblins watched, but at the sight of the three trolls, they began backing off. Then they seemed to recognize Tusk Bas and fled.

Green Rock laughed, and Tusk Bas stared after the goblins impassively. Thomas and Lucy left the three trolls at the base of the tower and raced to the top. Thomas almost ran into the ferryman who stood on the gangplank, a cowl covering his face. Thomas gathered his breath. "We seek passage across the inner sea to the core."

"And back," Lucy added.

"Can you pay the fare?"

"What is the fare?" Lucy asked. Thomas glanced back at the port, to see Frore racing back to the tower. He was carrying something.

"Three tokens and a piece of gold."

Thomas still had the gold he'd found in the crust of Prometheus. He gave it to the ferryman. "What tokens?"

"Tokens of truth, power, and love." That was not what Thomas had expected. "The inner sun tests spirit—the tokens are symbols of the tests. The Fire is not given freely; it's earned, and the price is high. The tokens are merely tests of potential, but be warned, the Fire might cost you all that you have. The first is truth. Why do you want the Fire?"

"We're called," Thomas said. "And I travel to see someone who was dead and may live."

"We bear the Spirit Keys," Lucy said. "We have to go."

The ferryman studied them for several seconds and nodded. "You speak the truth." Thomas wondered if it could really be this easy. "What's easy for you is not easy for all."

Thomas felt uncomfortable when people, especially strangers, could read his mind. "For power?"

"Swim in the inner sea."

"You don't want us to waste your time if we're going to die there," Lucy said.

He nodded.

Thomas stepped through the invisible barrier and swam again, waving at Lucy to join him. Lucy looked nervous but jumped into the swirling orange and red sea. Several seconds later they climbed out.

Loud sounds came from the base of the tower. "The trolls!" Lucy said. "We must help them."

Thomas nodded. "Can you wait?" he asked the ferryman.

"You would return for your friends?"

"Yes," they said.

"They're alive, if bruised. It would take a truly powerful sorcerer to seriously hurt those particular trolls."

Sounds came from the stairwell. Frore was dragging a protesting goat up the steps.

"And for love?" Lucy asked.

"A living mascot freely offered."

Lord Frore dragged the bleating goat onto the platform and thrust it in front of the ferryman. "My living mascot!"

"The living mascot must be freely offered. This animal is unwilling." Frore glared at the ferryman who seemed unconcerned and turned to Thomas and Lucy. "You may board the boat. Your mascot has already offered himself and awaits you on the ferry. We sail shortly."

Thomas crossed the boarding plank before anyone could speak.

"Our mascot?" Lucy whispered.

He shrugged. He didn't care as long as they were going. He turned to see Frore being blocked by the ferryman. The sorcerer flashed with bursts of light. Then he screamed, slamming the ferryman with magic. His force rocked the boat, but the ferryman remained unmoved. The black magic rebounded and sent the sorcerer spinning over the edge of the tower. From the ferry, they watched him hit the docks; his magic scorching the ground. He pulled himself up and limped away.

Lucy spoke the True Language to the terrified goat, calming it, and directing it back down the steps. The boarding plank retracted into the boat, and the ferryman stood at the stern. The ferry slipped into the rolling red sea. "Look!" she said. A grey cat sat at the bows—its deep purring vibrated the wood of the boat, sending ripples out into the sea.

THE SHORE FADED FROM VIEW, and they sailed deeper into the red sea, towards the bright yellow sphere in the centre of the planet. As they sailed, the colours of the sea constantly changed. They sat with Tu in the bows. Lucy interpreted his story. "Frore left him for dead, but he'd survived, making himself invisible and crawling onto the back of one of the hounds—the misshapen one we saw in the mantle."

"He's scarred," Thomas said.

"He's handsome," Lucy replied, stroking his head to the sound of loud purring.

The ferryman stood behind them at the stern. A long

black cloak and hood covered every part of his body, and black gloves covered his hands. Thomas wondered whether he was human. "Who will test us?" he asked.

"The Spirit of Prometheus."

"Tell us about the tests." Lucy said.

"The tests might deceive, but they are real. If you die in the test, your body will die."

Thomas felt a heaviness in his stomach. "What happens if we fail one of the tests?" he asked.

The ferryman shifted slightly as he steered his barge around an orange whale. "Partial success results in partial power."

"What if we fail all three?" Lucy asked.

"You die."

She glanced at Thomas. "How do you know these things?" she asked.

The ferryman didn't answer immediately, but later he spoke again. "The power of the Fire is loaned—no one holds it forever."

As the voyage progressed, they lapsed into even longer periods of silence. They passed their time sitting in the bows and talking. Many hours later, Thomas noticed Lucy looking at him. "What?"

He waited while she thought. "What if the test of truth asks about Aina? What will you say?"

"That I believe she lives." He wondered whether it was a belief or a wish, and what the difference between the two was.

She looked down. "We've had no time to prepare for these tests."

Her worry was obvious, and he shared it. "What preparation could we do?" He watched another pod of orange whales swim past. "Perhaps our lives have been our preparation." Thomas looked around the sea. In the distance was a dark speck. He watched it for the next few minutes as it slowly became bigger. He sat up and looked more carefully. "We're being followed."

"Goblin barges," the ferryman said.

Thomas scanned the sea. It was Lucy who saw the second one. "There."

"They're both following us," he said. He wondered how the crew had been forced to sail, because he was sure no sailors would willingly travel to the core. For several hours they watched the dots get larger. Eventually, they saw the silhouettes of the sorcerers in the boats. The goblin's boat trailed behind Frore's.

"They might catch us up," Lucy said. Then she turned and stared into the sea again.

"What?" Thomas asked. He sensed her changing mood.

"I'm worried about what I'm becoming." He waited for her to continue. "The way I stopped Frank's heart with just a thought. Thomas, what does that make me?"

"Human." He'd thought about her new power, and he'd wondered whether he'd be able to the same, but it was not the type of thing you could just go around practicing. "It was self-defence. You prevented Frore from possessing the body of an assassin who was about to die anyway. You did the right thing."

"I caused Victor's death."

"Lucy, you did what you had to do. No one could know the Alain would try to kill you, or that Victor would try to save your life. I don't believe that Victor would blame you."

The yellow disc of the core shone brightly before them and now took up most of their field of vision, but it was still hard to judge the distance. He was about to ask the ferryman how much further it was when he spoke.

"Each test has a different colour: blue for truth, dark blue for power, and violet for love." The boat shook, and they grabbed the sides. It ran up onto a scorched orange beach, surprising Thomas. At the top of the beach was a burning red forest where trees and plants of wild energy flickered and mutated from form to form. "The forest will speak to you in its language—listen for its messages. I'll wait here," the ferryman said. "Leave your possessions in the ferry." Thomas placed his knives on the deck, and Lucy put her oracle deck beside them. "The keys, too."

Thomas looked at Lucy, and he gave his head a slight shake. "That's too much." To step into this world without their magic was death. A scratching sound came from along the beach as Frore's goblin barge rushed up onto the abrasive sand. Frore leapt onto the beach and burst into flames.

"We need the Keys," Lucy said as she watched the burning Frore in horror.

They jumped onto the beach. The heat was intense. Thomas almost jumped back onto the boat. Even with their magical protection, their clothes caught fire and fell away, and the Spirit Keys dropped into the burning core.

"You're meant to be here," the ferryman said from the boat. "Your natural magic will be enough for the first test, and if you pass it, the Fire will start to seep into you."

Clothed in light, they ran into the bright forest.

33

Thomas found himself alone in a forest of burning colours. Anarchic flowers of flame burst from nowhere, danced in the hot wind, then vanished. For a moment, he doubted his ability to walk through the fire, and searing pain ripped up his legs and body, but on pushing away his doubts, the pain subsided. *"Lesson learnt—never doubt your magic."*

There was shade in the forest, too; some of the larger fiery plants flickered in darker colours. And the landscape changed, morphing from valleys to hills and back again. At first Thomas followed his feelings, wandering towards anything that attracted him. He touched a large pink fern of flames. It brightened and turned towards him, stroking his hand. The fern brightened again, and a frond of gentle fire reached out and touched him.

The flames turned blue. *"The Test of Truth?"* He walked deeper into the forest. Some flames burnt hot, some cold, and some allowed him to pass through them.

A bright blue vine touched his face, and he brushed it away, but it wrapped itself around his wrist. Its head lifted and two jewelled eyes watched him. *"What are you?"* he asked the serpent. An image of cool blue flames flashed into his mind. The scene changed, and he saw a mountain path. The blue snake crawled down his back, then slid down his leg, dropping to the forest floor. It crawled along the path, and he followed until it disappeared under a pile of rocks.

The vegetation here was sparse, hardly reaching his ankles. He kept to the glowing rocks, avoiding the darker ones that poured out heat of an intensity that scared even him. A tree grew in front of him. Its branches were heavy with crystals of fruit; each glittered with reflections.

A face reflected in the crystal fruit. He looked behind, but there was no one there. He picked the fruit and was surprised to see his own face. He frowned, not liking what he saw: a harder, grimmer man, but he knew it was true. The image vanished, and the crystal shone blue.

Ahead was a fork in the path, and from the right-hand path he saw a pair of turquoise eyes. The grey cat descended into a valley, but he chose the higher path. Rocks became crystals, reflecting the blasted ravine with its ragged trees. Then scenes from other places appeared: he saw an image of Aina in the polished rock. He gently touched the smooth surface; he knew it wasn't her. He'd seen no sign of her. Crackling flames bursting from the flowers growing higher up caught his attention, but he remained on the path, which was now no more than a ledge clinging to the side of a steep gorge.

Sensing a presence, Thomas stopped and waited. Xart stood by a boulder, searching for something. Thomas wanted to kill him, but was this another test of truth? Was he really looking at his enemy? He looked down at his own body of blue flame, and then at Xart, burning in black and red.

Thomas moved and Xart turned, his eyes widening. The goblin leapt forward, tiny grey talons of magic extending from each finger, and slashed. Still feeling as if this were all a dream, Thomas tried to block.

Intense pain woke him up to the reality of his situation. Thomas looked at his left hand, the one he'd held up to protect himself. One of his fingers was gone; he smelt it burning on the ground. The goblin picked it up, sniffing it. Thomas attacked, but the goblin fought fiercely, and his magic talons caught him again. Thomas was now wide awake. His ring finger was a throbbing stub, and the pain from the cut across his chest had focussed his mind.

Without the force of the pentacle, he was forced to remember the basics of rock magic, and one of these was using attractive force in the rocks and minerals of the planet. He sensed a large amount of iron around him. He called it as he stumbled backwards, and shards of iron flew at Xart. The goblin screamed and fell backwards.

Thomas ran along the mountain path, and now it was very real to him, including the scary drop into the valley below. He thought he heard his name being called, but he ignored it, running to escape the sorcerer.

"Thomas."

It came from a lower path. He looked around; it sounded like Aina, but it couldn't be, and he saw no sign of her. He cursed this test, suspecting Xart's trickery, and continued to run, looking over his shoulder until pain seared across his face.

"I have you," Xart said.

Thomas had no idea how the goblin had moved so fast or been able to get in front of him. There must have been a shortcut. Xart struck him hard, sending him backwards. Thomas tripped; his hand throbbed as he tried to break his fall. He called up a magical shield to block the goblin's attack, but the sorcerer rushed around him, striking the ground. Sword-like blades of magic rushed from the ground and arched above over his head. When Thomas touched one, it cut his hand and sent a shock into his body.

The goblin looked at him from the outside of his prison; his speckled grey and silver eyes catching the light from the fires around them. *"If I were Frore, I may have wasted my time finishing you off, but I'm not."*

"What do you want?"

"The Fire." Xart laughed and ran down the path. *"And I don't want competition."* The goblin disappeared around a corner and was gone.

He stood alone inside his radiant cage. He now believed that the voice he'd heard had been Aina, but he'd refused to listen. He pushed his hands between the shining blades of light, but when he touched one of them, intense pain made him pull away.

He tested each part of his cage, but each part was alive with biting magic. Sitting down, he examined his wounds. They were real, but he didn't care about them. He had to escape, but did nothing except sit and stare at the changing flames beyond the bright blades that formed the bars of his prison.

He'd failed so close to the finish. All he could do was wonder about the images he'd seen, and the whispers he'd heard. Were they really of Aina? Or was this cruel world tricking him? Determined to get out, he stood, but again, the cage caused only pain.

A flash of light made him look up. A tiny bird hovered above his cage. He knew that in seconds it would disappear, like most things in this world. Again he doubted his hopes that Aina could still be alive. After all, he'd seen her die. But again the colourful bird caught his eye. He watched it, becoming mesmerised by its bright colours. It was certainly the most beautiful thing he'd seen in this strange world.

It now hovered directly above and in front of him, moving forwards and backwards. He stood and reached out between his bars. The tiny bird landed on his outstretched hand. Unthinkingly, he'd reached out with his left hand, and the bird touched his bloody stump, but instead of pain, Thomas's eyes widened.

"Aina?"

The bird lifted from his hand and entered the cage. Then, as soon as it had come, it flew through the narrow gap and towards the rock.

"Stay," he said, feeling sad to lose his companion.

The bird returned, then flew back out to the burning rocks again.

"What are you trying to tell me?" Then he knew. He called the burning iron in the rocks and felt its force extend outwards. The bars of his prison shook. He tried again, and again they moved. The bird sang excitedly, and Thomas pulled on the magnetic force in the metal, bending the bars backwards and forwards; soon there was enough space, and he stepped out.

"I'm free," he said to the bird. But it was gone. He left the cage on the path and ran, but he was thinking about the bright bird. He wanted to believe that Aina had sent it, but he still doubted. *"Aina,"* he called in the True Language; he seemed to hear a whisper of his name.

For the first time in a long time, Thomas felt joy, and he ran around a corner grinning broadly. But his grin disappeared when he saw the goblin.

Xart gave an incredulous stare. *"How did you escape?"*

But Thomas had no intention of being distracted again.

Calling his magic, he imagined himself dashing past Xart; the sorcerer chased the illusion, laughing as he sent jets of fire into the false Thomas. The false image screamed and fell from the mountain. Thomas carefully created the suggestion of grey ground beneath his image's feet. Xart followed and fell into the valley below.

LUCY WALKED through the forest and spoke to the plants and trees. When they did answer, they were harder to understand and their life more intense than the life of plants on the surface. A single bush burnt on the edge of the glade; the rest of the forest was dark. A whispering from behind her made her freeze. A trail of white mushrooms grew along the path she'd walked; more grew around her feet. Although the branches that curved above her were dark and grey, the mushrooms were bathed in golden light. She brushed a white spore from her legs. Somehow tiny spores must have clung to her body. *"I transported you here."* She was a little surprised.

Small bright creatures moved around by her feet. They appeared to be tending the forest; she watched the tiny creatures flit about, and then she noticed a shadow move within the trees. She knew her test would be about more than truth.

"The Queen of the Underworld," Frore said. She watched him approach. He looked both fascinated and repulsed by the sight of her, and she imagined how she looked, bathed in the golden light of the mushrooms. It appeared a world of decay, but she knew it was fertile. She was already listening to the web of life around her, and it listened to her, too.

"What do you want?" He'd invaded her personal space

again.

"I'm taking another look into your mind."

"Is that what you think this is?" She wondered how true that was. Was this dark forest a part of her, and if so, could she ask it to rid her of this man? If that's what he was. Aina had once told her that the Imperial Order had altered themselves through technology and black magic. *"Are you human?"*

She shivered at his crooked smile. *"A new being, stronger than before."* It was probably true. He walked closer, and she readied herself to fight, if that was even possible against this man. *"You have something I want."*

"I know, but I won't share it." She was sure he meant information on her world. On Earth.

"You shared it before."

"You took it, until we threw you out."

"What's the difference?" Already he was twisting the truth. *"And your friend is not here now. Perhaps Xart has killed him."*

"Perhaps Thomas has killed Xart."

Frore nodded. *"Perhaps, but the goblin is tough to kill."* He took her hands, but she pulled away. *"Lucy, you misunderstand me."*

She shuddered when he used her name. *"I don't think so."* Now he was becoming weird; he seemed to want more than information. *"What am I to you?"*

"You're wasted. I need a queen to rule the Empire with me."

He was insane. *"I prefer my mushrooms."* She shared some true feelings in the True Language. He bared his teeth, and she laughed.

The sorcerer took hold of her hands. *"I tried to be nice."*

She stared at his empty socket. *"No, you didn't; you tried the easy way."* She sent a shock of magic into his hands, but he just grinned.

"You're perceptive—a good quality in a queen." She called to the forest but had to stop her search for life when he pushed into her mind. This time she was stronger, and she pushed back, telling his heart to stop, but it seemed to have no effect. *"You can't kill me, you don't have the strength to finish me off."* Again, he was right, she lacked the strength to fully exert her power, and she dreaded that test.

Several fiery insects flew through the trees and made her think of her purpose here. *"Do you think you can take the Fire?"* She'd distracted him and, pulling one hand away, she pointed at the fire bush.

"I already have. I can show you."

She knew then that he'd misunderstood the nature of the Fire. It was more than the physical fire around them; it was something internal.

Frore dragged her to the fiery bush and put his hand into the flames. His one eye focussed on the flowers of flame, and again she looked into the socket Tu had created. An aggressive fire wasp buzzed around her, and she spoke to it, an idea forming in her mind as more of them buzzed around her, attracted by the magic.

She showed the fire wasps a cosy home of warmth and magic. And a dozen wasps flew into Frore's empty socket. He screamed, letting go of Lucy, and she quickly ran across the glade and into the trees, stopping to watch from the cover of the forest.

Then something changed. He'd forgotten her and stood with a beatific smile on his face—his socket full of swirling fire wasps. He really seemed to believe he'd been gifted with the Fire. She turned and ran, soon finding herself deeper in the darkening forest. A dark blue light was permeating the trees. *"The Test of Power,"* she said to the forest with a chill feeling of dread.

34

Thomas dropped through the core, but the heat was replaced by coolness. He hit something soft, and it moved, cursing. Opening his eyes, he saw dark blue paintings of flowers covering the ceiling. He lay in a perfumed bed, and two naked figures stared at him.

The woman moved quickly off the bed, grasping a sword and turning to face him. A slender man with a painted face glared at him. "Get out!" He spoke with a Tartarean accent.

Still feeling disoriented, Thomas sat up slowly, noticing more weapons on the stone floor. The painted boy beside him didn't seem the sort to use a sword. He looked back at the woman, who stood watching them with a complete lack of self-consciousness.

"Now!" the young man shouted.

"Not so fast." The woman grinned, studying them both carefully. "My favourites: an ironman and a bellflower boy. I don't know how you ended up here, but I never look a gift man in the mouth." She rested her sword point down on the ground.

"I'm calling the madam," the young man said. Thomas realized he'd fallen into a brothel.

"Call all you want," the woman said. "She's my friend, and I'm the one paying." The boy huffed.

"I'm leaving," Thomas said. He just needed some clothes, and preferably a sword. He stood, but stopped at the sound of men approaching from outside the door. The look on the woman's face told him enough; he picked up a sword.

The door burst open and armed men ran in, the first into the woman's sword. Thomas thrust his sword into a surprised man as three more men rushed into the room.

They were brawlers, and thankfully they lacked skills with a sword. One jabbed awkwardly at Thomas and lost a finger for his efforts; Thomas finished him off with a thrust through his throat. The woman beside him finished another; the final man dropped his weapon and ran out of the door and down a set of stairs.

The bellflower boy whimpered on the bed. "Their uses are limited," she said. Turning to face Thomas, she asked, "Who are you?"

"Thomas Brand. And I think I'm wanted in this city."

She laughed. "Who isn't?"

"Who were they?" She told him about the gangs of assassins wandering Tartaros as they dressed. He chose the cleanest pants, boots, and shirts from the dead men. And the best of their weapons. He told her a few choice parts of his story.

"Did you lose your finger recently?"

He looked at his left hand and nodded, noticing the throbbing pain again. So it was real. He'd hoped it had all been a dream. Perhaps not all.

"And you don't know how you got here?" she asked.

"No."

"Nor why you're here?"

"I have a test of strength."

"You've passed."

"I wish it were that simple," Thomas said. "Why were they trying to kill you?"

She finished strapping her swords to her belt. "I killed one of the king's men, but I had good reason."

"I don't doubt it," Thomas said. "King Val?"

She nodded. They left the boy alone in the room and walked down the stone stairs of the brothel and into the street. "I'm leaving Tartaros," she said, "I hear there's work in the marsh towns. Why don't you join me? There's always opportunity for someone who can use a sword."

He shook his head. "My job's here."

"Then I bid you farewell. I'm Sora." She stretched out her hand.

"Thomas." They shook, and she slipped into a nearby alley.

Following his nose to the river, he continued down the street. He'd been transported back to Tartaros, and it still stank. The only difference was the way people looked at him, until he realized it was the bloody sword in his hand.

When he entered one of the main streets that led to Dock Square, just above the Old Port, he heard sounds of a disturbance behind. He turned and cursed when he saw Sora pelting down the street, chased by about twenty men. She ran straight towards him, shouting something.

Thomas ran, but more slowly, allowing her to catch up. The two nearest men lunged with their swords. Sora sidestepped one of them, piercing his shoulder. Screaming, the man dropped his sword to the cobblestones and backed off. Thomas was faster than his opponent, stepping inside and thrusting his sword through the man's heart.

"Not bad," she said as they continued to run towards the square.

"What was it you were shouting?" he asked.

She narrowed her eyes. "I said keep away from Dock Square. It's full of the king's men."

He cursed as he saw a company of king's soldiers running through the crowd towards them.

"I know a way," Sora said, running along the side of the square. They ran fast, but he still had time to notice the twitching bodies suspended from gallows in the centre of the square.

A crowd of children ran from a side street, pushing them towards the gallows. Thomas tried to force his way out of the square, but it was too late. The king's men grinned as they approached.

"You should have cut your way through," a sergeant said, kicking a child out of the way. There was little they could do. Thomas and Sora dropped their swords, and the soldiers tied their wrists together, then roughly dragged them towards the platform in front of the gallows. "Today's hanging day."

Lucy breathed the magic of the core, but a different smell mingled with the magic. It was familiar, and then she recognized the fragrant sewer of Tartaros. The magic tugged at her. She resisted, not wanting to return to that stinking city, but the pull was too strong. Letting go, she rushed to a cooler, darker place, yet she felt that her feet were still firmly planted in the flames, and the fire rising through her soles and into her body transmuted into power; she felt it pulsing through her.

She stood in the Old Port—in the square close to the docks. To the side was a circular cage that sat on a platform between the royal building and the gallows. She pushed through the crowd until she stood beneath the cage. Chloris was chained inside.

Only then did she become aware of people laughing at her, and she realized she had no clothes. Snatching a cloak from a sniggering woman, she wrapped it around herself and leapt onto the stage. Ignoring the woman's shouts, she walked up to the cage door and tried to open it.

"I can help you," a man said. Chloris hissed a warning, but it was too late. The man opened the door and pushed her in, pulling away the cloak at the same time.

Lucy didn't care. None of this seemed real, although she knew it was. Chloris was disoriented, and Lucy felt the bruises and wounds to her body as if they were her own. "Luce . . ." she whispered, unable to speak. And Lucy felt the binding at her mouth and the soreness to her throat.

"Chloris, what happened?"

"Can it speak?" an officer asked.

"They can imitate speech—like mynah birds," the showman said. "We can teach it to sing as it fights." The officer nodded.

"Coming here was a mistake. The basilisk caught me with his magic. How did they catch you?" Chloris said.

"I've come from the inner sun."

"Can you get us out?"

"I don't know." She walked up to Chloris, and many in the crowd gasped. She tested the iron ring she was chained to. Outside the cage, the crowd was becoming excited.

"This has never been seen before!" the showman announced. "The demon and its lover!" He started selling tickets for a place on the circular platform, and families scrambled up to watch the spectacle. "Will it love her or eat her?" the showman shouted.

"This is ridiculous," Lucy said. Then she noticed movement by the gallows about twenty yards to the left of her cage. *"Thomas?"*

"We're sharing our test of power," he said.

"And I'm naked."

"Clothe yourself in fire," he said.

"Is that what you're doing?" She wasn't exactly sure how to do that.

"Soon. I think the power is coming back. Can you free Chloris?"

"I can try," she said.

Ignoring the cruel taunts, she turned back to the ring. Knowing that the power she needed was not physical, she relaxed and called her inner power, but noise from the large porch of the royal building on the opposite side to the gallows made her turn.

"The king of Tartaros!" a crier announced. King Val looked towards them and laughed.

"Ignore it," Chloris hissed. "Help me, and we'll kill it."

Some people turned to listen to the demon speak, but others were listening to the king.

She felt her magic, but exerting her power still felt wrong to her. A block.

"Help me!" Chloris struggled with her chains.

Doing nothing would be worse, and she didn't feel much for the crowd that pushed against her cage. She only felt slightly uncomfortable when she realized that she identified more with an ice demon than with these people. She reached for Chloris's chains. She knew the magic she had could snap them in a second. Her test was her will to act.

A man threw rotten fungus at Chloris, mocking the

demon. Lucy slipped her mind into the lock and released her power. The chains fell away from Chloris. "Thank you."

"I'll try the door," Lucy said.

"No need."

Lucy felt Chloris's hatred of the men, and her energy rising as she limped forward. She ripped the door from its hinges, and the crowd panicked, many of them falling from the round platform, but the showman tried to prod her with an electric stick. Chloris snapped it in two and bit half the man's head off.

Lucy noticed that Thomas was clothed in fire and walking across the square towards her with a woman at his side. Behind him were burning gallows—an executioner stared after him. "I can do that," she said. Seconds later her magic flared, and she was clothed in flames.

Chloris looked up at her. "This is getting better."

Lucy nodded. She felt fine. Her energy pulsed through her; she felt stronger than she'd ever felt. A soldier stabbed at her with a sword, but she grabbed hold of the blade and let the fire burning inside her leap into the man. He screamed, and then his body was reduced to a pile of smoking ash on the ground.

"I didn't mean to do that," she said, more surprised than upset.

"It served him right," Chloris said.

Thomas and a woman stared up at her and Chloris. "Who are your friends?" the woman asked.

Thomas gave a fiery grin. "Sora, Lucy, and Chloris."

Sora nodded at them, and then pointed to the king. He was organizing his soldiers. "I think we should leave."

"We have one more task," Thomas said.

"Kill the king," Chloris hissed happily.

"You certainly have unusual friends," Sora said, looking

at them all. "As unusual as you." She hesitated. "It's not often that I'm one to back out of a fight, but have you seen how many there are?"

Lucy had counted about fifty soldiers and assassins. "Let's just do it." She jumped from the stage, and all four of them walked towards the royal building and the king. When they got closer, the soldiers attacked. Chloris charged into them, injuring several at once. A sergeant shouted at her, and she spat acid in his face.

Thomas fought with a flaming sword; corpses lay around him.

"Here," Sora said, giving Lucy a sword. "Can you use it?"

"A little, but I have other skills."

"I believe you." Sora stayed close to her, dealing with any blades that came too close, while Lucy tried the new magic she'd discovered, and through sound vibrations, sent soldiers to their knees.

Soon they stood beneath the porch, looking up at King Val and his personal guard.

"Kill them!" the king ordered. But his guard looked at the two flaming figures, the ice demon, and the warrior. And then at each other. The king's guards fled.

Val drew his sword, but before he could attack, Lucy whipped a strand of magic around the basilisk's neck. She pulled and he sprawled to the ground in front of the porch.

"Shall I kill it?" Chloris asked.

"No. I'll deal with it," Lucy said. *"I'm ready to leave,"* she said to Thomas.

He nodded and turned to Chloris and Sora. "I hope you two can make friends," he said, grinning, "and when we return, you're welcome to join our army."

"Army?" Sora raised an eyebrow.

"We're going to destroy the Empire."

"You don't think small, do you?" She looked at them both. "You mean it?"

"They have to be stopped," Lucy said. "And if we can take the Fire, then we have the chance."

"It looks like you have it now."

"We have a final test," Lucy said. She tightened the magical strand as the basilisk struggled. "Will you be all right?" she asked Chloris.

"Yes," she hissed. "They won't catch me again."

There was a confidence in her voice, reassuring Lucy. "When I return, we'll travel to the surface."

"We can hunt together," she hissed.

Lucy felt the satisfaction in her words; she felt less sure about the hunting part. Again she felt the pull of the core of the planet, and keeping a firm grip on the king, she sank into the earth. She felt Thomas's presence beside her and the struggles of the king cease. Then the darkness was replaced by light, and she stood in the inner sun.

35

The flames burnt violet, indicating the final test. Lucy feared this test less than the previous one, but that made her nervous, too. Complacency could kill as much as the struggles she'd gone through. She walked through the shining forest, watching the shadows move, and then she felt a change: something was following her.

Moving quickly away from the darkness, she wondered how such a dark feeling could be related to a test of love, unless it was a test of her ability to love something unlovable. She shook her head at her stupidity—as if the test would be about bunnies. As if responding to her thoughts, a red rabbit hopped across her path and over a bridge. She followed, wondering if it was a warning.

When she stepped off the far side of the bridge, the rabbit was gone, and she was in a wood. Violet flowers grew in small groups around her. The sounds of the inner sun had disappeared. It would have been perfect, except that each time she left the core, she lost her clothes. Wishing she had the comfortable jeans, jacket, and boots she used to have, her skin tingled. The clothes materialized on her body, and she felt the magical link with the distant core. But this wasn't Prometheus; it was a much more temperate planet. The forest was full of birdsong and the sounds of insects, but there were no signs of human activity. The air was rich with oxygen.

Animals watched her from the trees, and she spoke to them. They answered her questions happily and explained that all the world was forest. She was the first human they'd seen.

She immediately loved this green world and wished that this love would be enough for her to pass the test, but she knew it would not. Sensing a change, she turned to look back. Something dark had entered the forest, and the smaller animals disappeared from sight. *"Predator,"* the grey bird warned. She already knew.

Lucy walked deeper into the forest, but she sensed Frore approaching. Instead of running, she chose a beautiful spot by the slow green river and waited. She knew that Frore would be part of her test of love, and she calmed her mind in readiness.

"None of this is real, you know." Frore walked from the trees towards her.

"It's very real." She felt the moss beneath her fingers and watched the dragonflies dance over the surface of the slowly moving water.

"It's the magic of the core. I thought you'd understood."

Lucy was curious. Was he trying to make her doubt herself? "We're in a forest on a different planet."

He shook his head. "You're wrong about me, too." She guessed where this was going. Again. "We could be good together on the throne in Palace Moon."

"Why do you want me?" she asked.

"With your magic, you'd make a suitable partner. And the Empire would follow you."

That held some truth. But she had no intention of allowing herself to be used to further this man's ambitions. "I'll stay here."

"You can't. When the test is over, this place will cease to exist." She didn't believe a word of it—she knew this world was very real, and that they'd been taken here for a reason.

"The answer is no."

Around her wrist a golden chain formed, linking them together. Frore admired his handiwork. "The chain is real and will keep you safe."

Everything he said was a lie. "Remove it."

"I just want you to think about what I've said."

"I have," she replied. "Is this your test of love?" The way he looked told her it was—but the desire in his eyes was of possession and control. She raised her eyebrows. "You'll fail, you know. Chaining someone down is not love."

He tried to smile but failed. If she'd not seen all of the things she had, she'd have been scared at his twisted face. Instead, she ignored him, and his grin disappeared. "Your friend has failed the test of love."

He was lying, and she took no notice of his attempts to sow seeds of doubt, nor his attempts to make her feel guilty for the deaths of those she loved. He tugged on the chain, but she was listening to the grey bird.

"It's only real if you believe it."

She smiled at the bird's words—she knew they were true. She felt her love for this green world growing, and as it did, the golden chain faded before her eyes. She walked along the riverbank, followed by Frore.

"What have you done?"

Puzzled by his behaviour, she asked, "Why don't you attack?"

"I'd never do that."

The lie was so blatant that she was about to ask why he persisted with it, but then she remembered that this was his test of love. He was trying to control himself—and failing. His face twitched with anger, perhaps because she was beyond his control. But his words didn't stop, and she noticed that some of them were tinged with magic.

"This forest is dangerous. You shouldn't wander here alone."

"I'm not alone," she said. "All the forest is with me." For the first time, he glared at her angrily. "Your scowls suit you better than your smiles." As she walked, a small flock of birds flew nearby, warning her of him. She thanked them in the True Language and sent them her love.

He grabbed her wrist, forcing her to turn and look at him. All she saw was the red eye with the swirling fire of the wasps. "I've already passed my tests, and I possess the Fire."

"Then what are you doing here?"

"I'm taking you back. Your knowledge and magic will benefit the Empire."

"You mean benefit you."

"They're the same."

"Does the Emperor agree?"

His magic swelled—and so did hers. She forced him to let go, and he only just resisted striking her with his power. But this time she was ready. Her connection to the core was still strong, but he changed his tactics.

"You love this forest, don't you?"

She did, but now, she was worried. "Leave it alone!"

He was alight with magic, and snakes of energy crawled from his body and wended their way into the woods, crackling as they moved. *"Leave!"* She spoke to all the small animals that watched, hidden in the vegetation. Some followed her instructions, but some were mesmerized by the magic. Fire was already leaping from the forest floor.

"My spell will stop the moment you leave the forest." He held out his hand, which she slapped away.

"Put out the fires."

"Only you can do that. What happens to the creatures of the forest is your responsibility."

She shook her head at his lies, and she reached out to the forest. The fire was spreading at an unnatural speed, and many of the creatures were panicking. *"It's sticking to everything,"* the grey bird said. It had flown deeper into the forest.

"Then I'll leave the forest," she said. Frore smirked, but she turned and walked to the river.

"The only way is with me."

But she ignored him and called all life for help. *"The giant turtles,"* the grey bird said. He was now flying away over the river.

Lucy sensed no giant turtles, but she visualized them anyway, and called. Then she waited while the forest burned. Leaving with Frore was possible, but she had an unpleasant feeling about it. Nothing he said could be trusted. Once he was absolutely sure the tests were over, everything would change. And his power was such that even with the Fire, she'd be challenged to defeat him. She needed time to learn its power, but she had to get away from this man.

She flinched as he took her hand, immediately sparking her magic. He let go with a laugh. "I can play that game too."

"I know," she said. "But your power is corrosive."

"I cleanse the world."

"Like the Goddess of Purification?"

He spat his words out at the mention of her name. "Nothing like her!" He glared at her, and Lucy preferred this expression. "She's evil, of the old faerie world. Nothing she says should be trusted, nor that wretched cat of hers that I killed."

Lucy grinned. "He's alive." Frore's eyes widened. "You must have seen him on the ferry. He's the ship's cat." Sensing movement beneath the surface of the river, she turned. A sharp pain flared in the back of her head. Frore was attacking with magic. She looked at him in shock.

He was scowling. "If you won't cooperate in a reasonable way, you'll remain and burn with your pets."

Another blast of magic forced her into the shallow water at the edge of the river. When he attacked again, she raised her defence, and his magic slipped from her shield.

"Why do you call the Turtles of Green?"

A large turtle lay half-submerged in the river. She explained her need, feeling anger emanating from the giant turtles. Unsure what risks they'd take, she spoke. *"He's hard to kill, and that's not your job."*

They agreed. *"We are your path to the other place, but you must open the portal."*

"Yes." She leapt onto the turtle's back, skipping from turtle to turtle as if they were giant blue stepping stones. After each step, the turtles swam ahead, forming a moving path across the river. Calling on the core, she saw a shimmering portal opening ahead of her.

"Thank you, Turtles of Green." She leapt into the bright portal. Behind her, Frore cursed as the fire sputtered out.

THE FOREST HAD COOLED, and the flames burnt in shades of blue and violet. A deer watched Thomas from the forest. Curious, he pushed through a patch of bracken and followed it deeper into the woods. It ran ahead, crossing a stream, and then moving further away until it was only just in view. It waited on the top of a rise. Something moving through the trees distracted him; when he looked up again, the deer was gone and Aina stood in its place. *"Thomas."*

"Thomas," Frore mocked from the forest.

Thomas's heartbeat increased as his hatred grew. "I thought you'd be dead by now." But Frore laughed as trumpets sounded, and with every note, the trees withered until they'd shrunk to yellow blades of grass on a vast plain. Tens of thousands of imperial soldiers marched past Frore, towards the towering figure of the Emperor. The triumphant music was greeted with cheers by large groups of lords and ladies.

He searched for Aina, but she'd gone.

"She's dead, and you know it," Frore said. "You made the wrong choices, and now you're here: so close and yet so far." Thomas sprang at the sorcerer, but a line of imperial knights appeared between them. "I've passed the tests of truth and love. Be warned, my test of power is about to commence."

"You have no love," Thomas said.

Frore pointed at the parades marching across the open space where the forest had been. "My love is a big love: a love of the Empire, a love of the imperial achievement, and a love of the order we bring to the nine planets." He conjured a distorted image of Aina. "While your love is a small and selfish lust for a dead woman."

"She lives." He prayed it was true.

"You know she's dead. What you saw was a memory.

You've failed the test of truth; you've misunderstood life and death. I know its secrets. I have eternal life."

"Through murder."

"The elixir of life has a cost, but the lives spent are insignificant relative to the gain; they are sacrifices to something greater."

"A twisted love of self," Thomas said.

"After I kill you, you will, through me, learn to love the greater good." The plain was replaced by a desert, and Frore attacked, blasting Thomas with fire. He flew through the air, gasping in pain. His lungs were burning, and he choked. The sorcerer towered over him. "You never had my power."

"Thomas!" Aina called. *"I'm in the forest."*

The desert disappeared, and Thomas lay on the ground in the humming forest. Aina watched him from the trees. There was no time to speak; he had to kill the sorcerer first. Frore attacked, and Thomas deflected the magic, rolling onto his feet, but he was still pushed back.

"She's dead—just a ghost," Frore said. His eyes, one metallic grey, one a fierce red, protruded; his apparent calmness had been replaced by anger. Thomas gathered power through the roots he felt connecting him to the fire of the core, and he knocked Frore to the ground with a thought. The sorcerer's eyes widened as he struggled to stand.

Thomas saw the lattice of energy that was the forest, and if he could study it, he could kill the sorcerer. He moved away from a solitary fire hornet, hoping that Frore would antagonize it, but he didn't. All he needed was a little time.

Aina called him. *"Thomas, I need you. I'm being pulled back to the other side."*

"Aina, I can kill him." He knew he was so close.

"I'm dying a second time! Thomas, I'll never be able to

return!" Aina searched for him with her eyes but didn't appear to see him. She was crying.

Thomas felt a deep chill spread through his body. He was losing her a second time.

Frore gave a short bark of laughter as he misunderstood Thomas. "You're scared!"

Thomas realized that although he hated the man, killing him was a deadly distraction. However, when the sorcerer attacked, he was forced to respond. His mouth was dry as desperation took hold; he was now willing to do anything. When Frore's magic touched him, he hardly felt the pain. Looking for a distraction, he saw the hornet again. He sent it a message, and it responded.

He ran to Aina, hearing laughter from behind. He moved close to her, scared she'd vanish as she always had in his dreams. A scream from behind told him the fire hornet had taken an interest in the sorcerer's red, swirling eye. He had a few moments with her.

"Choose me, Thomas!"

"Aina, I love you." He felt his legs go weak, and the forest faded around him. *"Where are we?"*

"We've not moved, but you're vibrating at a higher level—he can't see you here." He automatically reached for his pentacle, but it was gone. *"You don't need it anymore, the Fire is inside you."*

"What's happened to him?"

"He passed a test, so he'll live, but he thinks he's passed all."

Thomas saw Frore smiling to himself. The hornet had gone, and he felt the fire in his eye. *"Lucy added a little of her own magic,"* Aina interrupted his thoughts, *"and now he thinks he has the Fire."*

"He thinks I'm dead," Thomas said.

The sorcerer walked to the beach, and the goblin barge was waiting for him. He was gone.

"Lucy?"

"She's passed all three tests; she waits for you."

Thomas studied Aina. "You look different."

She grinned. *"Of course. It's a complex pattern of energies; I fashioned this body especially for you. Do you like it?"*

"Come back!" His eyes moistened.

"It's not so easy," she said.

"But you came here."

"This place is special, but even here I can't remain long. Thomas, I'm real, but my body has gone."

"But you're coming back?"

"Not as I was."

"What do you mean?"

"I don't have any more time here."

"Aina, come back to me!"

She grinned. *"I love you too."* The image of Aina flickered before him, and her expression became more serious. *"Thomas, raise the Fire, and I'll return!"* And then she was gone.

EPILOGUE

Thomas stood deep beneath the surface of Prometheus when his vision came. The black dragon flew from the forest and landed beside him. Its eyes burnt red. *"Now it's you who disturbs my dreams."*

"I saw Aina."

"And now do you believe she lives?"

"Yes. But how can the dead return?"

"They're reborn." Smoke came from its nostrils. *"Do you have the Fire of Prometheus?"*

"Yes."

The dragon roared, leaving Thomas feeling uneasy. He looked up. Dark dots appeared on the horizon. They were moving fast, and soon filled the sky. Hundreds of dragons flew towards him, a golden dragon leading the group.

As the vision faded, Thomas glanced at Lucy. Her forehead creased as she said, "I saw, but I don't understand."

"Chloris warned me about dragons."

"Not trusting is her nature," Lucy said. "It seems we have dragons in our futures."

Thomas stood silently with his magic alight—the image of the golden dragon burning brightly in his mind.

PLEASE LEAVE A REVIEW

If you enjoyed The Darkling Odyssey, please leave a review. Reviews can help a writer's work be read by more readers and help promote their career, so allowing more books to be written. Thank you!

FREE STORIES!

Find out about Aina's young life in the forests of Prometheus. Visit NedMarcus.com and sign-up to my newsletter to get two exciting prequels to Blue Prometheus for free.

BOOKS BY NED MARCUS

Blue Prometheus Series

- Young Aina (#0)
- Blue Prometheus (#1)
- The Darkling Odyssey (#2)
- Fire Rising (#3)

Orange Storm Series

- Orange Storm #1
- The Orange Witch #2 (forthcoming)

ABOUT THE AUTHOR

Ned Marcus is an author of fantasy and science fiction. He lives and writes in the mountains of northern Taiwan.

NedMarcus.com

ACKNOWLEDGMENTS

Thank you to my editor, Parisa Zolfaghari; my proofreader, Deborah Dove; and to Taipei Fantasy & Sci-fi Writers' Group for their help with this novel.

www.ingramcontent.com/pod-product-compliance
Lightning Source LLC
LaVergne TN
LVHW041744060526
838201LV00046B/909